At The Cart's Tayle

Mysti Spiel

Copyrights & Disclaimers

The story in this book is a work of fiction. The names, characters, and events are the product of the Author's imagination and are used fictitiously. Any resemblance to actual events or persons is coincidental.

The historical events contained within are believed by the Author to be accurate at the time of writing. References are often provided for such events, including but not limited to references to books and internet sources. The links contained within the book were accurate to the best of the Author's abilities at the time of writing. The Author is not responsible for any URLs that may have expired or changed. The Author reserves the right to shut down the Author's website at any time and is not obligated to maintain it. No warranties are provided regarding the accuracy of historical content and references.

No part of this publication may be reproduced, distributed, or transmitted in any form or by any means, including photocopying, recording, or other electronic or mechanical methods, without the prior written permission of the Author. The only exception to this prohibition is limited "fair use" as strictly defined by U.S. copyright law.

There is no monetary value or reward associated with any of the potential mysteries, games, un-games, or puzzles that may or may not exist within this work, online, and/or elsewhere.

This is a work of fiction set in a real town and includes historical references. Readers who choose to visit or explore any of the places mentioned do so entirely *"at their own risk."* The Author does not encourage or condone trespassing, theft, vandalism, or any behavior that may endanger personal safety or otherwise violate the law. The dangerous and/or illegal acts of the fictional characters that are part of the story are not condoned by the Author in real life.

"At your own risk" means that any decision to visit any location within this book (real or imagined), or to follow any clue leading to any other locations (real or imagined) from the website www.MystiSpiel.com, or from any clues found along the way (real or imagined) are made voluntarily and with full personal responsibility for any outcomes, including but not limited to physical injury, property damage, and/or legal consequences. This includes any injury, accident, and/or loss occurring while traveling to, from, or within any location, and/or while at such location.

"At your own risk" includes, without limitation, following any directions, paths, or clues (whether real or imagined), interpreting or acting on anything within or outside this work (real or imagined), visiting any physical locations, accessing any websites, or engaging with any related materials or activities (real or imagined). You (the reader) assume full responsibility for all of your actions and any outcomes that may result.

ISBN 9798218790509

Moorefield Press

YA & Adult readers

- This book was written for high school age and up. It's not recommended for middle grades or younger.

- It's a fictional mystery novel with true local historical intrigue and a touch of sci-fi/fantasy.

- As a mystery, this story includes themes commonly found in mystery and true-crime series. I don't want to include spoilers, but if you typically avoid such themes, this book is not for you.

Author's Note

Visit: Why did I chose to use the names of real towns in a work of fiction? The answer is simple: when weaving real history into a fictional narrative, place matters. And when history is forgotten, cycles of inhumanity inevitably repeat.

Second: Moorestown, Burlington, and Burlington County hold a special place in my heart. I am grateful to be a speck of sand within this wonderful community. None of the characters in the fictional portions of this book represent real people, nor do they reflect this beloved community.

Time: I had planned and looked forward to refining this book over an additional year. However, the need for this story, the need for remembering our past, exists now. I release it into the world as it is today.

Books: My hope is that future authors will provide clear references for historical elements they incorporate into their fictional works. Readers should not have to struggle to distinguish between documented history and the author's imagination.

Inquire: To my family and friends, thank you for your support, patience, blessings, and love. And for pretending to believe me every time I said it was "almost finished."

"Speak up for those who cannot speak for themselves,
for the rights of all who are destitute.
Speak up and judge fairly;
defend the rights of the poor and needy."

Proverbs 31:8-9

"The ultimate tragedy is not the oppression and cruelty by the bad people, but the silence over that by the good people."

Martin Luther King Jr.

If your forefather was an enslaver, that is not your shame. If your forefather was on a jury that punished someone wrongly, that is not your shame.

But what about those who hide, destroy, or prevent others from learning history? What happens when their actions lead to future ignorant generations repeating atrocities such as genocide, racism, and slavery?

Will those individuals who claim they were just following their employers' instructions be excused from the moral guilt?

Mysti Spiel

Contents

Welcome to the Hunt!

Chapter 1

Dear Reader,

Here you will find a fictional mystery, yet **all the historical references before 2000 are true**. Don't believe me? Dare to jump down the linked rabbit holes? The story of South Jersey is not the sweet one you were taught.

Happy hunting!

Mysti Spiel

Day 1, Monday, September 19, 2022

Chapter 2

Rex zigzagged along the water's edge through the trees, the mist drifting off the lake in the cool air of the fading night. I followed at an easy pace, letting his unrestrained joy pull me along. When he caught sight of movement ahead, he slowed into a quiet sit, soaking it all in. A majestic buck stepped out from the bushes, fully aware of us, and stopped with quiet authority.

Feeling safe, his family followed. They emerged from the honeysuckle and moved with unhurried grace, nibbling berries and sweet grass as they passed.

In moments like these, I felt in harmony with the lake, the trees, the birds, and everything around me. My spirit danced. I was free.

Catching those magical minutes of morning twilight at Strawbridge Lake was heaven. I stood beside Rex in awe as the deer drifted past and crossed Kings Highway.

Rex stood up and waded into the water, sniffing along the bank for hidden animal dens. I glanced around. It was still too early for other walkers to be out. Later, when they came, most would stay on the path by the road, missing the peaceful energy that flowed through everything here.

I heard an owl hooting and felt the pull of the archival stone beckoning as we neared. *Stone, what have you seen over your many years?* I wondered as I neared.

The stone stayed silent, recording history, but never revealing its secrets. I glanced around. So much had happened here at Strawbridge Lake, where Haines Drive intersects Kings Highway. Dinosaurs roamed. Native Americans lived. Colonial soldiers camped. Freedom seekers on the Underground Railroad passed through, stopping up the road. Even Alice Paul walked this path before she fought for women's right to vote.

I glanced at the stone lying gently between the two sister trees, their intertwining roots slowly pushing it up from its hiding place. I'd always felt drawn to old places and to nature, but this spot with the stone was different. Not that the stone itself was anything special. It was wider than both of my feet, rough and brown. It might contain a small amount of iron in its mix.

I stepped between the two trees, placed a hand on each trunk, and moved my right foot from the grass onto the stone.

Warmth spread from the tree's bark, up my fingertips, and traveled up my arms. Waves of peace traveled up my legs and spine. My whole body was abuzz.

I tilted my head back toward the canopies high above me. "Good morning, friends," I said.

After soaking it in, I let go of the trees and headed closer to the lake, passing Donna's bench.

Honestly, who knew if the energy and vibrations I felt were real? For those few moments, I was happy and worry-free. All was well, and I was smiling. Better than any medication. Rex, dripping with lake water and mud, barreled past me, jumped over the stone, and returned to my side. Maybe Rex felt it too, whatever made this spot special.

No matter what important history happened here, currently it was where Rex was taking his morning swim, watched over by the great blue heron. My thoughts drifted.

What important thing will happen here today?

BANG!

My brain rattled as 165 pounds of wet, ecstatic Great Dane collided with my legs.

I looked down. "Rex. You play too hard." I swiped at the mud he had smeared on my jeans. Just the flair I needed for school.

And so it began. Freedom lost.

Chapter 3

Walking up the steps, I took care to be quiet.

Creeeeak!

Darn that last step.

"Lottie, is that you? You're early again."

I slid Avalon's bedroom door open. Scattered about were the outfits she had already tried on. Her daily quest to find the perfect outfit. The air was thick with a mix of vanilla body spray and the familiar scent of her cucumber face mask. "Any new journal entries last night?" she asked, examining her profile in the mirror.

"No. They come when they please."

She tossed her top on the floor. "Your gift is literally insane. I would be telling everyone, like actually everyone."

"It's not a gift. There's a logical explanation for it. I'm not some special weirdo."

Avalon's phone vibrated with a whirlwind of notifications. She muted her phone and skimmed the messages. A social butterfly at work. "Then let's get Wulf in on it and figure it out."

"I'm not becoming his guinea pig."

Avalon, with one eye still on her phone, grabbed an Eagles shirt. "For someone who would like to be invisible, you were blessed with a gift that would make you stand out."

"We've been through this," I groaned. "Whatever this is, it's not something to celebrate."

Avalon glanced at her reflection. Satisfied, she looked up at me. "Oh no, you don't. After three years, you need to burn that sweatshirt."

I gently placed my backpack on the floor and sat down on her bed; the springs faintly squeaked beneath me. Hyde and Jess Benko's 'Kiss Me Before You Go' hummed softly from her speaker.

"Lottie, please. We need to expand this wardrobe situation. Where's your sense of adventure? At least let's go out and pierce your ears or something."

"Change is overrated." I pulled out my phone and skimmed the headlines, trying to ignore her. A floor caved in at a wedding reception on Long Beach Island. Another reason to avoid crowds. Catalytic converters were stolen from 9 Moorestown High School buses. *That explained today's text from the school.* And the New Jersey State Police were asking for help regarding the two young women who were murdered in the last month in South Jersey; one was found in the woods near the Delaware River, and the other was found just off the walking path in the state park.

My stomach tightened. Both were found near places I knew. The police were asking for anyone with information, including about the white dresses both victims were found wearing, to call.

"How about after school, we add some style to your closet?" Avalon pleaded and made her puppy face. "Please?"

I shook my head.

Avalon grabbed a navy halter top from her closet. "How about we make a deal? If you wear this today, I will not pester or poke you about anything for a month." Avalon turned away to put on lip gloss. "You loved this top when we were shopping, and you looked great in it."

But people would see me, I thought. My chest tightened. *Invisibility is survival.* I pulled a long-sleeved cream shirt from her closet. "What about this? It's daring."

Avalon rolled her eyes. "Nope, it's got to be this one."

I smirked, remembering school policy. "I can't. Halter tops are against the dress code."

"I've already worn this top this year, and no one cared. Nobody gets dress-coded anymore. It's not 2014."

My body tightened while my mind weighed the offer. It would be nice to be left in peace for a whole month. "Our agreement would cover anything that makes me sweat? No pushing me to call and order the pizza? No challenging me to enter a store with seniors inside?"

"Yes. I promise."

"Hmmmm." It was a good deal. It was just a top without sleeves that was cinched in at the waist and would have shown a little bit of back had my hair not been long and highly conditioned today to keep it from fuzzing up. *Six and a half hours of anxiety in exchange for a month of peace*, I thought. I grabbed the top, pulled it on, and zipped it up the side. "It's too tight. Too bad," I smirked.

"It's supposed to hug your curves. It fits you better than me."

"Hey." Wulf barged in, making us jump. He always skipped that last step. "Did you see that Senator Manchin thinks fusion energy could actually bring world peace? It's theoretically possible, but the economics make it pretty unlikely. Greedy corporations and power-hungry governments will never allow free energy."

"Sorry, I missed that," Avalon said, rolling her eyes. "Do you notice anything different about Lottie?"

I slouched. Wulf glared at me from head to toe, wringing his hands.

"No significant changes detected," he said with a slight grin.

"See. Nobody will see any difference. You'll be as invisible as ever." Avalon glanced at her phone. "We need to move or we're going to miss the bus."

I looked at the time and started sweating. "Avalon, you know that being at the bus stop ten minutes early is on time. We're cutting it way too close." I glanced at the mirror. My hair had a mind of its own. I grabbed Avalon's hairspray and put on another layer, hoping it would hold it back for at least an hour.

Avalon grabbed for her black jacket and tried to pull it out from under my backpack, but it wouldn't budge. I ran to grab my backpack's handle before she did, but I lost.

"Whoa," Avalon winced as she struggled with the heavy bag. "You got bricks in this monster?"

"Hey, I see a lot of others with the Zuftz' Trekier backpack," I said.

"Yeah, the entire boys' varsity rugby team," she snarked.

I glanced out the window. Three people were already at the bus stop. I rushed to the door.

"What do you have in there that's so heavy?"

"Avalon! Remember, no picking for a month."

"This is going to be difficult," she whined.

As we ran down the steps, metal on metal clanked from within my backpack. My heart sank.

Avalon scrunched her face and ran an imaginary zipper across her lips.

Note to self: Reorganize my backpack for stealth mode. There were things even Avalon didn't need to know.

Chapter 4

"Why don't they offer freshmen an Honors World History Course?" I asked Wulf. "They offer honors courses in everything else, including choir."

"Maybe because you'd be the only person who would take that class."

"Not true." I glanced up at the security camera. My tension eased knowing that someone might be watching. *At least those eyes were there to protect.*

The hallway was a whirlwind of students. The fluorescent lights flickered briefly overhead, casting strange, shadow-selves that followed each person along the chaotic corridors. I spotted Eris approaching, fake-smiling eyes tossing evil daggers in my direction. We veered off to avoid contact.

"Why does she hate you so much?"

I shrugged and walked into class, bee-lining for my seat in the back corner. The seat furthest from the door. The safest seat.

Keefan turned around. "You look nice, Lottie." His smile started gently. One side lifted slightly higher than the other, creating that single dimple that always appeared when he was being charming. But then his eyebrows lifted, and a spark of something playful flashed in his eyes as they briefly dropped to take me fully

in. He tapped his pencil twice on my desk, a gesture between friendly and...
something else.

A red flush traveled up my face. Not a cute slight blush, but a bright red-hot
my feet are on fire look. I tried to whisper "thanks," but the word wouldn't come
out. I smiled. My pulse hammered in my ears, drowning out the sounds of the
classroom.

Idiot. My body betrayed me again. Sara said I was making progress, but I didn't
see it. Why couldn't I just attend school from home?

Mr. Ogden started class by continuing yesterday's lecture on racism during
World War I. Specifically, he focused on America, where at least 10 of the 77
lynchings in 1919 were of black veterans, some wearing their uniforms at the time.
I shuddered at the statistics.

It was common knowledge that slavery was primarily a Southern problem,
while the North worked to free the few enslaved that were here. Moorestown
and the surrounding areas seemed far removed from the horrors of racism, both
geographically and historically, I thought.

Mr. O moved on to current events. "I'm having trouble imagining how some
of the articles you submitted to me last night foreshadow a potential repeat of
major historical world events."

"Tiffina, you submitted the New York Times article from Saturday titled 'After
Temporary Break, Line to View Queen's Coffin is Reopened.' Can you explain
how that article could foreshadow the potential repeat of a notable past world
event?"

Tiff stood and walked toward the front of the class. She wore a Phillies shirt. My
eyes darted around the class. Everyone was wearing various team shirts. *Crap, it's
Spirit Day.* Specifically, wear your favorite team's shirt day. Between the Philly's
hot streak, the Eagles' win yesterday, and seniors with early acceptance showing
off their college pride, participation was high. Avalon should have warned me.

"This article is about the heavy traffic and lines people were willing to wait in to see the queen's coffin. She reigned for 70 years, and her approval rating was resoundingly positive among her subjects," said Tiff.

"That's all good and true, but how does that foreshadow a possible repeat of a major historical world event? Please defend," said Mr. Ogden.

"Because the United Kingdom is a constitutional monarchy, King Charles will have no role in politics or running the government. He will only remain a celebrity figurehead as long as the citizens agree. France, Greece, Italy, and Germany are just a few countries that threw over their monarchies. While Queen Elizabeth was wildly popular, her son Charles was not. The question is whether his recent bump can be maintained and whether the monarchy can survive."

"I'll accept that," said Mr. Ogden. He turned and said, "Sabielo, you're up next. You submitted the Washington Post article from the 16th, 'Iranian woman dies after detention by 'morality police,' stirring outrage.'"

Sabielo stood. "This is the story of Iranian women fighting for their rights. In the 1960s, Iranian women were able to wear miniskirts and go to college. Then they lost those rights to a group of men who saw women as incompetent, weak, and inherently sinful. Women had to cover up their bodies for fear of tempting men, putting the responsibility on women for men's thoughts and actions. While this Post article is about women again fighting for their rights to be free from tyranny, it's also a reminder to American women not to become complacent in our rights.

"Mr. Ogden, can you pull up my next link? This is the Southern Poverty Law Center website, which tracks hate organizations and groups advocating for male supremacy. Those groups' agendas often include reducing women to their reproductive function. They shame women for having sex while claiming the purpose of women is to have children. They espouse that wives are obligated to their husbands to look beautiful, while not causing other men to lust for them. These groups also place the responsibility for men's thoughts and actions on women."

Mr. O nodded. "Any comments?"

Foster stood up. "I'm not buying any of this. It's just feminist propaganda. It's overblown whining."

Wulf leaned over and whispered to me. "People who don't think shouldn't talk."

"Feminists speak about liberation, but their real agenda is to put down men." Foster sat down.

"Do we have any comments on this?" Mr. O looked around the class. "Lottie?"

CRAP! I forgot our deal. Mr. O was allowed to call on me this week. I rose, reminding myself to breathe. My heart pounded against my ribs, and my mouth went dry. Yet, my updated 504 plan didn't allow transient tachycardias due to a panic attack as a reason for not speaking in class anymore. My therapist and doctor agreed. *Traitors.* "Can you repeat that p-p-please?"

The class quieted down, which made it even worse. My eyes were getting moist as if I wasn't different enough already.

Mr. O smiled. "Do you have anything to add?"

"I agree with Sa-Sabielo." I dropped into my seat.

"As I believe many here do. Thank you," said Mr. O.

Crap. Crap. Crap. I had so much to say. My 504 plan used to protect me. It used to allow alternatives, including video presentations. But in high school, my 504 recently became my nemesis under the guise of preparing me for the real world. They just didn't understand. The changes were called "minor." I disagreed, but here we were.

I wished they'd let me be happy in my bubble. I wished they'd be open to my eventually going to college online and ultimately working from home. The bell rang.

"I'll see you at lunch," said Wulf.

I nodded, unsure if my shaking vocal cords had settled down.

I stopped at my locker to grab my notebook for my next class when I heard from behind, "Look, it's Turkel." It was Dax's voice. With that, a symphony of lockers clanged shut as other students' survival instincts kicked in as they fled the area.

As I glanced up, I saw Oscar was with Dax. That was even worse. They weren't interested in me, but that never stopped my mind from panicking and mentally figuring out escape plans and hiding spots.

Even when in the grocery store, I evaluated each person as to their being a potential predator. My plans were reevaluated on each visit. It was exhausting, yet it's where my mind went. I had plans for flight. I had plans for fight, knowing I'd never have the nerve to do that. My brain created thousands of plans over the years, yet I knew in an emergency, I'd likely freeze, or worse … I'd go into fawn mode again.

Oscar always raised my fear level whenever he was around. He was supposed to graduate this year. *God, I hope he graduates this year.* He was a bully in Elementary School, and he was still in High School.

I shut my locker and turned toward the commotion. Dax opened Tuck's locker, and Oscar tossed in Liquid Skunk. "Oops, sorry Turkel. I opened the wrong one," said Dax.

Jerks. I turned my back, guilt washing over me for not speaking up for Tuck. Full of shame, I walked down the hall.

Click click click.

Mrs. Grum jumped in front of me. *Could this day get any worse?*

As a freshman, I didn't have any classes with Mrs. Grum. She didn't know me, but we all knew her. We all avoided her. She stared at me, blocking my path. A sweat bead slid down the side of my face. I would have thought she was old by her bitter and tight-cheeked nature, but she was only in her late twenties. The longer she silently glared, the more I shook inside. Her outfit, posture, and attitude screamed, *"High-strung, uptight, and pain in the ...."*

"The student handbook on page 23 contains the Board of Education Code 5511 on student attire. It forbids students from wearing clothing that is a "distraction," she clucked. "All clothing must have sleeves. Specifically, halter tops are not allowed. You think you can waltz around here, distracting every boy in sight? Cover up. You should be ashamed of yourself." Mrs. Grum started to write me up.

I froze, unable to move, a tear dangled from my eye. I dared not blink or it might escape. A warm, friendly hand slid onto my shoulder. Tap tap tap tap. Tap tap. Morse code for Hi. I took a deep breath, relieved Parisol was here. My champion. We used to use Morse code, tapping lightly behind our plates during dinners when we didn't want our parents to know what we were up to.

"Mrs. Grum, I agree," said Parisol, dripping with sweetness, her head tilted slightly to an angle. "I just read this morning that men are losing their minds over women's scapulas and humerus heads this season. And really, there should be a different set of rules for girls who are .... hmmmm.... endowed, requiring them to hide their bodies." Parisol moved to my side and winked.

Not a real sister, but Parisol was the closest I had. She was sweet, kind, and a force to be reckoned with, even when she was just two years old. The story I heard over the years was that my mother, fully pregnant with me, was walking around the block. Parisol saw my mother and ran up to her, and blurted out, "You're fat." Parisol's mom was mortified. My mother laughed and told Parisol I would be coming soon. That's when Parisol proclaimed herself my big sister. Our moms grew close, and Dad cut an old wooden gate in half and installed it in the slim twenty inches where the corners of our backyards touched. Pavers were added when the well-worn path became a muddy mess during the rainy season. Soon thereafter came a flower garden and a white bench swing.

"Did I hear you mention scapula?" Dax asked, raising his eyebrows up and down.

What did Parisol see in him? Opposites? Maybe she'd find someone nice when he went away to college in the fall. Dax proudly wore his Preddington University Quillocrane shirt with the ravenous-looking bird, and put his arm around her. "I can't take you home after the game. I've got to pick up my mom from work. Her car's in the shop and she's chairing some big conference on P.R. for the doctors at Saint Rita's," said Dax.

Parisol smiled at me as they walked away. Dax never glanced in my direction. Dax never acknowledged my presence, even when I was at Parisol's house. After nine months of being around, he never said a word to me.

As they walked past Galen, his head followed her. Palmer put his hand on top of Galen's head, turned it back, and mouthed, "*Not for you.*" Galen had a thing for Parisol ever since first grade, when he proposed with a ring-pop on her first day of Kindergarten. The deal held for an hour until Parisol got hungry.

"Cover yourself up with something," Mrs. Grum snapped. "Next time I'll write you up." My shoulders drooped and rounded as I tried to make my chest smaller. She shoved her notepad in her pocket and walked away, her heels clicking down the hall.

Note to self: Kill Avalon.

Chapter 5

I wanted to sleep. My head throbbed, and my fingers burned from the cold. I needed to tell Mom to turn off the air conditioning. My wet toes dug into the carpet, and I inched forward. The walls of my room looked so strange. It was unusually dark, but I could make out my pillow beckoning to me. "Ouch." My knee landed on a sharp pebble. Crawling, crawling, dragging. Never had my bed felt so far or my room so dark.

My earring caught on a rough blanket. I hoped it wouldn't rip my ear. I lay on my side, took my earring out, and tossed it. *I'll find it tomorrow.* Eyes tired and fuzzy, sleep would help. I wormed over to my pillow, but it was freezing cold, wet, and rock hard.

A bright light came on in the hallway. "Mom, something's wrong with my pillow." Her silhouette continued to get bigger and bigger... until all I could see was a big hand coming at my face. It slammed down over my mouth. I tried to fight.

"Rrrrp." Tape was pressed over my mouth. I tasted blood from where my retainer jammed into my lip. My skin cracked and tore as I tried to scream underneath the tape. Fighting, I dug my fingernails in deep and pulled. "Bam". Something hit my chin. Searing pain, spinning, and nausea enveloped me.

I was lifted, carried a few steps, and tossed in. "Crrnch." I felt a door hit the top of my head. Up came a volcano of puke trying to escape my mouth, to no avail, with the tape holding strong. The vomit burned my throat, mouth, and nose as it spewed out my nostrils. I couldn't breathe. Choking. A haze swirled around....

I moved my arm and felt my fuzzy blanket underneath. No longer participating, my eyes popped open, and I sat up. The warmth of my bedroom enveloped me, chasing away the lingering chill. While still remembering, I grabbed my pencil and journal and wrote:

Taken. Wet. Head hurts.

Emotion: Panic.

Monday, September 19, 2022, 8:46 pm.

That's all there was that I could still remember. The rest was gone. I took a picture of the journal entry and looked around. My lights were on and my books were scattered on my bed. Rex opened one eye for half a second and then went back to sleep. Kami's green eyes peered from the top of the hutch above my desk. Always watching, never cuddling. I put the picture in a text to Avalon and scheduled it for a delayed send at 6:00 a.m. I needed to get back to studying and didn't need her calling.

Day 2, Tuesday, September 20, 2022

Chapter 6

Rex sprang out the door, bouncing with every step. Morning twilight was our favorite time of day, for different reasons. Rex loved any time he could romp and swim at the lake. I loved the stillness ... the peace of no people and no cars rushing about. As we walked along the lake on clear days and the sun came closer to the horizon, there were moments when the lake mirrored the prism of colors in the sky before any people interrupted the silence. Perfection.

We turned off our street and walked up Kings Highway towards the lake. Rex stopped and lifted his leg on a utility pole. No dog in the neighborhood could challenge the height of Rex's aim. Innate overmarking rules, alpha status, and bounding with joy; I smiled at the simplicity of Rex's life.

Looking up, I noticed the siding of a house at the top of the ridge pulsated with flashing police lights. Another step forward and several more houses danced with lights to varying beats. This was no little police presence.

An inner debate broke out between my anxiety and my curiosity. Rex broke the stalemate with his obstinacy against turning around. I pushed him, but he wouldn't budge. I assured myself we could walk around, whatever was going on, without human contact. So, on we went.

As we got closer to the top of the ridge, I saw dozens of police cars and vans parked at the corner of King's Highway and Haines Drive. On one side of Haines Drive were houses; on the other side, there was a paved walking path where the green grass sloped down to the water. Strawbridge Lake traveled along Haines Drive for 1.5 miles. I always thought of highways as being big thoroughfares. But in our town, Kings Highway was a street with one lane going in each direction. Suburbia.

Officers set up cones and detour signs. Two state police cars passed by silently with lights on.

A rescue team in a canoe shone a bright spotlight into the water. I saw enough. I dug around in the bottom of Rex's bag, past the XL poop bags, and found the emergency dog treat. I was about to bribe Rex to turn around when I saw Sabielo wrestling with a white tent. Everybody was too busy to notice she needed help.

I looked up at the dark sky, imagined breathing in courage, and continued to walk toward the lake. While those tents are advertised as an easy one-person setup, I've never found that to be the case.

Sabielo, while not a good friend, was more than an acquaintance. Teachers often partnered us up on projects over the years. She was assertive and fierce. *Hmmm... Sneaky buggers.* As if everyone around me for the last seven years wasn't a role model of someone less anxious than me.

"Need help?" I asked.

Rex watched the police while Sabielo and I put up the tent. We grabbed three tables from her father's car and unfolded the legs. Only then did I ask. "What's going on?"

"Oh, my God. You don't know? I presumed you knew." Sabielo took in a deep breath. "Parisol is missing."

I took a step back. Waves of black pulled me under. My heartbeat thundered in my ears, drowning out all other sounds. "What?"

My mind raced. *That can't be right. Mom would have told me.* I had trouble processing what Sabielo was saying. My heart ached.

Mom left me a note this morning that she'd be back soon, but I thought she was out getting donuts. She must be with Aunt June, Parisol's mom. It's not unusual for Dad to be out before me on Tuesdays for his weekly day trip to NYC for corporate meetings.

"What did you just say?" I asked.

"Parisol met Dax at the lake yesterday. He planned to drive her home, but Parisol had plans with Eris. She was in a lyric-writing state."

I knew what she meant. When lyrics came to Parisol, she had to get them out. She'd write on sticky notes, napkins, or her arm... whatever was available. Her room was filled. The inside of her closet had her lyrics written all over the walls. Even my black trampoline hadn't escaped Parisol's gold sharpied lyrics. As she got older, she moved to writing in an app on her phone.

Sabielo continued. "The plan was that Eris would pick up Parisol at 9 p.m. and then they'd head to Ice Cream on Main. But when Eris arrived, Parisol wasn't there. When she texted and called Parisol and didn't get an answer after a time, she called Dax and then Parisol's mom."

My world was spinning. Parisol, my sister, my first friend, was missing. *NO, NO, NO... this can't be true.*

A white van pulled up to the tent. Sabielo rushed toward it. I eyed the man to make sure he wasn't a threat. Rex seemed calm. The man was there to donate bottles of water and orange juice.

I felt confused and overwhelmed. I started tidying the area when I noticed two men fifty feet from us shining their lights on the archival stone. They brushed a swab against the stone and put it in a container, and the container into a bag. Then they did the unforgivable. They picked up the archival stone and put it in a plastic tub. I wanted to shout, "You better return that when you're done." But I didn't.

I pointed my arms towards the men and stuttered, "What d-do you think they are doing?"

Sabielo bit her bottom lip in thought. She then walked to the yellow tape, lifted it up, and walked over to her father, Detective Huerta. "Papi. ¿Qué están haciendo?"

After they chatted for a minute, she returned. "The state forensics team took a sample off the rock of some sticky substance." She paused and swallowed. "It tested positive for blood. They're taking the stone to the lab for further analysis." She then turned and pointed. "They found Parisol's cell phone over there in the brush near the water. And there was a gold earring two feet away."

I was losing my mind. *I must be in a nightmare. Wait ... last night's dream. FUP!*

My stomach lurched. "I've got to go." Rex and I ran home as more donations from local businesses arrived.

Chapter 7

Avalon grabbed the blanket off her bed and put it around me. "Is there anything I can do? Seriously, name it. A shoulder? A distraction? I'm totally here for whatever you need." *She reached over to tuck a strand of hair behind my ear that had escaped.*

"Stop being so nice."

"Don't you think it's time you let the police in on what you know?"

I wiped my eyes. "What do I know that will help the police? I had a dream last night where I woke and wrote the words 'Taken. Wet. Head hurts. Emotion: Panic.' And then quickly forgot the rest of the dream."

"You and I both know the dream remnants in your journal aren't normal dreams. Remember the RSVP dream. That was spooky," said Avalon.

"But I don't see how these eerie connections will help the police."

"We could bring in Wulf."

"Never. I am not going to turn into his science experiment."

"What? You always made a great guinea pig," said Wulf. Avalon and I jumped.

"You need a bell," I said. "How long were you standing there?"

"Long enough to know you two are hiding a secret. Something the police would want to know." He jokingly rubbed his hands together, mimicking an evil scientist. "Come on. Spill it."

"Seriously, Wulf, you need to vibe check the room," said Avalon.

There was something too upbeat in Wulf's demeanor. Did he not know about Parisol? Wulf wasn't a people person, pompous and bored by most, but he did understand social decorum and faithfully followed through on etiquette. In fact, he was an etiquette snob, ... well, when it pleased him to be.

After Avalon updated Wulf on Parisol, Wulf walked over and awkwardly hugged me. My arms remained at my sides as he encircled me with his arms. I must have grown, as my eyes now saw over the top of Wulf's head... well, just barely.

Wulf began pacing Avalon's room back and forth... back and forth. "I'm missing something here," he finally said. What secret are you hiding from me?"

Avalon looked at Wulf. "It's not my secret to share." Both of them turned and stared at me, the room falling silent for far too long.

"I'm thinking," I said. "How do I explain the unexplainable? How do I put into words things for which words have yet to be created?"

"Grrrgle." My stomach could be heard across the room. I tried to ignore it. "Grrrrrgggggle."

"I suppose I ought to eat or drink something or other; but the great question is, what?" I didn't feel hungry. My appetite was off. But I also didn't want to crash from not eating.

Avalon headed towards her door. "Let's see what my mom left. Wulf, you could go in late with us."

I made a mental note. Avalon hadn't mentioned that her mom was back. But then, she never did. But she also never mentioned when she went to the psychiatric retreats, either.

The grandfather clock in the hallway chimed the half-hour as we made our way to the kitchen, its familiar tone echoing through the otherwise quiet house. On the kitchen island was a white bag with a sticky note. I handed the note to Avalon. On it was a pink heart encircling the words "Love Mom." Parents across town were being overly attentive and huggy this morning.

I opened the white bag and peeked inside. The delicious smell drifted into the air.

"Scones?" Avalon asked while sliding plates around.

"Yes. It looks like Butterscotch, Lemon Blueberry, and Chocolate Chip," I said.

"Isn't Pie Lady closed on Tuesdays?" Wulf asked.

"I thought I saw their pastries on the donation table for the emergency workers this morning," I replied.

Wulf grabbed the tea box and pulled out Lemon Zinger.

"Tea?" I asked, surprised at his choice. My speech was muddled by the dark shadow hanging over every cell in my body.

"It's always tea time," said Wulf. He opened the cabinet with mugs. "Anyone joining me?"

I picked out a mocha coffee pod and held it up, but it felt fake. The corners of my mouth hung lower than I knew they could go. Just yesterday, my cheeks had ached from laughing with Parisol. Now those same muscles felt atrophied, useless. *I'm not sure I'll ever smile again,* I thought.

Wulf handed me a mug. "How's Parisol's mom holding up?"

"Mom said Aunt June is not doing well. Not that that is surprising. Mom and Dad are over there now, handling the phone and getting pictures out to the media. The next 48 to 72 hours are critical." I lay my head on the counter, emotionally empty, exhausted, and out of tears. The cool marble against my cheek was the only sensation that felt real. Avalon's phone vibrated, making a little buzzing sound that traveled along the counter and tickled my cheek. Avalon glanced at her phone. "The school brought in counselors, and everyone's posting about it. There's like a whole setup in the library and the chorus room."

Wulf looked up from his cup and directly at me. He looked hurt. "What I don't get is why you'd tell Avalon your secret and not me."

I picked up my head and met his gaze. I took a deep breath in and slowly let the air pass out over my lips. I had no words. I took in another breath. And then another.

"You've got to promise that you won't tell anyone what I tell you today, I said."

"Of course."

"No, I really want you to know what you're getting into. You cannot tell anyone. Not your parents, not the police, and not your online science buddies who tell you they are from CERN or NASA. No one." My chest tightened. I picked at the hem of my sleeve. "The only way to guarantee a secret stays secret is to tell no one." Ironically, I was telling Wulf.

Wulf stood up and put his hand over his heart. "I promise I will not breathe a word of this to anyone. While this friendship was forced on me seven years ago..."

Avalon cleared her throat. "Ahhh hmmm."

Wulf continued, "forced on all three of us. But you two... you're it for me. The only friends I have, or want. I'd never break your trust."

"Awwww." Avalon went over and hugged him.

Sharing secrets didn't come easy for me. They were to be hidden and pushed down to where no light could get to them. Dark secrets kept in little boxes, hidden from the world, ... hidden from myself at times. Sara, my therapist, tried to open the vault for years. My standard answer, *I'm fine. Nothing's wrong.*

"The only reason Avalon knows about this secret is because she was there when it was a nothing and then it turned into a something."

"Hmmm. I will tell you. But as I do, please be patient. Imagine if you had never tasted anything in your life, and then you tasted your first cookie. You'd suddenly experience not just the individual flavors of warm chocolate, sugar, and vanilla for the first time. But their synergy. How they combine into something more meaningful and decadent than any ingredient alone. If you were asked to describe that to someone who had never tasted anything before, you'd stumble and fall short. That's how it is for me, trying to put this into words."

I continued, "You should also know, being let into this secret, there will be times when you'll question your sanity."

"Oh, you can't help that," said Avalon. "We're all mad here."

Wulf wasn't deterred. "Excellent. The best scientists always are."

Chapter 8

My coffee cup was empty, yet I wasn't ready. I ran my finger around the edge over and over again. Avalon took it away and started to make me a cup of decaf.

Would I ever be ready to share all my secrets? I shook my head.

I looked at Wulf. "The year after Mrs. M put the three of us together, I guess that would have been second grade, ... do you remember the lunch meeting in guidance where she tried to get the three of us to meditate?"

Avalon butted in. "Yes. I couldn't get my brain to stop jumping around."

I looked at Avalon with crossed eyes and scrunched my face.

"Yes, I remember," said Wulf.

"Well, I told Sara about it, thinking she'd laugh. Instead, she thought meditation was a good idea. She had me meditate at the end of a few therapy sessions and had me practice at home.

"One of the visualizations she had me doing was walking towards a cottage. I was supposed to imagine leaving my worries as I went through the cottage gate. I could pick those worries back up later when I walked back out the gate if I chose to. But until then, she said the universe would hold onto those worries for me while I was resting.

"Over the years, I knew every detail of my cottage. The quilt was made by my grandmother. Love and blessings were sewn into every stitch. Walking behind the cottage, the animals played along the stream. I added everything that brought me peace to my infinite cottage property. It's endless.

"Then this past March or April, something changed. It's as if I had rested into a deeper zone. A place of restful consciousness and peace. A place that feels realer than here, and yet there is nothing physical to that location, despite its existing everywhere. In that zone, the closer I looked, the farther I found my consciousness reaching out in every direction.

When I'm there, I'm floating in perfect weightlessness, in harmony with everything and part of everything. Not merely the feeling of floating in a swimming pool, but complete freedom. Pure awareness that transcends physical boundaries.

"Initially, when I came back from that zone, I'd feel complete peace and love. Over time, I began to come back with a few words. I wouldn't remember the context, but I'd remember the overall emotion of how I felt while I was there. I could come back knowing I had been quieted, excited, at total peace, or terrified while there. The overall substance was peace and love in the one consciousness that envelops everything. However, there were times when I would visit areas where limitations and imperfections could be experienced."

One time, I came back with the word 'Liber' and knew that's where I was. When I looked up liber online, I found that in Latin it could mean inner bark, to liberate, or a place where things were recorded.

"All knowledge exists in Liber. It's pure consciousness. While there, I can think of any question and immediately know the answer. Without having a background in something, I can understand the depth and breadth of information light-years beyond what experts know today. Yet, the substance disappears upon waking.

"It always seemed so real, but as long as I was only bringing back a few words, how real could it be? I began to journal each experience, dating back to early May of this year."

"My Nanna gifted me this beautiful journal several years ago. I had no need for it until these experiences began. Now, its pages chronicle my journeys to Liber." I hesitantly opened it and showed Wulf the first time I recorded one of these."

Moorestown. Little kids trafficked.

1851. Emotions- Fear.

May 4, 2022, 9:04 p.m.

"In looking it up, I found this 1851 ad placed by Joseph Davis of Hartford, near Moorestown, advertising girls and boys, including some small girls, that he had a constant supply of from New York who could be had at his residence."

Monmouth Inquirer
Sat, Jun 14, 1851 ·Page 3

Freehold, May 31, 1851.   3w

NOTICE.—The subscriber has made arrangements with the Commissioners of New York, to furnish him with a constant supply of domestic help, such as hired girls and boys, and some small girls, which can be had at his residence, in the village of Hartford, near Moorestown, Burlington Co., N. J. All letters post paid.   JOSEPH DAVIS.
May 1st, 1851.   6m

Newpapers.com

"While I could sometimes make sense of the words I brought back, at other times there was no information, or the words were nonsensical. And sometimes, I didn't bring back any words at all."

I looked at Avalon. "At that point, I started questioning if I was going nuts."

Avalon looked up from her phone. "I just thought she was reading too much into her dreams. Well, that was until the night I slept over."

Silence dropped over the room when it was mentioned. I took a sip of my coffee.

"That's when everything changed. Avalon was sleeping over at my house, and she mentioned just before we nodded off that she was excited about Keefan Doyle's potion-making party at the Cauldron the following weekend. That's when I remembered that I hadn't emailed my RSVP to Keef yet. It really bothered me. The Cauldron had just opened, and I wanted to go. I asked Avalon to remind me to email him as soon as we woke up. As I was falling asleep, I kept reminding myself to email Keefan.

"That night, I was in Liber, but it was different. In it, I was floating in consciousness and typed an email RSVPing "yes" to Keefan's party in that one consciousness, and then I pushed the 'Send' button. When I realized I had just pushed 'Send' in that consciousness zone, I was kicked out of the dream. I sat up in bed and said to Avalon, "Oh my God. I just sent an RSVP by email to Keefan in that dream state, ... in that one zone.""

I took another sip of coffee. Wulf's elbow was on the counter, and his pointer finger was curled around his top lip in concentration. I couldn't tell if he thought I was nuts.

"Avalon was sort of pissed I had woken her up and said, 'What are you talking about?'"

"No, literally, I was thinking you just had weird dreams and I should never be woken up for them. But now this is actually insane."

"I told her again that I had sent an email RSVP to Keefan's party in that dream zone. I pushed the send button, and it was sent." I showed Wulf my journal entry from that day.

I emailed Keefan Doyle "yes" to his party.

Emotion – it was so real.

5:23 a.m., Saturday, May 14, 2022

"After eating breakfast, totally forgetting to really email Keefan, Avalon and I biked to Sunnybrook. While sitting next to the upper pool, Keefan's mom, Mrs. Doyle, came up to us laughing. She's usually put together, but this time she was laughing so hard that she was having trouble getting the words out. She sat down on the chaise lounge next to us and composed herself. 'Keefan would kill me, but I have to tell you… It's too funny,' she whispered.

"Shaking her head in disbelief, she said, 'This morning Keefan came downstairs and told me you emailed him 'Yes' to his party."

"At this point, I thought, *Holy Crap!*"

"Mrs. Doyle continued, "So, I marked you down as a yes. An hour later, Keefan returned to me and said, I think I just dreamed I received an email from Lottie, but it was so real… so very real. He went back and checked his emails, and there were no emails from you." She laughed and laughed."

"This was our moment of confirmation that what I was experiencing in that zone was real. The same night I sent an email RSVPing in that zone, Keefan received an email in his dream from me RSVPing, and he thought it was real. That is when Avalon joined me on the crazy train."

Wulf opened his mouth to say something. Then he closed it as Ozzy's "Crazy Train" began to play from Avalon's phone. "ALL ABOARD!" Ozzy sang.

Wulf glared, and she turned it off.

Finally, Wulf opened his mouth, and words came out. "I didn't think you'd want to go to a party in Philadelphia. Isn't that way outside your comfort zone?"

"Wulf. I tell you this story, and that's your first question? Yes, it was outside my comfort zone. That's why I procrastinated sending the RSVP."

Wulf started pacing the room and mumbling to himself. I caught words and pieces "... but Penrose thought ... then again LQG... mumble mumble mumble...MIT's Dormio Device... Hmmm, PEAR...cumulative deviation where x is the deviation from expected and n is the number of trials...."

Wulf stopped in front of me and turned. "You said you were kicked out of the dream. What did you mean by that?"

"When in this sleep state, where I'm just consciousness, there comes a point where I realize I'm watching my consciousness. Where I separate from being the consciousness, and instead I become aware of watching it. As soon as that happens, I get booted from sleep and am pushed into this half-asleep, half-awake zone. But that only lasts a second or two, and then I'm fully awake."

"Why do you think you have all this information and knowledge when in consciousness, but you don't bring it all back with you?"

"I don't know. I've tried and tried to take more with me, but it doesn't work. And if I don't write it down while still hanging in that hazy sleepish zone, the information... the memory disappears like smoke."

"Very interesting," said Wulf.

"That brings me to last night's journal entry." I opened the journal and showed him the entry.

Taken. Wet. Head hurts.

Emotion: Panic.

Monday, September 19, 2022, 8:46 pm.

"I immediately texted Avalon about it and then went to sleep. I didn't know Parisol was missing until this morning."

"Wait, that's so weird though," Avalon said, immediately checking her notifications. "I literally didn't get your text until 6 AM."

I opened up the text app's history, which showed when texts were sent. On the bottom right, I clicked on "More", "Options," and "Delayed History," and showed them I entered the text to Avalon at 8:48 p.m., but set it to send at 6 a.m.

Wulf looked up. "Let me get this right. You woke up from your dream and immediately wrote in your journal at 8:46 p.m. At 8:48, you entered the delayed text into the app. And Parisol was supposed to be picked up by Eris at 9 p.m., but she didn't show up. Did I get that right?"

"Yes."

I turned to Wulf. "Am I reading too much into this? Have I gone mad?"

He smiled. "I'm afraid so. You're entirely bonkers." Wulf nudged, "In the gardens of memory. In the palace of dreams. That is where you and Keefan met," said Wulf.

"But a dream is not reality," I said.

"Who's to say which is which?"

We heard a car door close. Avalon's mom was home.

"You're right, there is not enough here to bring to the police. Yet, there is a scientific explanation. It's just a matter of whether scientists today have progressed enough to know it. How about I marinate on it, and we talk at lunch?" asked Wulf.

Mrs. Duvois popped her head in the back door. "How's everybody doing?" she asked, looking at me. "Are you ready to go to school?"

Chapter 9

The cafeteria, which was usually very loud, was eerily quiet.

Our lunch period was generally the one that got in trouble for being the most raucous. Not the lunch that someone like me, who craved silence, wanted to be in. If I could go around throughout life wearing noise-canceling earbuds, I would. Especially since we sat at the table bordering the senior section. Too close to the action for me.

Wulf joined me at our table. He put down his backpack and whispered, "I was thinking about your dreams..."

"Hold that thought for a sec," I said.

Avalon was checking out at the lunch line and made her way toward us. She usually sat at the more popular freshman tables, bouncing around like a bee, but today she made a beeline for us.

Avalon sat down. "I've got news." She turned to me. "Can I share details about Parisol's case?"

I bit my bottom lip and nodded yes. I held my breath.

"Parisol found out yesterday that Dax was cheating on her. She had texted him to meet her at the lake because she planned to break up with him."

My blood boiled. *What an @#$%!.*

I had never trusted Dax, but I'd kept my opinions to myself. Now Parisol was missing, and her last hours had been spent dealing with his crap.

"No wonder she was in a lyric-writing mood. How did she find out?" I asked.

"Eris has been telling people that Parisol and she were watching the varsity boys' rugby game yesterday. Dax was in, and his phone dinged with a text message that made his phone glow through the side pocket of his backpack. Parisol grabbed his phone, and saw the message was from someone labeled 'Whisp,' and the text read 'I'm ready. Game over?' with a red lip print emoji. Parisol entered his password and read through all of Whisp's texts and pictures. She left the game without talking to Dax. When he later texted her asking where she went, that's when she asked him to meet her at the lake." Avalon took a breath.

Whisp. The nickname bugged me; it was not one I'd heard before. I mentally scrolled through possibilities. Maybe a nickname just between the two of them? Maybe she was from another school? Whoever this person was, I hated her. I filed the name away for later research. Parisol would have wanted answers, and so did I.

"Do you think Dax was involved in Parisol's disappearance?" asked Wulf.

"That's the thing," said Avalon. "Dax has been cleared."

Avalon stopped talking when she heard Galen's voice. Her crush of the month. Full stalker mode engaged. While only a junior, Galen generally sat with the Varsity Rugby players who claimed the table just inside the senior section.

I watched her attention shift. How quickly Avalon pivoted from crisis to crush. What she didn't seem to realize was that Galen had barely taken his eyes off the empty seat where Parisol usually sat with friends at lunch ... as if Parisol might still sit down. The same hopeful desire he'd maintained since first grade. Well, maybe not quite the same. A first grade ring-pop proposal wasn't in the same league as Galen's longing that echoed from his eyes over the past year. The tangled web of who liked whom in our school was almost as complicated as brain surgery.

"Yeah, my parents are blaming me and won't submit it to the insurance because of the deductible. I've left that bike leaning against the side of the house, charging under the overhang, for two years, and it's only been stolen this once. Nobody could have foreseen it would have been stolen," said Galen. But when Palmer started talking, Avalon lost interest and continued whispering.

"Sabielo told me that after Eris spoke with the police, they were looking at Dax as a suspect. But his phone's GPS showed that he left the lake and arrived at home, and stayed there long before Parisol and Eris had one of their text exchanges about going for ice cream. So Parisol must have been at the lake after Dax left her in order to text with Eris."

Oscar walked past and sat at the senior table, which was getting louder. Avalon lowered her voice even further. "Also, Sabielo overheard her dad say Dax's home security footage confirmed he arrived home at the same time his GPS showed him arriving home."

It's not surprising Sabielo would be all over these details. It fit with her wanting to be an FBI agent. She's been focused on the FBI since Career Day in first grade.

"What kind of idiot even uses an e-bike when you have a car?" Oscar asked loudly, breaking through all the soft conversations.

Galen picked up his waffle and flung it at Oscar's head. Oscar tossed one back, triggering a waffle war in the senior section. Palmer sent one whizzing past Rory's ear and into the back of Wulf's head.

Wulf turned to glance at Palmer. "Oh, what a delightful child!" He touched the back of his head. "Gross. Maple syrup." He walked off to find some napkins.

The war ended quickly due to a lack of ammo.

Wulf came back and poured water over a few napkins. "I've been thinking about that RSVP you sent to Keefan," he said, rubbing the napkins over the syrup in his hair. "What you experienced aligns with quantum entanglement. Einstein called it 'spooky action at a distance,' so you're in good company thinking it's eerie. But you are not crazy."

"I've put a few quantum theories together in a rough draft to explain some of what you experienced." He handed us his Latin notebook and turned to a formula that took up an entire page. "This science is in its infancy, and I'm taking leaps between theories, but there is something here. The preliminary correlations suggest a viable hypothesis."

It looked Greek to me.

Quantum Consciousness Transfer Formula

$$\Delta\Psi_c(t) = \int_{\tau_0}^{\tau_1} \exp\left(-\int_0^t \gamma(t')\,dt'\right) \cdot \langle\hat{O}(t)\rangle \cdot \hat{M} \cdot \hat{E} \cdot \eta(\lambda)\,d\tau$$

Where:

- $\Delta\Psi_c(t)$ = Non-local consciousness state change
  (probability amplitude for transfer)

- $\exp(-\int_0^t \gamma(t')dt')$ = Decoherence survival factor
  (how long coherence lasts before collapse)

- $\langle\hat{O}(t)\rangle$ = Self-observation operator
  (the act of awareness affecting the state)

- $\hat{M}$ = Quantum memory encoding operator
  (determines what information 'sticks')

- $\hat{E}$ = Entanglement preservation factor
  (strength of non-local linkage between minds or states)

- $\eta(\lambda)$ = Penrose-Hameroff microtubule coherence function
  (supports quantum-level integration in microtubules)

- λ = Planck-scale orchestrated objective reduction threshold
  (the fundamental limit for consciousness collapse)

Understanding nothing, I turned the page. More gobbledygook.

Core Theoretical Framework

This formula models consciousness as a non-local quantum field phenomenon utilizing AdS/CFT correspondence, where information exists holographically encoded on the boundary of spacetime. The key insight bridges Penrose-Hameroff's orchestrated objective reduction with Von Neumann-Wigner consciousness-induced collapse.

The temporal integration suggests certain brain states reduce decoherence enough to allow brief non-local access to information.

The microtubule coherence function $\eta(\lambda)$ accounts for Penrose's quantum gravity threshold, while the entanglement preservation factor $\hat{E}$ prevents information loss during consciousness state transitions, consistent with quantum error correction principles.

The formula suggests consciousness operates via quantum entanglement with the holographic boundary of spacetime itself, making all historical information theoretically accessible during specific brain states when decoherence is minimized.

"When did you have time to do this?" I asked.

"Health class." Wulf looked up. "As you know in quantum mechanics, information is never lost due to the holographic principle."

"No." Avalon and I said in unison, pretending to be shocked ... and to care. Wulf tried again.

"Lottie, you mentioned that there was a place where all information exists. That is suggestive of the holographic principle, where information is never lost."

"You also mentioned that the deeper you go within yourself, within your consciousness, the larger you find you spread out in every direction. That is suggestive of the quantum string, where the closer you look at the string and the deeper you go, the farther you find it spreads out.

"You mentioned that when you would go from participating in the action to realizing you were watching the action, being the observer, you were then booted out. That is suggestive of wave-particle duality."

"Think of it this way... Here we see a table." Wulf knocked on the table. "Classical physics tells us that this table, this matter, is made up of particles. In quantum physics, it also finds that it is made up of particles. The difference with quantum physics is that when we stop observing it, we find it's not made up of particles, but instead, it's made up of waves. The act of observation changes its form. If you observe it, it's a particle. If you don't observe it, it's a wave."

I glanced at Avalon. She was already zoned out and paging through her phone.

Wulf could tell my attention was wandering. "I'll give you just two more examples," said Wulf. His special form of torture.

"I'll try to hold on. But no promises."

"The storage of information in quantum physics is also different from classical physics. For example, quantum computers have qubits instead of bits. Bits in normal computers are either set to a zero or a one. However, a qubit is in a state of all possibilities. Think of the thought experiment of Schrodinger's Cat. You put a cat in a box with poison and put the lid on the box. You don't know if the cat is alive or dead or in some range of possibilities between until you take off the lid and observe the cat. But once you observe it, that's it."

"You also mentioned having trouble remembering everything when you went from being part of the larger consciousness to being Lottie in this physical form. That is suggestive of the connection being lost and the entanglement ending. Imagine infinite knowledge on any subject trying to come back into your brain with limited RAM, processing speeds, and memory. There is no way what you experienced is ever coming back here fully intact. Your experience was in qubits, but you are trying to remember it in bits. It will never be fully retained, except when in your quantum consciousness."

"Thanks, Wulf! That actually made sense to me, sort of. Well almost. It's as if coming back, I'm trying to pour the ocean through a straw. No wonder I can only bring back fragments. Like trying to describe a symphony when I can only remember a few notes and I don't play any instruments."

With that, Avalon snapped a picture of her lunch and quickly sent it off into her social ether.

I understood a quarter of what Wulf said. Maybe not that much. Thankfully, Mrs. M stopped Wulf from quizzing us on science back in third grade. Not a character trait for maintaining friendships.

"I do believe quantum physics is where the answer to your experiences lies. While it seems magical, it's just science. Physicists have begun to find quantum elements in studies of human brains. We all must have this ability."

"I told you," I said as I nudged Avalon.

"I have an idea of how you might be able to enter this zone more consistently," Wulf said, his voice dropping to barely above a whisper. His eyes held that intense focus I'd only seen when he was onto something significant.

I leaned forward despite myself. "What kind of idea?"

"Maybe getting back into that state will help you remember something about Parisol or even connect with her." The words hung in the air between us.

A shiver ran up my spine. The thought of deliberately seeking that connection, of possibly reaching Parisol somehow through the quantum field, was both terrifying and compelling.

The bell signaling the end of lunch period rang, but none of us moved. Whatever Wulf was about to suggest, I knew our afternoon was about to take an unexpected turn.

Chapter 10

Avalon and I let ourselves in Wulf's back door. It was always unlocked, having not survived the lock-picking experiments of 2017.

Mr. Biko should have suspected we were the culprits when we jumped in the car to go to Home Depot with him. It wasn't until we examined the available locks and started discussing cylinder bumping, a way to force the tiny pin-and-tumbler parts into position without a key, that he realized what we'd been up to. At that point, he decided to forego lock replacement until the 'phase was over.'

Avalon shouted, "Wulf, where are you?"

"Down here."

Walking down the basement steps, I heard the hum of the ancient dehumidifier and breathed in the distinct scents of 1970s wooden paneling and recent soldering. These sounds and smells were both familiar and comforting. The remnant of smoky soot in the corner of his basement and the dent in the wall stood as physical reminders of our failed experiments over the years. While we usually succeeded eventually... well, most times; on first tries, we had our share of calamities.

Looking around the basement, Wulf had moved the old La-Z-Boy into the middle of the floor. He stood on the couch, pulling the shade down over the cellar window, and motioned for me to sit in the chair.

"Aristotle wrote that sleep is the borderland between being and not being. A place between living and not living where a person who is asleep is neither completely non-existent nor completely existent," said Wulf.

Avalon looked up from her phone. "Sort of like Schrodinger's Cat before the lid is taken off."

Our eyes darted to Avalon in disbelief.

"What? Just because I actually have a social life doesn't mean I don't listen. I can multitask."

Wulf jumped off the couch. "Many people throughout history have claimed that waking while in the hypnogogic zone, what we now call the N1 sleep state, is when people are able to access unique and creative ideas.

"Albert Einstein, Thomas Edison, and Salvador Dali all practiced rousing themselves out of the hypnagogic state in order to find answers and creativity. Salvador Dali took naps sitting up in a chair while holding a key. When he'd start to fall asleep, he'd drop the key, and the clank would wake him. He said waking at the moment of falling asleep 'revivified' him.

"Albert Einstein napped in a favorite chair, holding a spoon to tap into inspiration. Edison said his mind was flooded with images when he woke from this zone."

Wulf's usual scientific detachment slipped for a moment as he handed me the metal balls. "I know it seems like I'm just excited about the experiment, but," he yanked his earlobe, a gesture I'd come to recognize as his way of hiding emotions. "Parisol's been a part of my life, too, over the years. Whatever I can do to help find her, even if it means working with Avalon on a social media campaign," he shuddered, "to bring her home. I'm all in."

The brief vulnerability disappeared as quickly as it had appeared. He straightened his posture, and his voice returned to its lecture tone. "There have been studies proving that waking during the N1 sleep stage provides more answers and creativity than either not sleeping at all or waking during the N2 stage. Since the N1 stage lasts only 1-5 minutes, you won't be in it for long."

"In one study, participants were given a problem to think about. Participants who spent at least 15 seconds in the N1 stage had an 83% chance of discovering the hidden rule. Participants who remained awake had only a 30% chance. Participants who were allowed to drift from N1 into N2 sleep had the boost disappear. Therefore, the sweet spot for answers and creativity exists in waking during the N1 stage."

"It would be nice to have MIT's Dormio Device. It's a wearable technology that tracks sleep transitions and wakes users during N1 to capture hypnogogic insights. Instead, we have metal cookie sheets and metal balls. Wulf placed the cookie sheets on the carpeted floor next to me to ensure a solid clanking sound when I fell asleep and dropped the balls. I placed my journal and pencil on my lap.

"Some people report that focusing on the problem as they enter sleep helps them to zero in on the issue. Similar to how you were thinking about emailing Keefan the RSVP when you fell asleep. Try to focus on Parisol as you doze off."

I felt them staring at me from the couch as Wulf turned off the light. The darkness transformed the familiar basement into a void where sounds seemed sharper and closer. The metal balls grew heavier in my hands, their surface cooling against my palms. A sudden glow illuminated the room, casting eerie shadows across Avalon's face.

"Avalon!" said Wulf.

She turned off the screen, plunging us back into complete darkness. I closed my eyes and tried to relax, though it hardly mattered in the pitch black. I knew they were watching. It was unnerving trying to fall asleep while being observed. The opposite of peaceful meditation.

Avalon flicked her nails.

Focus, I told myself.

Flick. Flick. Flick.

"Avalon. Shhhh."

"Sorry."

Being disconnected from her phone, Avalon couldn't stop fidgeting.

Creeeeak. The springs in the old couch let me know every time a butt shifted.

I tried focusing on the spot in the middle of my forehead that sometimes tingles during meditation. I focused on that spot opening and getting larger and larger.

Tap Tap Tap came from Avalon's direction.

"You two, upstairs," I said.

Avalon turned on her phone's flashlight and sprang up the stairs, relieved to be back online. Wulf followed her and shut the door.

I closed my eyes and moved around in the chair to get comfortable. Holding the balls over the arms of the chair was not natural and a bit awkward.

The weight of what we were attempting pressed in on me. If I actually managed to connect with Parisol, what state would I find her in? My mind threw up pictures of the worst possibilities. I shook my head to clear these images of doom and refocused on peace, love, and past joyful times with Parisol, imagining her safe and well.

This mental shift worked, replacing fear with positive, happy memories in my mind's eye. But what could I even do to help her from inside that consciousness zone? Still, just knowing where she was would be something, a direction, a purpose. Anything would be better than this helpless waiting.

I changed strategies. I focused on tightening and releasing each muscle in my body, starting with my toes and working up to my head.

Minutes later, muscles more relaxed, I imagined Parisol and me walking down the dirt path toward my cottage. But unlike the past, when I chose someone to occasionally join me at my cottage, this time it felt forced. It wasn't spontaneous. Rather than being natural like the ebb and flow of soft ocean waves, this time I paddled against the tide, trying to make it happen.

The wall I had built to contain my emotions crumbled. A tsunami of tears streamed down my cheeks as my chest heaved with short, desperate breaths. "This isn't going to work," I gasped between sobs. "I'm failing her!"

Chapter 11

Time passed before I felt composed enough to face anyone. Glancing at my reflection on my phone, I winced. My red nose and streaked cheeks practically shouted "emotional breakdown." I wished I had some powder. My backpack held many things, but makeup wasn't among them. Avalon's purse was upstairs. With no way to hide the evidence of my tears, I opened Candy Crush Saga and gave my face time to return to normal.

Eventually, I gathered the metal balls and cookie sheets. I heard Mrs. Biko talking in the kitchen upstairs and made my way up from the basement.

Seeing me come up the basement steps holding cookie sheets, fear crept into Mrs. Biko's face. "Don't worry. No messy experiments today," I assured her.

She nodded and came over for a hug, a long one that spoke volumes. When she finally let go, she headed upstairs, passing the window ledge lined with mason jars of thriving herb plants. Beyond them, her beehives stood in the backyard, their white boxes gleaming in the afternoon sun. Even in crisis, the Biko household maintained its gentle rhythm of composting, conserving, and nurturing.

A few moments later, settled in the Bikos' living room, we faced the reality of our failed attempt. I looked at Wulf and Avalon. "I'm sorry, no success. It felt unnatural."

Avalon's thumbs paused over her phone screen, and she glanced up. Something in her expression softened. "We'll figure something else out," she said with unusual gentleness. She tucked her phone away, a rare gesture of her full attention that spoke volumes about her concern.

"Hmmm." Wulf knitted his brows. "Was there anything that changed back in April when you went from having your normal meditation practice to when you started coming back with words?"

"I can't think of anything. Wait." I tapped my fingers against my temple, searching my memory. "We learned from Mrs. M that we shouldn't get so comfortable during meditation that we'd fall asleep. Sara agreed with that, as did the articles and videos I watched on meditation. I followed that advice ... well until...."

I leaned forward, the realization dawning. "One day, I was so tired sitting in the chair meditating that my head nodded down for a second and popped back up. I tried to stay awake, but my head kept nodding, and then I'd wake with a jerk. I was so tired and craved sleep so badly that I allowed myself to slide off the chair onto the floor and to float into delicious sleep." My voice softened with the memory. "I'm not sure I brought back a word that first time. It was sometime around then when I noticed that there were a few seconds when I remembered a few words. From then on, meditations often transitioned into a blissful light nap."

Wulf's eyes lit up with that familiar spark of scientific discovery. "In order to trigger quantum entanglement for you, you might need to be lying down. Not everyone can relax or sleep everywhere like Avalon," he said, gesturing toward her.

Avalon looked up from her phone. "What? It's my superpower."

Wulf stood up, back in full lecture mode. "Tonight, you'll have a few chances of waking during the N1 stage. The stages of sleep are N1 (1-5 minutes), N2, N3, and REM. The total cycle lasts 90-120 minutes, and it repeats 4-6 times per night." His expression grew serious. "And don't forget to think about Parisol as you fall asleep."

As if I could stop thinking about Parisol.

Chapter 12

I floated lazily on a stream, bobbing up and down as the current meandered, when I realized I was floating in Liber. Conscious that I was half in the zone and soon to be booted out, I wondered what I should take back with me.

The cool night air on my skin and Rex's soft snoring in my ear pulled me back to my bedroom reality. I sat up, grabbed my pencil, and wrote as fast as I could.

"Cart's Tayle...Parisol." *Think, think, think. Crap.* It's gone.

I wrote:

Cart's Tayle...Parisol.

I was with Parisol. She's alive!

Emotion: Petrified

Tuesday, September 20, 2022, 11:59 p.m.

I wanted to scream. A sob of relief caught in my throat, quickly followed by a wave of helplessness that made my stomach clench. She was alive ... the single most important fact in the universe right now. But "petrified" echoed in my mind, a counterpoint to my relief. The space between knowing she existed and being able to bring her home felt like an uncrossable chasm.

I took a picture of the journal entry and texted it to Avalon and Wulf. No response.

I sent a 2nd text message, "Meet 15m b4 bus"

I jumped out of bed. Kami's two green eyes glowed from the top shelf of my closet. Thank goodness Rex didn't try to follow our cat up to her perches. On my desk, the framed photo of Parisol and me at last summer's block party sparkled in the moonlight, her smile frozen in time. I grabbed my computer and hopped back in bed.

What the heck is a "Cart's Tayle?"

Day 3, Wednesday, September 21, 2022

Chapter 13

Rex put his paw on my arm and lay his head on my stomach. For the first time, I didn't look forward to our morning twilight walk. Parisol was missing, and the place where I cleared my mind and which gave me energy was now a crime scene. Every cell in my body whispered, *Stay in bed until this nightmare is over.*

I pulled the blanket over my head and repositioned for hibernation when the extra-large drooler rolled in my direction and slid me onto the floor. *Rex must be an operative for Sara.*

I hesitantly dressed for our walk and opened the front door. *Yet, better not.* I took off my backpack and pulled out the pepper spray from one side pocket and the loud siren alarm from the other. With an assailant around, best to have them in hand while walking before sunrise. Rex ignored my gloom and sprang out the door.

It wasn't until we arrived at the corner across from the lake that I saw the police tape was still up. Rex let out a vocal whine as we walked in the street along the shoulder of Haines Drive. He longed to chase the geese sleeping near the dam into the water. Not that he ever caught them. He pretended to try, and they pretended to be startled. Their daily game. I patted his head and kept walking.

Coming upon the sister trees, I wasn't able to jump through them, nor touch them to say *good morning*. Instead, I stopped and bowed my head. The earth had an open wound of dirt where, up until yesterday, the archival stone had rested between them. The outline of the missing stone was visible where the grass had grown up around its edges.

This spot, where I'd had so many peaceful moments, where past and present seemed to merge, now felt violated and incomplete. My mind briefly imagined Parisol lying here, but I quickly shook the thought away. No time to shatter into a million pieces.

The water's edge was closed to us today. We couldn't go out on the L-dock or take the secret path through the brush and jump across the little stream. The straight dock was also off-limits, but the yellow tape appeared to end ahead, where the thicket of trees came close to the road.

Finally, at the section known to locals as Whispering Waters, no yellow tape in sight, I was able to release Rex. After a half mile of being denied his independence, he zoomied around the old trees. His face pulled back into a huge smile with his jowls pinned to his ears. He ran past the tree with the long limb, where many Moorestownians sat for romantic pictures. Not so much recently though, with branches haphazardly falling from old age. With my very incomplete knowledge of dendrology, it looked to me like a turkey oak tree with birch tree leaves. But that couldn't be right.

The tall brush at this time of year limited Rex from finding an entrance to the lake. We walked through the little meadow and around the hidden bend to the pebble beach where the lake makes a sharp turn. Depending upon who from the township was operating the tractor, this path could be cut narrow and come in at an angle and be invisible from the street, or it could be cut wide and visible from the street. It was narrow and angled on this visit. My preference is always invisibility.

Rex ran into the water; his vision of heaven. Next to having a moment of unrestrained joy oneself, was there anything better than watching an animal playing joyfully without a worry in its head? Watching others in unencumbered, bubbly states rejuvenated me. Better yet were those moments when nobody was around and I let the joy that bubbled up from within, where my inner light was free to dance. There would be none of that today.

Looking down at the pebbles under my feet, the water just an inch from my toes, I realized how clean the park was. Usually, there would be a few pieces of trash around that lazy people left; but after the police scoured for, picked up, bagged, and mapped every man-made item on the ground, it was immaculate.

After following a turtle twenty feet out into the lake, it disappeared before Rex's eyes. After a few minutes of looking for his friend, Rex returned to the lake edge, where he stood in four inches of water. Nudging the lily pads and floating leaves with his nose, he hoped to find a frog to pester.

While most trees wouldn't lose their leaves for a month or two, some leaves had already fallen and were clumping together at the water's edge. Rex loved digging into this dark brown mess of decaying leaves and mud. Sometimes, he'd find a snake wanting to be left alone, and other times, little tadpoles. He turned over some muck, and what initially looked like leaves was a flip-flop. He left it alone and went out for one more swim. When he came back, we continued our walk at a faster pace. I needed to be back early to update Avalon and Wulf.

Walking at the water's edge, I could see people beginning to appear on the path. First a dog walker, then a jogger. Then, a thought popped into my head. *What if the flip-flop was left by Parisol's abductor? And what if somebody disturbs it after we leave?* We kept walking. *No time to think about that now.*

A minute later, with it still weighing on my mind, we turned around, and I took a picture of the flip-flop lying in the water. I flipped it over with the help of a stick and took a picture of the other side. It was stamped on the sole with a 10 with a circle around it. My conscience was clear; I had the evidence that a flip-flop was here, and Rex and I continued our walk.

But if it was evidence, the police wouldn't know I had a picture of it, I thought. *Don't be stupid. There is no way it is evidence....*

But what if it was? What if the flip-flop could help the police find Parisol? But then I'd have to call the police. No way. Never. Can't do it.

And even if I could call them, and even if I could talk to them, they'd roll their eyes at how idiotic I was being. A flip-flop. All settled, we kept walking.

But what if this piece of evidence had a one-in-a-million chance of leading the police to Parisol? She'd be calling right now if I were missing. Frick. I was going to have to call the police.

I HATE THIS!

My hands shook so badly I nearly dropped my phone. Sweat broke out across my forehead despite the cool morning air. I pulled out my phone and stared at it for a minute or three. Then the voice in my head said *Just do it!*

I pushed the buttons and heard. "911. What is your emergency?"

"This is Lottie Aaraniah. I'm at Straw... Strawbridge Lake, where the police were yesterday." I took a deep breath, "and picking up and bagging. Walking my d-d-dog, flip-flop. Probably nothing." Long pause. My brain froze.

"I'll send an officer out to you shortly."

Not what I wanted to hear. What I wanted was, *it's nothing. You can go about your business.* More likely, the dispatcher thought I was having a stroke or was on drugs.

It was getting later. A father showed up with his little boy, setting up for a morning of fishing. Dad had his oversized chair and heavy pole, his son had a tiny folding chair and toy pole to match. Adorable.

An elderly couple strolled past and waved. I waved back like it was just another ordinary morning.

Then I looked down at my feet. At Rex. Back at my feet. This really, really sucked.

Then I heard it... ""Eee-ow, Eee-ow." A siren.

JUST KILL ME NOW!!!!

Sara's voice popped in my head. *Breath. Feel the breeze on your cheeks and the angle of the ground beneath your feet. Smell the autumn leaves in the air. Use your senses.*

As the officer walked towards me, I realized the pepper spray was still in my hand. I jammed it into the back pocket of my jean shorts. *Great! Now I'll be charged with carrying pepper spray while underage.* Rex, sensing my anxiety, circled around me, letting me know I was safe.

The officer introduced himself. I opened my mouth, but nothing came out. I swallowed and tried again, but my brain was truncating everything. "Walking Rex... Flip-flop... Thought of Parisol. But unlikely."

I sounded like an idiot. Rex put a paw on my foot. I shifted my weight from one foot to the other and leaned back on my heels. Anything to help me from spiraling.

"Can you explain it more thoroughly?" He asked.

Another car drove up behind the police car and parked. It was Sabielo's dad, Detective Huerta.

"Oye Lottie, I'm glad you called. Hola Rex." He leaned down and petted Rex, who was very happy to see him.

He looked at the officer and said, "I'll take it from here."

The officer nodded, took a step back, and stood there waiting for Detective Huerta to take over the questioning. After Detective Huerta stared at the officer and the officer didn't get the hint, he motioned for him to head to his car. The officer nodded and walked away.

When out of earshot, he said, "Newbies, eh?"

I nodded.

He looked around. "Do you want to go sit on that bench?"

I nodded. We walked back to the bench under the old trees, but this time there were no zoomies. Rex sat on the grass between us, making himself available for pets from both sides. We must have stared out at the water for five minutes before

I realized he was waiting for me to be comfortable. It took another minute for me to find my voice.

"On our morning walk, Rex turned up a flip-flop at the water's edge. It's likely nothing. But just in case, I wanted to let you know about it after all the work you did scouring the lake yesterday."

"Sounds like we missed something. Can you show me where it is?"

We went over and he bagged it. I figured he was just being nice.

As he was gearing up to leave, he wrote down his cell phone number and handed it to me. "Just in case. I know you and Parisol are very close. Call with anything, and I do mean anything, you think might be of interest."

He headed back to his car, and I looked at my phone. Three missed calls from Avalon and a text asking if I was running late. *Maybe if I cut through Mrs. Dikastis' yard.*

Chapter 14

Sneaking through the hole in the split rail fence was easy. I knew it well. What I hadn't counted on was how tall and thorny the rose bushes in Avalon's backyard had grown.

My phone vibrated and I ignored it. The lingering scent of fresh-cut grass mixed with the sweet perfume of late-blooming roses, a stark contrast to the bag of Rex poo I was now carrying. As we stepped out of the bushes, I pulled a branch of tiny thorns from Rex's coat. I hoped Mrs. Dikastis didn't see me walk through her yard with Rex.

"Should we call Lottie's mom?" I heard Avalon ask from within her garage.

"NO," I said. They both jumped.

My hair was a bigger mess than usual, which is hard to imagine. I was blessed or cursed, depending upon how you looked at it, with troll doll hair. Lightweight blond frizz that went in every direction, especially up .... as if my hand was on the static electricity machine at the Franklin Institute. Someone told me I had Einstein's hair, just longer. Actually, right now, it was just taller after rising while going through the rose bushes.

"Sorry, I'm late," I said, trying to straighten and push down my fluff. I looked across the street to the bus stop. "You saw my text?" I asked.

They nodded.

"I looked up Cart's Tayle, and it's just the old English way of writing at the tail end of the cart. Some places used the old spelling up until the mid-1700s."

Wulf walked up close, within my personal space. "I found the same thing," he said while picking what I hoped was a leaf out of my hair.

"I'm going to take the day off and head up to the Burlington County Historical Society to see if I can find something on Cart's Tayle, but I don't have high hopes." Visiting historical societies and rummaging through old books and diaries were my passions. The one in Burlington City was especially nice, consisting of four buildings.

"I'm surprised your mom is leaving Parisol's mom to take you there," said Avalon.

"Actually, I'm going to take the NJ Transit bus. No need to take Mom away from Aunt June. And no need to concern her."

"WHAT?" Wulf and Avalon said in unison.

"You, Lottie Aaraniah, are going to take the public bus?" asked Avalon.

Hopefully. Honestly,.... not likely. I would try. But, I nodded "yes" anyway. I busied myself with brushing imaginary dirt from my sleeve, avoiding their eyes that might see right through my false confidence.

Wulf handed me a few sheets of paper. "I've updated the Quantum Consciousness Transfer Formula to take into account the sudden collapse when observation occurs, that is, when you get booted upon realizing you are watching, rather than being the consciousness."

I looked down at the pages and thanked him, knowing full well that I would never look at these pages again. But I appreciated that he thought I might be able to comprehend it.

Quantum Consciousness Transfer Formula, Ver. 2 and the Enhancement of The "Observer Paradox" Resolution:

$$\Delta\Psi_c(t) = \int_{\tau_0}^{\tau_s} \exp\left(-\int_0^t \gamma(t')dt'\right) \cdot \langle \hat{O}(t)\rangle \cdot \hat{M} \cdot \hat{E} \cdot \eta(\lambda) \cdot \Theta(\tau_s - t)\, d\tau$$

$$\Delta\Psi_c = \lim_{\varepsilon\to 0}\int_{\tau_0}^{\tau_s - \varepsilon} \exp\left(-\int_0^t \gamma(t')dt'\right) \cdot \hat{M} \cdot \hat{E} \cdot \eta(\lambda) \cdot \psi_{GHZ}(t)\, d\tau$$

Where:

- $\tau_s =$ Spontaneous collapse time
  (when metacognitive awareness 'boots' you out)

- $\langle \hat{O}(t)\rangle =$ Self-observation operator
  (≈ 0 during unified superposition, $\to \infty$ at self-awareness)

- $\gamma(t) =$ Dynamic decoherence coefficient
  ($\gamma(t) = \gamma_0 + \beta\langle \hat{O}(t)\rangle^2$)

- $\Theta(\tau_s - t) =$ Heaviside step function
  (sharp cutoff at collapse moment)

- $\hat{M} =$ Quantum memory encoding operator
  (determines what information 'sticks')

- $\hat{E} =$ Entanglement preservation factor
  (maintains non-local linkage between states)

- $\eta(\lambda) =$ Penrose-Hameroff microtubule coherence function

- $\gamma_0 =$ Base decoherence rate

- $\beta =$ Coupling constant for self-observation strength

- $\psi_{GHZ}(t) =$ Greenberger-Horne-Zeilinger entangled state
  (maximal entanglement with historical information)

Enhancement - The "Observer Paradox" Resolution

New Elements:

- $\psi_{GHZ}(t) =$ Greenberger-Horne-Zeilinger entangled state (maximal entanglement with historical information)

- $\lim_{\varepsilon \to 0} =$ Captures the infinitesimal instant before collapse

- $\int_0^t \gamma(t')dt' =$ Cumulative decoherence loss

Framework Addition:

- The Consciousness-History Entanglement Principle:
  The formula incorporates quantum archaeology — the theoretical ability to reconstruct past quantum states through entanglement with the universal wavefunction. During deep consciousness states, individual awareness becomes entangled with Everett's many-worlds branches containing historical information.

- The Metacognitive Collapse Theorem:
  Self-awareness acts as a quantum measurement, instantly collapsing the superposition of temporal states. Increased self-observation terminates the experience — a quantum measurement destroying the coherent historical superposition.

"This is exciting because it suggests a testable mechanism," said Wulf, bouncing. "We might actually prove how consciousness can access non-local information through entanglement with the holographic structure of spacetime."

"Squeeeeeeeak." The unmistakable sound of the brakes on our bus coming around the corner. Wulf and Avalon started jogging to the bus stop. Wulf stopped mid-street and turned around. "Should I go with you today?"

Avalon spun around, too. "You'd better text me hourly updates, or I'm posting that picture of you falling in the mud at Johnson's Farm!"

"Stop worrying. I'll be fine." I lied.

Chapter 15

Cars passed by every few seconds as I walked up Kings Highway towards the bus stop located between Foxwood Drive and Lenola Road. This was not my usual time for a walk. It was too people-y and I was Rex-less.

On top of that, I had never taken a public bus. The school bus was scary enough.

Mrs. Ross from the corner house waved from her garden, calling out, 'Tell your mom I have extra tomatoes!'

"Will do!"

While walking, I downloaded the NJ Transit app and bought a $2.75 one-way ticket.

I was trying to navigate the app, as I walked down the road and crossed over Strawbridge Lake, when a bird flew off a nearby branch and made me flinch. My hypervigilant nervous system fully engaged. *No time to give in. Keep walking.*

My heart beat slowed down, remembering I lived in a storybook town where people waved, parades still mattered, children rode their bikes to the library, and occasionally Mrs. Claus read *the Night Before Christmas* at the tree lighting on the Community House mansion's expansive lawn.

The peace lasted a half block before my brain got in the way.

Dozens of questions about the bus ran through my mind. *What if someone sits next to me? What if the bus has no air conditioning? What if I get off at the wrong stop?*

I could hear Sara's words ringing in my ears: "Stop catastrophizing. Use your senses. What is around you when you get on the bus? How does the back of the bus seat feel? What are the smells?"

The transit website emphasized activating one's ticket before getting on the bus, so I activated my ticket for bus #413. It was scheduled to arrive in Moorestown at 8:19 a.m. and in Burlington City at 9:30; three times as long as it would have taken by car. I took a drink from my water bottle and put it back in my backpack.

At the bus stop, I sat on the stone wall, my feet dangling over the edge. I continued to read the transit instructions. "Tickets expire 30 minutes after activation." Wait what? Maybe that should have been written at the top of the page.

I had activated my ticket ten minutes before the bus was scheduled to arrive, and it was now 8:38. The ticket would expire in less than a minute.

My phone vibrated. "How's the bus?" Texted Wulf.

"Running late."

"And how is your anxiety?"

"What anxiety?" I spotted the bus coming. "GTG bus."

"Farefaren."

I was so worried about my ticket expiring that when I stepped up onto the bus, I forgot all my bus worries. Thankfully, the ticket reader was down, and the Driver said, "You're good."

I sat towards the front of the bus, figuring it was a safer spot. I was surprised. It was clean, had good air conditioning, didn't smell, and most importantly, there were only three other passengers on board. It wasn't anywhere near as scary as I had imagined. More passengers did get on board over time, but not enough for people to need to share rows. I'm glad I didn't go during rush hour.

As more people got on board, my stomach knotted, and my pulse thudded in my ears. I ran through each of my senses. I saw the color of the seats was grey. They felt hard, but I wouldn't be uncomfortable in them for a trip that was less than an hour. I heard people chatting behind me.

When I drew in a breath to smell, I discovered the man sitting in front of me reeked of weed. *I'm glad he's not driving*, I thought. I pulled out my water bottle and drank some more.

I always loved going to Burlington City. It was chock-full of history, having been settled five years before William Penn even arrived across the Delaware River to create Philadelphia. People think of William Penn as being the first to conduct his "Holy Experiment" where people experienced freedom of religion. But, such ideas were actually in place five years earlier when Quakers moved into Burlington in West Jersey.

I chugged more water. Panic attacks always left me thirsty. I pulled out my phone, wanting to see if there were any updates on Parisol. One article suggested the police were investigating whether Parisol's disappearance was related to the two murdered women found in the white dresses. It made me nauseous to think about. I took another drink of water.

I flipped to the other local news. The Moorestown Business Association was planning an upcoming event, the township wanted to remind residents not to put raked leaves in the street, and the e-bike stolen from a house that backs up to the Moorestown Friends School was found in the woods near Strawbridge Lake, just east of Church Street.

When the bus finally announced the next stop was at the corner of Broad Street and High Street, I pushed the yellow strip above the window, and "Stop Requested" lit up at the front of the bus. I stood up as the bus passed by two of the BCHS buildings. There was the Victorian home of James Fenimore Cooper, the author of "The Last of the Mohicans," and the Captain James Lawrence House, who when mortally wounded, he was credited with shouting to his men, "Don't give up the ship!" Today, this is the Navy's battle cry and the motto of the City of Burlington.

The bus arrived almost on time, having skipped all of those empty bus stops.

The BCHS, Burlington County Historical Society, offered morning and afternoon research reservations from 10:00-12:00 and 1:30-3:30. I reserved both time slots for today. There were 28 minutes to kill before I could get into the BCHS. *I do wish I hadn't drunk quite so much!*

While the historic section of town near the Delaware River was fairly safe, BCHS, just a few blocks away from the water, encroached on a higher crime section of town ... well, compared to my Moorestown bubble. No time to fret, I needed to find a clean, safe restroom.

Evermore Coffee Roasters, just a few streets up, looked promising. Within held a clue to what the day held for me. Their slogan, "Roasted for Adventurers, Brewed for the Journey," was apropos for the day. I laughed at the thought of being an adventurer.

Parisol would have enjoyed this. She was always up for a good adventure. When I was two years old, she decided it was time to take me to Friendly's for some ice cream. The walk was long, but the ice cream was good, that is, until they called our parents when she tried to pay with play money ... that was right before it closed.

I took my coffee with me as I walked up High Street. Touring the old Burlington Quaker Meeting House had been on my to-do list, but it was closed today. I walked up the driveway to get a closer look at the building and roamed around back. Not a soul was in sight, just the way I liked all places. The energy of this historic site was palpable.

On a large boulder, just before the cemetery, there was an old copper plaque that long ago turned green. On it was written: "Near this spot lies the body of the Indian Chief Ockanickon, friend of the white man, whose last words were: 'Be plain and fair to all, both Indian and Christian, as I have been. 1681.'"

Dammit. It was 10:05. I had dallied too long.

Chapter 16

Mr. Hartshorn unlocked the door. "Lottie! It's great to see you. Is your mom parking the car?"

I looked at the floor as I entered. "No. She's meeting me at Francesco's for lunch." He locked the deadbolt behind me, and I followed him into the main research room.

"What are you researching today?" He excitedly asked.

"What can you tell me about Cart's Tayle? The spelling is T, A, Y, L, E."

"Nothing off the top of my head. If you want to start looking in the card catalog, I'll pull some books."

In the few minutes it took me to look in the card catalog, Mr. Hartshorn had already placed eight books on my table.

The first book was on woodworking and cart building in early America. I checked the index and found no reference to "Cart's Tayle." Skimming the book, nothing stuck out.

"Ding-dong." He placed two more books on my stack and went to let in another researcher. I knew I needed to work quickly as he'd soon be back with more books.

A few books in, I was making good time. Yet glancing at the next book, with its dark maroon leather cover with gold embossing, I knew I could easily get lost in its pages for hours. It was five inches thick and of archival museum quality.

No time for a rabbit hole. Focus. I told myself.

The precious work was titled "The History of Burlington and Mercer Counties, New Jersey" by Woodward and Hageman, 1883. While the average person would look at this book and yawn, I knew it contained stories of exploration and intrigue. I just needed to connect the pieces.

Opening the book, I found it to be no ordinary rabbit hole. It was an entire fluffle's warren. Everywhere I looked, there was another rabbit asking to be chased. I pulled out my phone and set the timer for ten minutes to keep me on task. A few seconds later, my phone vibrated. *No way that was 600 seconds.*

I hadn't found anything on Cart's Tayle in the book during that quick skim, but I did find Daniel Leeds' Map of Burlington Township from 1696 redone – "Engraved expressly for this Work." I made a copy of it to add to my collection of early maps. *What a geek*, I thought.

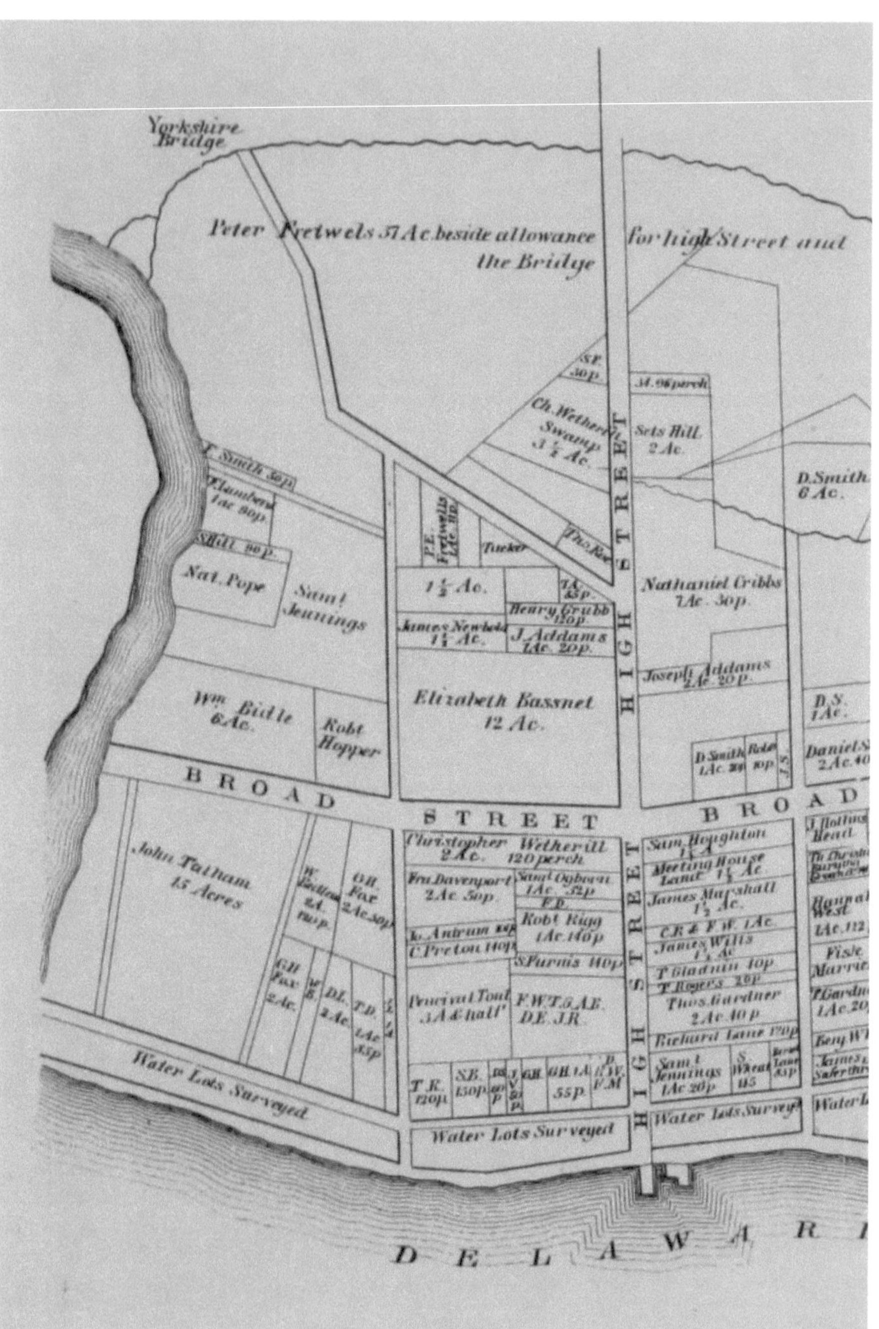

Yorkshire Bridge
Peter Fretwels 57 Ac. beside allowance for High Street and the Bridge
T. Smith 36p.
Plumbers 1Ac 80p.
Hill 90p.
Nat. Pope
Sam.t Jennings
Wm. Biddle 6. Ac.
Rob.t Hopper
Ch. Wetherill Swamp 3½ Ac.
St. 30p.
Tucker
P.E. Fretwells 1Ac 80p.
1½ Ac.
James Newbold 1½ Ac.
Henry Grubb 120p.
1Ac 45p.
J. Addams 1Ac. 20p.
Elizabeth Bassnet 12 Ac.
Tho. Read
HIGH STREET
34. 96 perch
Sets Hill 2 Ac.
D. Smith 6 Ac.
Nathaniel Cribbs 1Ac. 30p.
Joseph Addams 2Ac. 20 P.
D.S. 1Ac.
D. Smith 1Ac. 30p.
Rob.t 30p.
ST.
Daniel S. 2Ac. 40
BROAD STREET
John Tatham 15 Acres
Water Lots Surveyed
Christopher Wetherill 2Ac. 120 perch
Fra. Davenport 2Ac 50p.
k. Antrum 14p.
C. Preton 110p.
Sam.l Osborn 1Ac. 32p. F.D.
Rob.t Rigg 1Ac 140p
S. Furnis 110p.
Percival Tout 3A & half
F.W.T.G.A.E. D.E. J.R.
T.R. 120p.
S.B. 130p.
G.H. Fox 2Ac.
D.L. 2Ac.
T.D. 1Ac 85p.
G.H. 1A. 55p.
B. F.W. F.M.
Water Lots Surveyed
Sam. Houghton 1½ A
Meeting House Land 1½ Ac.
James Marshall 1½ Ac.
C.R. & F.W. 1Ac.
James Willis 1½ Ac.
T. Gladwin 10p.
T. Rogers 20p.
Thos. Gardner 2Ac 40 p.
Richard Lane 170p.
Sam.t Jennings 1Ac 20p.
S. Wheat 115
Water Lots Surveyed
J. Hollins Head
Th. Christ Burgess
Hannah West 1Ac. 112
Fisk Marrie
T. Gardner 1Ac. 20
Beny W.
James Saberthr
Water L.
HIGH STREET
BROAD
DELAWARE

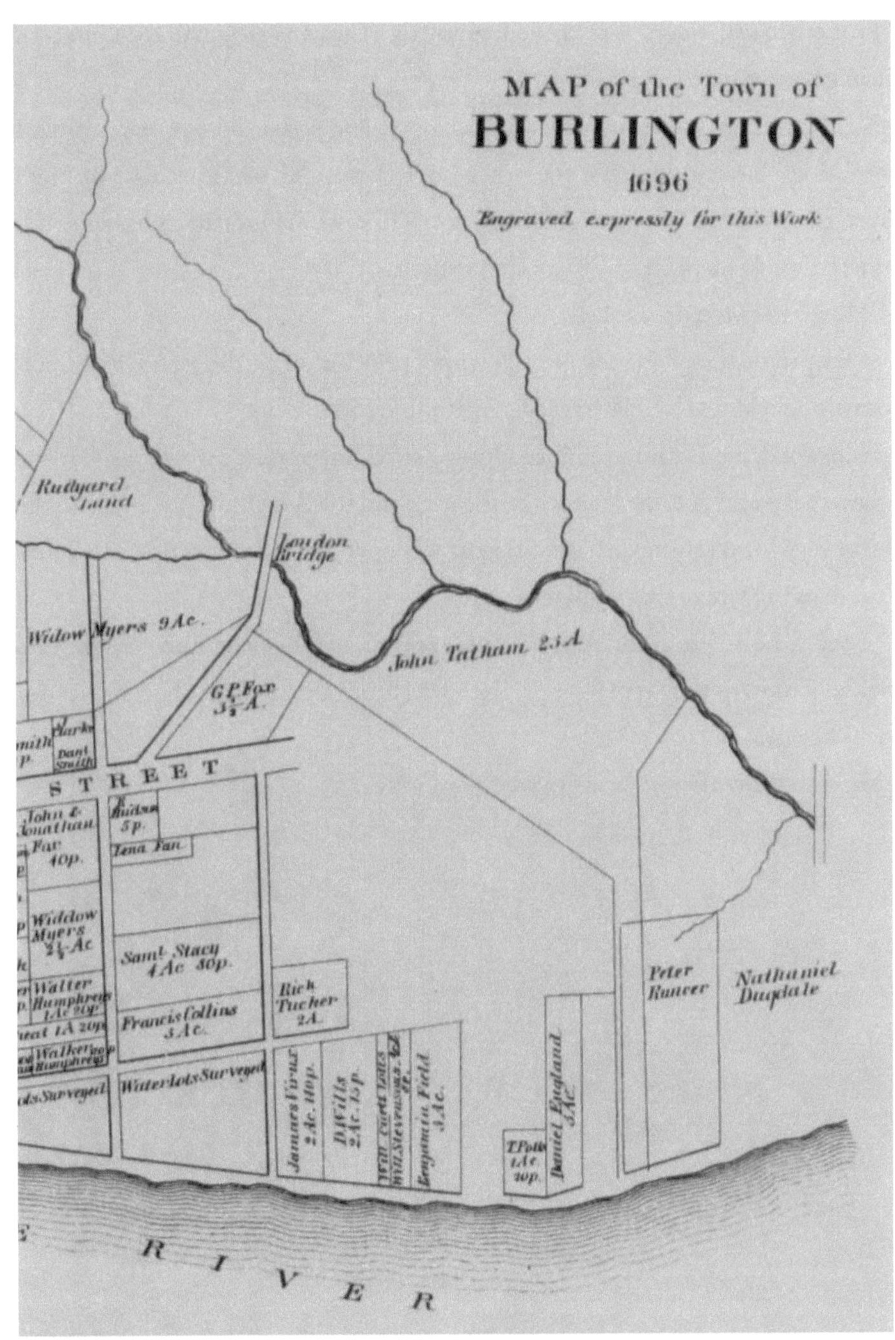

MAP of the Town of
BURLINGTON
1696
Engraved expressly for this Work
Rudyard Land
London Bridge
Widow Myers 9 Ac.
John Tatham 23 A.
G.P. Fox 3½ A.
Clark
Dan.l Smith
STREET
John & Jonathan Fox 40p.
Hudson 5p.
Tena Fan.
Widdow Myers 2½ Ac.
Walter Humphrey 1 Ac. 20p.
Sam.l Stacy 4 Ac. 30p.
Rich Tucker 2 A.
Walker & Humphrey
Francis Collins 3 Ac.
Surveyed
Waterlots Surveyed
James Virour 2 Ac. 10p.
D. Wills 2 Ac. 15p.
Will. Stevenson Field
Benjamin Field 3 Ac.
T. Pott 1 Ac. 10p.
Daniel England 3 Ac.
Peter Runver
Nathaniel Duplate
RIVER

Hopefully, this map was copied correctly from the original 1696 map of Burlington for that 1883 book.

Mr. Hartshorn came by with another book and spied the old map. "That's interesting," he said, putting the other book down. "If you look East of High Street, that is to the left of High Street, you'll find we are located right here on J. Addams' lot and a piece of Elizabeth Bassnet's lot."

"How can you tell?" I asked.

"I'll be right back." He reappeared with a printout of Burlington City Streets from Google Maps. BCHS was located at the arrow.

He turned the Burlington City Google street map upside down so that the Delaware River was at the bottom of the map and the Assicunk Creek was on the left for easy comparison with the old map. He drew the old streets on the current map, showing where the old blocks were.

"I see it now." It all lined up. It was amazing. Once the dirt streets were originally drawn, they remained in the same location and kept their names for over 300 years.

He then drew arrows showing where we were.

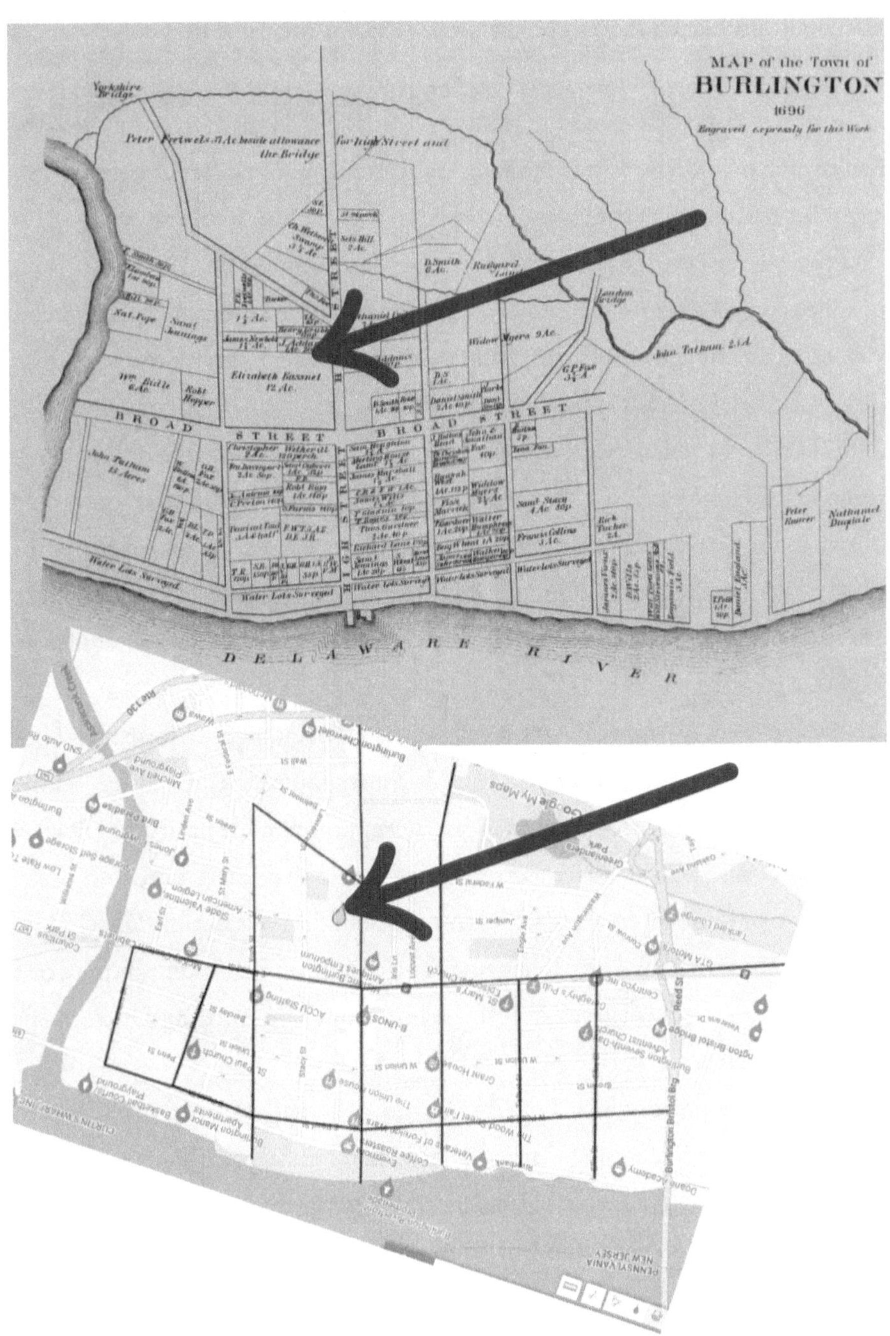
MAP of the Town of
BURLINGTON
1696
Engraved expressly for this Work
Yorkshire Bridge
Peter Fretwels 5 Ac beside allowance for High Street and the Bridge
DELAWARE RIVER
BROAD STREET
BROAD STREET
Elizabeth Bassnet 12 Ac.
Nat. Pope
Wm Biddle
Robt Hopper
John Tatham
Water Lots Surveyed
Widow Myers 9 Ac.
John Tatham 25 A.
Samt Stacy
Francis Collins
Peter Rawcer
Nathaniel Duplaie
PENNSYLVANIA
NEW JERSEY

The arrows indicating the area of the four BCHS buildings, lined up with the old map; it did indeed look to be on the J. Addams lot and a piece of Elizabeth Bassnet's lot."

Pointing to the old map, Mr. Hartshorn continued, "This map shows how the town ownership looked almost twenty years after the initial settlement. That is presuming the map was copied correctly from the original 1696 map."

We geeked out over the old map for another few minutes, until Mr. Hartshorn was called away by another researcher. I went online and searched the state of New Jersey's Early Land Records database for J. Addams. It took me a few tries as it was spelled with only one "d" in the database.

"THUMP." Mr. Hartshorn dropped two more books on my pile. That's when I realized I was off track. I glanced at the twelve books I had already skimmed through in the first hour, with no references to "Cart's Tayle". The task before me looked futile. I needed to keep going. I had only gone a little astray ... well, that was until I came to Jean Soderlund's book "Separate Paths: Lenapes and Colonists in West New Jersey."

In my experience, ADHD (Attention Deficit Hyperactivity Disorder) did not mean "attention deficit" or "no focus." It meant quite the opposite. I easily hyperfocused on things that interested me, never noticing the hours that flew by when in the zone. Yet, it was a torture much worse than mere boredom when forced to pay attention to things I wasn't interested in. Attention-Deficit/Hyperactivity Disorder was a horrible name for a condition that didn't require one to have ever been hyperactive. A better name would be Alluring Distractions Hyperfocus Deftness.

I started out on track when I opened up Jean's book. I skipped to the Index. There wasn't any reference to "Cart's Tayle". Then I did a quick scan of the book that led to a glimpse of a spell-binding rabbit that triggered my chase drive.

I had no idea that when the British arrived in Burlington, they found the Lenape women "savages" owning property, old and young both going around topless in the sun without any feeling of shame, obtaining divorces from spouses on demand, in the highest positions as Sakimaòk (Chiefs) themselves at land deals, and having a voice in choosing and removing leaders.

The irony wasn't lost on me. These "women savages" had more freedom in the 1600s than American women would have for the next two hundred and fifty years. When Britain established its laws here, Lenni-Lenape women lost their freedoms.

I felt a tap on my arm and jumped out of my skin. I looked up and realized I was in the research room. Mr. Hartshorn smiled, having knocked me out of my fixation ... again. "Lunch is 12:00-1:30."

Ughhh, another hour gone. I would need to be extra careful with the two hours I had left after lunch.

On my way out the door, he handed me a historical society map with sites within walking distance. I gulped as I headed out of my safe bubble, map in hand, down High Street for a slice. The pizza parlor was only a block away, and I walked quickly up the brick sidewalk, always aware of who was around.

Upon opening the door to Francesco's, I heard a loud "CRAACK".

The hair on my arms stood straight up. My head jerked down the street in the direction of the sound. Hypervigilance engaged.

Chapter 17

Despite the loud "CRAACK" that made me jump out of my skin, people continued walking down the street and chatting. Nobody seemed to notice the sharp sound. The people in line behind me to get into Francesco's continued in deep conversation. *False alarm?*

I sat down at a table and put on my headphones. I chose headphones over earbuds in public because people could see them. Yet, despite the fact that they were bright blue and clearly over my ears, a man asked to sit with me. Ughhh. It was a truth universally acknowledged that a single woman sitting alone in a restaurant must be in want of company.

I said yes because being assertive was harder than being a "nice girl." There ought to be a class on being direct and blunt without feeling guilty. I put my headphones back on and focused on eating my pizza and the historical tour map.

The map showed that the Revell House was just a block away. The house dated back to 1685. Yet, I would always remember it as the Gingerbread House. At 17 years old, indentured servant Benjamin Franklin illegally ran away from his Master and brother James due to a lack of control and beatings. On his way from Boston to Philadelphia, Ben stopped in Burlington and bought gingerbread from a woman who lived in the Revell House. She later gave him supper.

Years later, Ben Franklin was an enslaver, and also received advertising revenue in his newspapers for ads regarding the return of runaway indentured servants and runaway enslaved persons. His views on slavery later evolved, and he became a vocal abolitionist as President of the Pennsylvania Society for Promoting the Abolition of Slavery.

I went onto Newspapers.com and searched Ben Franklin's early newspapers. It was easy to find ads for runaway slaves and indentured servants both during and after his ownership. The below example was for a runaway "mulattoe" enslaved by Elizabeth Leconey of Cinnaminson (Senemenfon) where she asks for him to be secured in any jail (gaol) until she could recover him.

The Pennsylvania Gazette
Wed, Jan 30, 1782 ·Page 5

SIXTEEN DOLLARS Reward.

RUN away the 17th inft. from Elizabeth Leconey, of Senemenfon, in Burlington county, and State of New-Jerfey, a Mulattoe MAN, about 23 years of age, named Levi, 5 feet 11 inches high; had on, when he went away, a white cloth coat, leather breeches, patched in the feat, a pair of white yarn ftockings, and a hat painted on the top. He took with him two tow fhirts, a brown coat, a hat, a gun and an axe, which he ftole. Whoever can give information of the faid Mulattoe, or get him fecured in any goal, fo that his owner may recover him, fhall receive the above reward, with all reafonable charges, paid by

Jan. 21, 1782.   ELIZABETH LECONEY.

Newspapers.com

The next one was for a runaway indentured servant from Abraham Matlack in Evesham.

RUN away from the Subscriber, living in Evesham, in Burlington County, New-Jersey, on the 6th of May last, an Irish Servant Man, named Alexander M'Donnugh (or M'Donnell) about 24 Years of Age, about 5 Feet 7 Inches high, slim built, thin Face, down Look, subject to Drink, wears his own dark Hair, a little curled, with a sandy Beard: Had on and took with him, a half worn Felt Hat, bluish coloured Broadcloth Coat, a scarlet Ditto Jacket, both half worn, o'd Buckskin Breeches, two Pair of Yarn Stockings, one Pair ribbed, the other plain, old fine Shirt, an Ozenbrigs Ditto, and old Shoes, with carved Metal Buckles; he came into the Country last Fall, and is supposed to be gone towards Lancaster, as he has a Brother in that Part of Pennsylvania. Whoever takes up and secures said Servant, in any Goal, so that his Master may have him again, shall have Five Pounds Reward, and reasonable Charges, paid by

ABRAHAM MATLACK.

N. B. All Masters of Vessels are forbid to carry him off.

Newspapers.com

When the server came around and asked about dessert, I skipped the cannoli I had been dreaming of all morning. Getting up from the table and regaining some personal space sadly beat out staying for dessert.

The first stop was the Burlington Pharmacy, a half block up High Street, the oldest continuously operating pharmacy in New Jersey. The oldest part of the building dates to 1731. As part of the Underground Railroad, this building hid runaway slaves. The owners of the property didn't hide their views on the abomination of slavery, as they allowed abolitionist speakers to make speeches from their doorstep.

I hesitantly walked in and asked the pharmacist, "C-can I see the location where the enslaved were hidden?"

"Sadly, that part of the building is no longer open to visitors. The Underground Railroad Museum was moved to Smithville," she said. She kindly answered many of my questions and handed me a document on the Underground Railroad that had been sent to her by the State.

On my way out the door, I felt a light breeze go through me. I closed my eyes and wished all who were here in the past, freedom seekers and residents, and all who came in the future, "peace." I touched the door frame and felt the waves of energy of the unseen underpinnings wash over me.

I stepped into the sunlight. The sunbeams sparkled. It was supposed to reach 84 degrees, but it felt more like 90. I wiped my brow and looked at the map. My next historical stop would be the Library Company of Burlington, but first, Ummm Ice Cream Parlor for a root beer float, my earlier cannoli plan having been foiled.

On my way across the street, I caught a glimpse of a beautiful blue hat in the millinery shop when I heard another "CRAACK."

I flinched. The sound came from near, very near. Just a little up Union Street. Curiously, nobody else seemed concerned or even to notice.

As I walked past the benches and up Union, I heard it again. "CRAACK." It was definitely the sound of a whip hitting something. I bit my bottom lip. *Maybe it's part of a historical show?* I followed the sound, loving good historical shows. Not the shows for the youngest of children, but the ones for people who were interested in history who weren't four-year-olds.

I walked past the benches and looked up. On the side of the building was a beautiful mural with a large paddleboat loading passengers from long ago. Just past the benches, I found the town's mini park with a small flower garden. A woman was sitting on a bench at the park entrance with two children, coloring the red brick path with chalk. She looked up and smiled.

"CRAACK." It came from the back of the park, maybe 25 feet off the street. The woman and children didn't look up from what they were doing despite the loud slap of the whip. She continued to read, and they continued to color.

Why is nobody concerned?

They must know something I don't know. I walked around the planter overflowing with white impatiens and tall pink zinnia and headed to the back of the park. *Maybe there were speakers or an open window in a nearby apartment. .... Maybe the sound came from a loud TV.* But after spending a minute looking up, down, and under, I found nothing.

"LAZY SOW" was yelled into my left ear. I jumped a foot to the right, my head snapping left, but there was nothing there.

"No," was sobbed by a young woman to my right. She pleaded, "No fum fum."

"You needest enoucouragement." I froze, fearful of what this invisible man might do to me. The air around me suddenly filled with the unique blend of coal smoke, sweat, and something like blood.

"CRAACK." The whip hit the woman to my right. She screeched out in pain. It sounded like the screams of a dying animal.

My mind raced to make sense of the disconnection between what I heard and what I wasn't seeing. But I couldn't.

I recoiled with the sound of the next blow as she begged for him to stop.

My actions startled the woman and children, who now stared at me. I had to get away from this brutality, this craziness. I ran out of the park, my backpack bounced with every stride.

As I got farther from the park, the blows were not as loud, yet they were coming more often, one after another. He was going to kill her.

I had run past five buildings when I saw the sign for The Library Company of Burlington. I ran past the black rod iron fence and up the steep old brownstone steps. I opened the door, and the wind picked up and slammed it with a "Bang."

Chapter 18

Or maybe I slammed it. I don't know.

Stepping foot into the entry was like stepping into Oz. It was unlike any library I had been in before. Or maybe I was different.

I spun around, the scent of mahogany and books wrapping around me, steeped in history past. Different from the mini park's horror, it was peaceful here, despite my heart still galloping from the adrenaline.

I could imagine the wealthy male members' ghosts of centuries past in this hall. The main floor appeared smaller than I expected. A wooden staircase, off to the side, with steep circular steps beckoned me to climb. I longed to sneak up those steps and explore the nooks and crannies, but a sign read, 'Staff Only.'

My brain was dancing among the living tapestry when the librarian appeared in the entryway, looking concerned. I must have been a sight ... just off my escape from hearing the beating. *Maybe the library has a book on hallucinations*, I thought.

"I'm sorry for shut ... shutting the door so hard." I held up the map I had received from the historical society and explained that I was trying to fit in as many sights as possible before my research time at the BCHS resumed at 1:30.

The librarian quickly realized I was a kindred spirit. Without hesitation, she whisked me on a quick tour of the main floor. As she spoke, I shook the last of the whipping from my head and listened in. She began by pointing up the steps and said, "That's where the Masonic meetings from long ago took place." I wanted to marinate on that fact, but she kept moving.

"Benjamin Franklin, who was then well established in Philadelphia, founded the first subscription library for men, known as the Library Company of Philadelphia. All the top politicians and businessmen of Philadelphia were members. In fact, when the national government was headquartered in Philadelphia from the time of the Revolutionary War until 1800, that is, before it moved to Washington, D.C., the Library Company of Philadelphia served as the Library of Congress.

"Many of these same all-male library members," she continued, "maintained second homes in Burlington, where they could escape the smells and diseases prevalent in the city with just a quick boat ride up the Delaware River, crossing into New Jersey. Longing to read great literature during their time spent in Burlington, they petitioned the King for another library."

The librarian motioned to the wall behind me, "Hanging there is the original Charter from 1757 with King George II's original seal establishing this, the Library Company of Burlington."

As I followed her, I noticed the second-floor balcony that circled the perimeter of the room, looking down upon us from above. Behind the bookshelves on the balcony were long windows that were rounded at the top.

She continued. "The first book checked out of the library in 1757 by these gentlemen was "The Invisible Spy" by Exploralibus. I made a note to myself to look it up. What types of books our forefathers were reading prior to the Revolutionary War might be enlightening.

"When first opened, the library was located in a room in Thomas Rodman's house, which the library rented from him. Over time the library moved from people's homes into it's own little building on Library Street. A little over a hundred years after it first opened, while Ulysses S. Grant was away fighting the Civil War, Mrs. Grant actively raised funds to outfit the new library building, the one we are standing in. It opened in 1864. I imagined the faint outline of Mrs. Grant brushing by me. I smelled sweet honeysuckles in a vase nearby; her presence quickly disappeared into the ether.

As the librarian continued to show me around the first floor, I noticed the computers in the library had spots for potential floppy drives. Such dinosaurs. Noticing my eyes hovering over the old computers, she acknowledged that Burlington didn't have the library budget that many other libraries did. New computers were far down on the list.

As with many old grand historical buildings, time passed them by, and the buildings themselves, with their gilded details, were in stark contrast to the funds available in the current day. It was a love of great proportions for the volunteers and staff to keep the library open for the community, while also attending to the duty and privilege of maintaining this gem's walls from cracking and the roof from leaking.

The tour ended at one of the little reading nooks. "I'll be right back with two books I believe you will be interested in." She walked away, leaving me next to a high-back, upholstered, Georgian chair. Behind the chair was a second wooden staircase. This one was not wide like the one in the front hall.

Instead, it tightly spiraled upwards, leading to the second-floor book balcony. At the far end of the second-floor balcony, there was a door that I presumed led to another room that was above the entry.

I let out a sigh. *I really want to explore up there.* I turned to look at the stairs. *Darn.* The sign also said 'Staff Only.'

The librarian returned with two books, "Moorestown, Old and New. A local sketch." By James Purdy, published in 1886. The second was "Moorestown and Her Neighbors" by George Decou, published in 1929. I had read quotes from these books over the years, but I had never seen the books themselves.

I sat down in the chair. It was well-worn, but comfortable. Fanning James Purdy's book, the mention of Job Cowperthwaite caught my attention. He was one of the pillars of Moorestown.

His house still stands today, originally built by his father in 1742. I wouldn't have remembered the date normally, but it's on the bricks outside of the home, across from BJ's. In fact, I was in sight of Job Cowperthwaite's home just this morning when I was sitting on the stone wall waiting for the public bus. The book discussed how Job was instrumental in the establishment of the first brick schoolhouse in Moorestown.

A few years ago, I was blessed to receive a personal tour of Job Cowperthwaite's home. During that tour, I was told that, prior to the building of the first school, Job had a schoolroom in this house, located in a bedroom on the second floor. Coat pegs for the students lined the perimeter of the room. Just another place where history was electrified.

Imagine the British and Hessians marching down Kings Highway from Haddonfield and stealing from the homes and commandeering many of them as they went along, staying the night where they pleased. That house was witness to that history. Not all good history. But then again, not to be forgotten.

My alarm beeped. I needed to leave soon and get back to BCHS and researching Cart's Tayle.

The thought of walking out the door and running into the person who had tortured that girl with a whip made my throat tighten. The sanctuary of these old books and solid walls called me to stay, to camp out here indefinitely. But then again, heading back to BCHS wasn't just about me. *It was for Parisol.* Still, my body wouldn't cooperate; anxiety rooted me to the chair.

I glanced toward the entrance, picturing that mini park where I'd heard the invisible horror. What if he was still there? What if those sounds weren't just in my head? Before I could venture back outside, I needed certainty.

I needed to see out a window to the street out front, to know that all was well. I looked up at the door at the end of the second-floor balcony. That room might have a window. *Hmmmm. If I could just sneak up and take a peek...*

But I could never. Breaking rules, sneaking around ... that was Parisol's forte, not mine. 'Staff only,' remember.

Parisol would do it for you in a heartbeat, whispered something inside me. *Parisol is worth it!*

In the end, I was more worried about the monster I heard in the mini park than the trouble I'd get in if I were found. The "Staff Only" sign stared back at me, a boundary I'd never imagined crossing. But Parisol wouldn't hesitate. She'd already be up those stairs, curious and determined.

For Parisol.

I slid my shoes off and tip-toed up the wooden stairs, each careful step a tiny rebellion against the scared, hypervigilant person I'd become after that summer of 2015.

My fingertips brushed against the wall, my toes felt the smooth worn steps under my socks that many soles had walked up over the centuries. The faint scent of lemon polish and old books drifted up from below.

At the top, I realized I'd have to crawl to not be seen above the railing lining the balcony. I stopped and listened. My muscles tensed, ready to bolt at the slightest sound from below.

The well-worn, uneven wooden floor, while beautiful, was hard on my knees. I peeked around the corner, no one in sight, and crawled at top speed.

Arriving at the door, I reached up and touched the knob. Cold brass. At first, I thought it was locked. But it was just old and needed effort to turn.

The room was a sight to behold. Bookcases stretched from floor to ceiling, filled with treasures in individual protective boxes. My bare feet stepped further within, the cool wooden floor beneath me a reminder that I was treading where few visitors were allowed ... where *I wasn't allowed.*

I approached the first bookshelf with reverence. The first row held the antiquarian books from the 1500s, silently waiting in their archival boxes. The spine of each box whispered of Renaissance thinking and world-changing ideas born a century before the English boats arrived, establishing Burlington.

I spun around. The room was organized chronologically. Next were the bookshelves filled with books from the 1600s. *Just Wow!* I thought. I took out my phone and captured this literary time capsule.

The next row of bookshelves contained first editions from the 1700s, the Age of Enlightenment. I ached to open just one box, to hold history in my hands, but dared not. To damage such an artifact would be sacrilege.

Instead, I stood in awe, surrounded by nearly five centuries of human thought, rabbit holes of curiosity multiplied in my mind faster than I could process them.

Remember the time! I heard in my head.

I pulled myself together and started to look around the room to see if there was a window from which I could look out onto the street for the man with the whip. As I tried to glance behind the bookcases that were flush with the front wall, I heard a tap on the shelf from behind me. I spun around. Nobody was there. I glanced in the direction of the noise and noticed a book titled "Treatise Proving Spirits, Witches, Etc. Casaubon. London. 1672."

The little hairs on my neck stood up. *Time to go.*

I decided to take one last picture of the room. In glancing up from my phone's camera out of the corner of my eye, I thought I saw an outline of a man standing between me and the door in clothing from past centuries.

He appeared to look upon the books, as if he were a librarian or caretaker from the past. But in moving my head from seeing the mist out of the corner of my eye to viewing the area straight on, no such apparition existed. *Just my imagination*, I told myself.

I took a breath and began my excursion back. I got low and crawled out the door. I turned and quietly closed it, the latch sliding closed with a soft, distinct click.

Halfway to the steps, the librarian's chair squeaked. I froze as I watched her head to the front desk. *It's now or never*, I told myself, and tiptoed the rest of the way and down the steps.

Seeing the edge of the back of my chair, I moved quickly and dashed to pick up the two books off my seat and to sit down.

"How are the books?" asked the librarian.

My toes tried to find their way back into my shoes without her noticing.

"Very interesting. Thanks."

She nodded and went back to her office.

I let the air slowly out of my mouth, like a balloon with a pinhole, happy at not being caught. I relaxed fully back into the chair. My eyes again wandered up to the second-floor balcony. That's when I realized that when I was outside earlier, there was a rectangular window on the side of the building above the windows with the rounded tops. *Was there a third floor?*

The Library Company of Burlington

She had mentioned a room where Masonic meetings had been held long ago. I neither saw the front staircase nor that room on my travels upstairs.

I wasn't sure whether looking out the front window was worth the effort. The sound I heard from within the mini park was likely just my imagination having gone wild. But when I again tried to get up to leave, I couldn't. I needed to find that window and know I was safe before venturing out.

The worn carpet on the first floor muffled my footsteps. I kept my shoes on and moved quickly, rehearsing excuses in my mind in case I was spotted. But I wasn't, and I arrived at the front entry by the steps.

The steps went up and up and up. I was much higher than I had been when on the second floor.

I eventually came to the top of a little hall. There was a door to my left, and down a long corridor, there was another door.

I took a few steps towards the room on my left, put my hand on the doorknob, and opened it. This room didn't have rows of bookshelves. Instead, bookshelves lined the perimeter of the walls with old books in various states of deterioration. There was an old wooden bench in the middle of the room with a pair of white gloves and a book that was being attended to.

I wanted to stay, but there was no window and little time. I kept going. I went down the long hall to the other door. There was a cane leaning to the side, just outside the door. I moved it slightly so it wouldn't fall and make a noise.

The room I entered was a little more modern. Set up as if they brought historical tours up here. There were historical paintings, furniture, clothing, and busts of important people from the past. Descriptions were enumerated by plaques around the room.

I wandered around exploring when I came across an old map on the wall. It was behind glass and appeared to be an original or an excellent scanned copy of the paper and ink used in the late 1600s. It drew me in.

I squinted and read in the Map notes 1696 and saw the initials D.L. Could this be the original Daniel Leeds map that was redone and typed for that book that I came across at the BCHS?

This map was handwritten and not typed like the one redone for the book. Or maybe it was a scanned copy. And if scanned, where was the original. I'd never seen this map in any book before.

I took out my phone and compared the picture I took of the map in the book from this morning with this map on the wall. The year, the lines, and the property owners all matched. The crease in the map hanging on the wall went right across the top of the 9 in 1696, displacing some of the ink, as it did in other areas of the map too. However, even if this map hanging on the wall was a copy, it was significant in verifying accuracy of the town layout in the redone map.

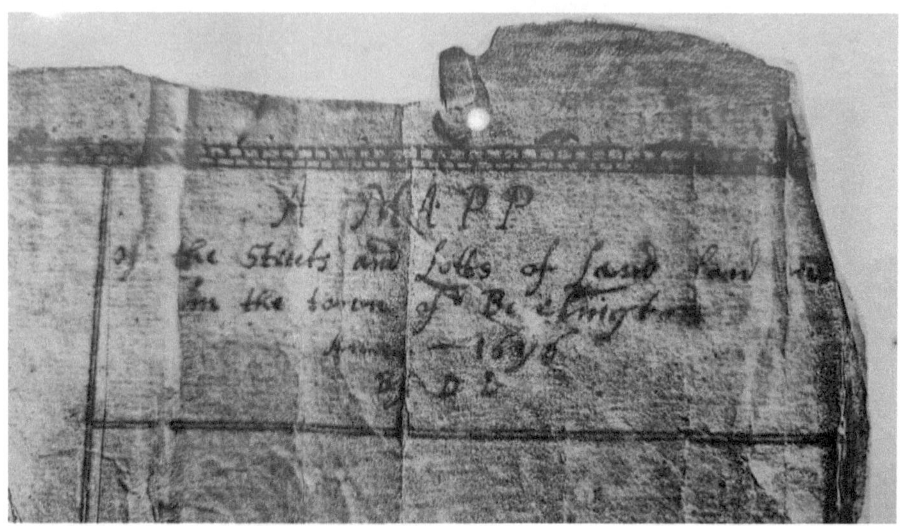

I looked at my phone and winced. I'd be late for my BCHS afternoon appointment. Leaving the room, I turned to shut the door and froze. The cane was missing. Horror shot through me. I was caught. I looked around the empty room, confused and alarmed, when I spotted it lying across a small table near the steps. A jolt of possibilities ran through my mind, the most frightening being that apparitions could somehow move physical objects.

Survival instincts kicked in, bypassing freeze, fawn, and fight responses and propelling me straight to flight. I descended the steps on silent feet, not daring to look toward the librarian's office as I passed. Moving swiftly but deliberately, I hoisted my backpack, placed the beloved books carefully on the front desk, and made my escape through the front door.

That's when I realized I'd never found the window overlooking the street. I came to a full stop at the top of the brownstone steps. I looked around, all my senses on red alert. The man from the mini park could still be around.

I listened carefully to the street sounds. A couple laughed nearby while a woman walked past, absorbed in a phone conversation. No whipping, no angry man yelling, no desperate voice crying, pleading for help. I relaxed enough to take in a deep breath of fresh air. Still, I chose an alternate route back to the BCHS, unwilling to pass the mini park again.

At the corner, I turned left and walked past a few row homes and came to the Ulysses S. Grant's House. Despite my hurry, my pace slowed as I took in the magnificent details and imagined hearing the sobs of history from within.

Ulysses S. Grant's House in Burlington, NJ during the Civil War

The Grants had been invited to attend the theater in the box with President Abe Lincoln and his wife, Mary Todd Lincoln, on that fateful April 14, 1865. However, with Mrs. Grant's intense dislike of Mrs. Lincoln, the Grants declined the invitation and took the train home to Burlington. When they arrived, they heard the news that President Lincoln had been shot. The guilt of not being there to protect his friend haunted Grant for the rest of his life.

I turned left, just past the house, down the little walking alley that ran along the Grants' side yard. I felt like an intruder, looking over the picket fence into that beautiful garden where the Grant children had played. The sweet scent of roses wafted over, tickling my nose. It was clear that the couple who currently owned the home loved and cherished it, as it deserved.

But as I came closer to the back of the mini park where I had heard the whipping, while separated by a fence, the hairs on my arms still rose. I made a sharp right through a parking lot to put some distance between the park and me, which brought me back behind the Quaker Meeting House.

I must be bat-crap-crazy, I ruminated. But there was no time to worry about the bat.... I mean bats, living in my belfry. There were fewer than two hours left to figure out what a "Cart's Tayle" was and what it had to do with Parisol.

Chapter 19

Mr. Hartshorn had been hard at work. The pile of books had grown into a small mountain while I was at lunch. I felt the familiar tightness in my chest as panic crept in. Overwhelmed didn't even begin to cover it. I couldn't fail Parisol, not after everything.

My mind pogoed wildly from Parisol to the whipping to the old library, bouncing between thoughts like a pinball machine gone haywire. Usually, when my brain gets this chaotic, I'd escape by zoning out with a Netflix binge or losing myself in a game on my phone. But today was different. Today, I couldn't just check out.

Mr. Hartshorn appeared and dropped off yet another book with a soft thud that felt more like a hammer to my nerves.

I needed a better plan to stop my brain from off-roading. I switched my alarm strategy, changing it from a single alert in ten minutes to gentle vibrations every ten minutes to snap me back to focus. Today, my brain was basically a bowling ball careening down the lane. I desperately needed those kiddie bumpers up to keep it from crashing into the gutter.

Doubts crept into my mind like unwelcome guests. *Was Cart's Tayle even related to Parisol?* I couldn't see how they connected. But the journal entry was literally all I had to go on. No other options existed.

I grabbed "The Burlington Court Book of West New Jersey, 1680-1709" from the top of the teetering pile of books.

Burlington County used to be way bigger than it is now. Back when East Jersey was established by the Puritans and West Jersey by the Quakers, Burlington County was the largest of all the counties in the Jerseys.

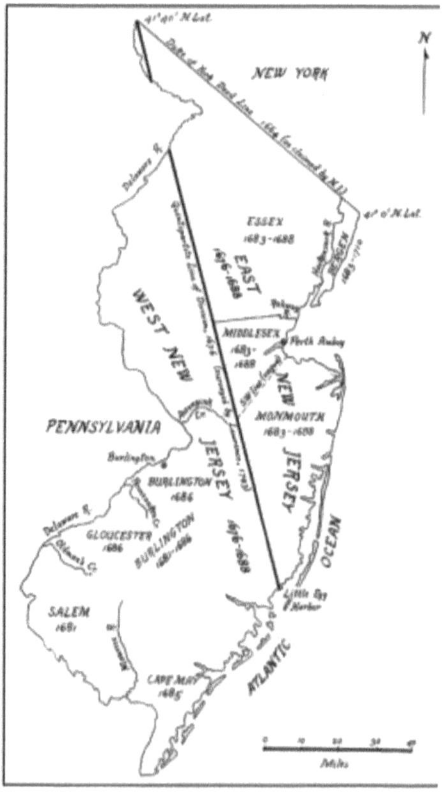

I pulled out my quick reference guide to early New Jersey boundaries and the years they were set up. Originally, Burlington County extended from the Assunpink Creek to Salem. This Court Book documented all the cases prosecuted in

Burlington for crimes committed anywhere in the massive original county, and some even farther north into the farthest sections of West Jersey.

I flipped straight to the back of the book, hunting for Cart's Tayle in the index. Nothing. Back to the front to start a quick skim. Not exactly easy-going at first. Early modern English wasn't quite as brain-melting as Shakespeare, but all those weird spellings definitely slowed me down. No sign of Cart's Tayle in the first dozen pages.

After what felt like forever, all the words started blurring together, and I had to slow my pace even more. Somewhere around page 18, my mind drifted, and I found myself actually reading instead of skimming.

"March 14th, 1682. John Carter of Elizabeth Towne in the Province of East Jersey being examined before John Cripps Justice, Deposeth, that hee lives at Elizabeth Towne aforesaid, And that hee the said Carter, and a woeman with whom hee is in Company (who hee calls Lydia Mosse, by the name of her Father) are marryed.

The said Lydia being then Examined before John Cripps, Deposeth, That the aforesaid Carter and shee the said Lydia were Marryed at Elizabeth Towne aforesaid, before the People called Quakers, at the House wherein one Samuell Groome Inhabitteth; And being then accused to be the wife of one John Toe of Elizabeth Towne aforesaid, Deposeth, and sayth that shee disownes the said Toe to bee her Husband.

One Alexander Callman being then examined consenting the premisses, solemnly Deposeth That hee knowes the said Carter, and the said Lydia, And that the said Lydia to his knowledge hath beene reputed and owned to bee the wife of the said John Toe for a Considerable tyme; And alsoe that hee the said Alexander the 4th instant was at the house of the said John Toe at Elizabeth Towne; And the said Lydia was then at home with her said Husband Toe. The said Carter thereupon deposeth. That hee knows not that the said Lydia is the Wife of the said John Toe: But aftenwards Confest it. And wished that the said Lydia was at home with her said husband.

Whereupon the said John Carter, and the said Lydia Mosse, alias Toe, were by Mittimus under the hand and Seale of the said John Cripps Justice Committed to the Custody of the sheriffe untill further order.

[March 22d.] The said John Carter and Lydia Mosse alias Toe, were had before Governour Samuell Jenings, and Robert Stacy and John Cripps Justices, And were (by them) ordered the next day by the Tenth hower in the Morning to be whipt on their naked bodies the said Carter to receive Thirty stripes, and the said Lydia Thirty Five stripes. And that the said Lydia should the same day be forthwith sent back by a passe to the next Constable home wards; And the said Carter should remain in Custody one day after the said Lydia, and then to bee dismissed, paying the Fees, per Thomas Revell Recorder."

I was stunned. Right here in Burlington, the government basically acted as morality police, handing out actual physical punishments. And to be whipped on their naked bodies? That's beyond insane.

Lydia Mosse had zero rights. She was literally her husband's property. I stared at the yellowed page of the old Court Book, my mind struggling to process what I was reading. I needed to go through the case again.

Forty years later, Thomas Revell's house became the place where Benjamin Franklin got gingerbread and supper. *History stumbles across itself in this town, layers upon layers.* "Bzzzz," my phone vibrated against my leg, snapping me out of my trance. *Right. Focus.* I needed to do a complete skim of the Court Book.

I switched up my technique. I placed my pointer finger at the top of each page and ran it straight down, scanning only for the words "Cart's Tayle" as I went. I forced myself not to actually read or understand anything else on the page. If

"Cart's Tayle" didn't jump out at me by the time my finger reached the bottom, I flipped to the next page.

Way faster process, but mind-numbingly boring. Finger at the top, eyes scanning down for "Cart's Tayle." Page 19. Page 20. Then the 30s. The 40s. Page 51. Page 52. I couldn't stop a massive yawn. Page 53. Page 54. BORING!

And then page 55. Four lines up from the bottom, sitting right there in the middle of the line: the words "Cart's Tayle." I felt a weird little thrill run through me. I honestly hadn't expected to actually find "Cart's Tayle" at all.

I backtracked to find the beginning of the sentence and read:

> "The Judgment of the Court therefore is That the said John Stanbanck shall be whipt on his bare back at a **Cart's Tayle**, and that hee shall have Thirty Nyne lashes well laid on, betwixt the howers of Nyne and Twelve upon the next Sixth day...".

So this man's punishment was to be whipped on his bare back at a Cart's Tayle. I grabbed my phone and searched "whipt at a Cart's Tayle." An illustration from Mark Twain's "The Prince and the Pauper," published in 1881, immediately popped up on my screen.

When I saw the image, actual shivers crawled up my spine. This horrific illustration was definitely not included in the kid-friendly version of "The Prince and the Pauper" I read growing up.

I flipped back to see what this John Stanbanck had done in 1686 to earn such a brutal punishment. My eyes focused on page 55, scanning for details, both dreading and needing to know what crime could possibly warrant being dragged through the streets tied to a cart while being whipped.

"John Stanbanck upon Indictment for our Lord the King on the Complaint of Maudlin Walter bound over to this Court appeares. The Grand Jury finde the Bill of Indictment, And the said Stanbanck called to the Barre pleads not Guilty and referres the Tryall to God and the Countrey.

The Traverse Jury last above Impannelled Attested. Evidence: Maudlin Walter Aged about Twelve yeares Attested Testyfyes to the Truth of the Indictment. Richard Russell Attested declares that the Evidence of Maudlin Walter formerly taken from her mouth and now read in Court, Testifying to the Truth of the Indictment was truly taken. And is the same that was then taken.

Hance Walter age about Eleaven yeares Attested sayth. The said Stanbanck did throw downe the said Maudlin Walter, in the house in the Indictment mentioned. And that hee also after heareing the said Maudlin Cry out aloud Severall tymes for helpe came to the windowe of the said house. And did then see the said Stanbanck lye upon the Belly of the said Maudlin with his Breeches downe, and his yard out. But did not see his yard in the said Maudlins Body.

George Lawrence aged about Twelve yeares Testifyes the truth thereof being also with the said Hance Walter.

The Sherifife for bringing his Prisoner Stanbanck into Court without Irons Contrary to the Command of the Magistrates Fyned Five pounds.

The Jury bring in their Verdict and finde the said Stanbanck Guilty of severall misdemeanours and abuses in Attempting the Ravishment of the said Maudlin Walter.

And the Jury with the Concurrence of the Bench Conclude upon this Judgment which is pronounced by the President, as followes.

Whereas the said John Stanbanck hath beene Indicted, and hath pleaded not guilty and referred himselfe for Tryall to God and the Countrey: And Whereas the Jury have found the said Stanbanck Guilty of severall Misdemeanours and abuses in Attempting the Ravishing of the said Maudlin Walter. The Judgment of the Court therefore is That the said John Stanbanck shall be whipt on his bare back at a Cart's Tayle, and that hee shall have Thirty Nyne lashes well laid on, betwixt the howers of Nyne and Twelve upon the next Sixth day; And that the said Stanbanck shall pay all Court charges, and other charges expended and accrueing by meanes thereof; And alsoe that hee give bond of one Hundred pounds for his good behaviour dureing life: And that hee shall remayne Prisoner untill hee performe the same."

Did this court actually hide a rape by calling it "attempted ravishment" to protect Maudlin's future? I wondered. And what exactly is a "well laid on" lash anyway? Stop it! I scolded myself. *Take the win.*

So there it was... "Cart's Tayle." The thing I'd been hunting for. But what on earth did this brutal punishment have to do with Parisol?

"Bzzz," my alarm vibrated against my leg, jerking me back to reality.

Chapter 20

I had ninety minutes left to research. There might be more examples of Cart's Tayle hidden in these pages. Maybe something that is actually connected to Parisol.

I flipped to the next page of the Court Book and went back to my mind-numbing technique of running my finger down page after page. I dragged myself through what felt like a million pages before I came across those words again... this time buried in a case from 1687.

> "Mary Driver! The Bench have Considered of thy Lewdnesse in defyleing thy Mothers bed, of which thou hast beene found guilty: And for the same doe order that tomorrowe being the 26th instant betweene the howers of Eleaven and Twelve in the forenoone, thou shall be severely whipt on thy naked back at a **Cart's Tayle** from the house of John Cripps in this Towne to the River side and that thou shall have thirty Nyne stripes well laid on."

That's completely insane. Whatever happened in her mother's bed got this woman thirty-nine lashes on her naked back while being dragged through the entire town. I went back and began reading the full case beginning on page 72.

> "Att a Special Court called and held on the Accompt of Henry Tradway the 23th 6th Mo. 1687. Robert Stacy, Edward Hunloke, James Marshall, Richard Basnett, John Wood, James Martin, William Myers Justices Present.
>
> Henry Tradway Indicted for haveing Carnall Copulation with his wifes daughter named Mary Driver."

Am I reading this right? Mary Driver's mother was married to Henry Tradway, which made him her stepfather. *Beyond gross.* I needed to know how old Mary was. I pulled up Grandma's ancestry account online, the one she'd transferred to me last year for that family tree project in history class.

A quick search for Mary Driver in New Jersey during the late 1600s brought up four links. The first showed her mother, Ann Driver, marrying Henry Tradway in Burlington on November 8, 1685. The second estimated Mary's birth year as 1672, which meant she was only 15 during the trial. Another had her as 17. The last source confirmed she was a teenager in 1687 when they carried out the sentence.

My stomach twisted into knots. In modern times, they'd call this exactly what it was, rape of a teenage girl by her guardian. Feeling slightly sick, I forced myself to keep reading.

> "Grand Jury Thomas Bowman, John Willis, William Stanley, Peter Jenings, Samuell OldAle, Thomas Gladwyn, Thomas Raper, Daniel England, John Kinsey, Abraham Senior, William Brightwen, Samuell Houghton, John Browne Attested.

Howard Ward and Elizabeth Salsbury Attested and sent to the Grand Jury. Alsoe the examination and Confession of Mary Driver taken before the Justices belowe, sent to the Grand Jury And Mary Driver alsoe Attested and sent to them.

The Grand Jury finde the Bill. And alsoe the Grand Jury present the County for want of a Prison, upon the Complaynt of the Sheriff. Alsoe the Grand Jury returne a Bill which is preferred to them concerning Henry Tradways uncivill actions with one Phillice Richards.

The Grand Jury returne Ignoramus upon the bill.

upon the first bill being found by the Grand Jury Henry Tradway Arraigned pleads Guilty. And referrs himselfe to God and the Countrey. Traverse Jury Thomas Gardner senr., Henry Grubb, Seth Smith, Seth Hill, James Satterthwait, Johosaphat Legrave, Samuell Herrott, Francis Isley, John Herrott, John Smith, John Cornish, Benjamin Holt Attested.

The Jury finde Henry Tradway Guilty upon the Evidence above.

And further the businesse and fact of said Mary Driver with Henry Tradway her father in Lawe appeareing by her owne Testimony and the Evidence above: The Grand Jury goe togeather againe. And present her, for that it appeares **by her keeping her said fact secrett that Shee was willing and assented thereunto."**

I steamed. The entire system was rigged against this girl who would've been a sophomore in high school if she lived today. Look at the setup: seven male Justices, thirteen men on the Grand Jury, and twelve men on the Traverse Jury. Thirty-two men total decided the fate of this girl who lived under the same roof as her rapist. What girl would have dared speak up? I wanted to take a switch to each one of these men myself. Complete lunacy. I forced myself to take a deep breath and kept reading.

I had to rest my forehead directly on the table, overwhelmed by the injustice Mary suffered. Girls back then were brainwashed into thinking these things were their fault.

I covered my eyes with my hands, realizing the horrible truth that even today, there are still girls raised right here in the United States who believe being raped is their own fault and that they're somehow "impure" because of it. With a heaviness in my chest, I looked back at the page and made myself continue.

"Thurla Sena preferrs a Bill of Complaynt against Henry Tradway on his owne behalfe, for the said Henryes abuse of him and declares and Attests in Court that hee is afraid of his life.

Elizabeth Salesbury upon her Attestation sayth that Henry Tradway said if hee could meet with the said Thurla that night (after hee had attempted to drawe up the said Thurla by the neck with a Rope) hee would either put him in the Creek or drowne him.

John Wood Attested sayth that to the best of his remembrance on the 19th of the 5th Mo. last Henry Tradway said that if the said Thurla came to his house, hee would scarr, or affright him.

The Court adjourne to the 5th day next at the 10th hower in the forenoone.

[63 1687] [5th day being 25th 6th Mo.] Henry Tradway and Mary Driver brought to the Barre.

The sentence of Court.

Henry Tradway! The Bench have Considered of the wickednesse of the Fact whereof by thy Jury thou hast been found guilty: And for the same doe fyne thee Fifty pounds: And also order thee to pay and discharge all Court charges and all other reasonable expenses and charges that are occasioned by reason of thy fact. And alsoe that thou be kept in prison untill the same shall be paid and discharged.

Mary Driver! The Bench have Considered of thy Lewdnesse in defyleing thy Mothers bed, of which thou hast beene found guilty: And for the same doe order that tomorrowe being the 26th instant betweene the howers of Eleaven and Twelve in the forenoone, thou shall be severely whipt on thy naked back at a Cart's Tayle from the house of John Cripps in this Towne to the River side and that thou shall have thirty Nyne stripes well laid on.

The Bench further order that as Concerning the Complaynt made by Thurla Sena against Henry Tradway, The said Henry Tradway shall remayne prisoner untill hee give sufficient security for his good behaviour:

And for the abuse of the said boy and losse of tyme said Henry shall pay him twenty Shillings."

So while Mary was physically punished for basically being a female victim of what today would absolutely be considered child rape, her step-father got off with a fine and temporary prison time until he could pay up. *Please let Henry Tradway be a dirt-poor man who rotted in prison forever*, I silently prayed.

I looked up Henry Tradway in the New Jersey Early Land Records database, and what I found made my blood boil.

Tradway owned 300 acres in Gloucester County. *Darn it all.* Tradway was one of the gentry, just like the men on the jury. No wonder they didn't sentence him to any physical punishment. They knew him. They were probably friends with him. The jury definitely knew he could easily pay the fine.

Maybe the Gloucester County Historical Society might have information on this case. I sent off a quick email and then my mind wandered to poor Mary being whipped while onlookers watched. Tears started to pool.

I stood up so fast my chair tipped over with a crash. The two other researchers in the room looked over at me with raised eyebrows. "Oops," I mumbled, trying to hide my frustration. I righted the chair and walked as calmly as I could to the ladies' room. Once inside, I turned on the faucet, cupped my hands under the stream, and splashed cold water on my burning face.

Parisol, I need you. I leaned against the cold bathroom wall, feeling its coolness seep through my shirt. My legs gave out, and I slid down to the floor, sobbing into my hands.

After what felt like forever, I heard footsteps approaching. I scrambled up and quickly splashed more water on my face to hide the tears. A woman working on her dissertation walked in. She took one look at my red eyes and asked, "Are you ok?"

I nodded unconvincingly. "No worries. I just read a story that troubled me."

"Real people, real stories affect me too." She handed me a tissue and gave me a gentle smile. "The things that bother us the most from history are the things we need to remember, and are the things we need to stop from ever happening again."

I nodded silently and walked out. Back at my table, I dropped into my chair and stared at the book still open to the Mary Driver case. My eyes kept returning to those same words: "well laid on stripes."

What the heck was a "well laid on stripe"?

Chapter 21

Was it so hard that it would leave welts? I pictured thirty-nine stripes so brutal they left thirty-nine angry black and blue welts across Mary's back. I wanted to vomit. I desperately hoped that wasn't what happened. I didn't want to dig deeper into this horrible punishment, but I felt like I owed it to Mary. Someone needed to know what had happened here in Burlington.

I typed "well laid on stripes or lashes" into the search bar. Several historical sites popped up immediately. As I read through them, my heart sank. "Well laid on lashes would not be held back" and would be "required to be done with such force as to slice open the skin until the blood flowed." I couldn't process it. Not here. Not in Burlington. I covered my eyes with my hands. This was what they did to a teenage girl who had been raped by her stepfather and then convicted by 32 wealthy, property-owning men. Completely, utterly shocking.

After taking a few deep breaths, I heard the woman's from the bathroom's voice echo in my head: "The things that bother us the most from history are the things we need to remember, and are the things we need to stop from ever happening again." I forced myself to continue searching and found an article on Harris A. Friedberg's site. He was an Associate Professor of English at Wesleyan with degrees from Harvard and Yale. His research would be legit. In his article

"Policing Sex: the Bawdy Courts," he mentioned something that made my skin crawl: "Well laid on till the blood come."

I kept digging. The earliest official record of this horrific punishment requirement I could find dated all the way back to 1578/79. According to Susan Brigden, a Fellow and Tutor in Modern History at Lincoln College, Oxford, in her book "New Worlds, Lost Worlds: The Rule of the Tudors 1485-1603":

> "Paternalist puritan Justices, driven by scripture and righteous indignation, exercised stern rule in their petty sessions. In 1578, the Justices in Bury St Edmunds drew up a new penal code. Women found guilty of fornication would receive thirty lashes 'well laid on till the blood come'."

But why were women like Mary Driver treated so differently from men like Henry Tradway? I found my answer in "Who was William Shakespeare? An Introduction to the Life and Works" by Dympna Callaghan (William L. Safire Professor of Modern Letters in the Department of English at Syracuse University) (2013). Page 166.

> "Some members of Parliament were concerned that whipping was "slavish," and thus an inappropriate punishment for gentlemen who had, at least from their point of view, like Lucio, but sown their wild oats. In 1593, objections were made to a proposal that the fathers of bastards be whipped along with their mothers. The concern was that the penalty "might chance upon gentlemen or men of quality, whom it were not fit to put to such a shame."

And there it was ... the ugly truth laid bare. Men often escaped whipping because they had merely "sown their wild oats," and obviously, a "gentleman" or "man of quality" shouldn't be subjected to such humiliation. But a teenage girl raped by her guardian? She was naturally shameful and therefore deserving of being whipped at the back of a cart and dragged through town while everyone watched and pointed?

I needed to know if this was standard practice. Did courts back then consistently follow this twisted logic? Were men and women routinely treated with such blatant double standards when it came to "morality" issues?

I kept skimming through Burlington County Court cases, searching for answers, when I stumbled across a case from 1691 on page 123:

> "[Henry Beck and Alice Rawood presented] The Grand Jury present Henry Beck and Alice Rawood the daughter in Lawe of William Black for Comitting Fornication. Henry Beck appeared on the behalfe of himself and said Alice (shee being not able to come) And acknowledged the aforeside Cryme: And on the behalfe of himselfe and said Alice submitted to the Judgment of the Bench.
>
> [Order of Court] The Court haveing thereupon Considered of the aforesaid Cryme, order as followes (vizt) That the said Henry Beck give security for the Indemnifying the Court of Burlington, And for mainteynance of the Bastard Child; And that the said Alice Rawood after shee shall be delivered and well, shall be whipt, or pay 5L."

So only Alice faced the possibility of being whipped, even though they were both clearly there at the time of conception. I kept digging and found countless similar cases throughout Burlington County where women were prosecuted for being unmarried and pregnant or for giving birth too soon after marriage. Then I came across a case from 1691 on page 129 that stopped me cold:

> "Thomas Peachee appeares and upon the Indictment ownes that hee gott Mary (now his wife) with child before Marriage and submitts to the Judgment of the Bench. The Bench order him to pay 5L. or his wife to be whipt.

Wait! What?! I had to reread it to make sure I wasn't hallucinating. **"The Bench order him to pay 5L. or his wife to be whipt."**

I couldn't wrap my head around it. I couldn't fathom a court actually saying something so twisted. Either the husband pays a fine, or they'll physically torture his wife for something they both did. I forced myself to keep reading.

> "Upon his further submission the Bench remitt their sentence upon his good behaviour hee paying Court Fees."

So she was spared a whipping because of her husband's "good behavior"? Not because it was a barbaric punishment or because she deserved basic human dignity?

"Sorry, Lottie," I heard someone whisper. I glanced up from the court book, startled. Half the lights in the room had been shut off. Mr. Hartshorn was standing there with keys in hand, ready to lock up for the day.

But there were so many more women who deserved to be remembered.

Chapter 22

The home-bound bus stop sat just across the street and a few feet down from the BCHS, right at the corner of High Street and West Federal Street. The area was pretty empty. No one was waiting for the bus but me.

I sat down on the old bench with its flaking green paint and found myself wondering: what stood on this exact spot back in the late 1600s?

I pulled out the redrawn 1696 map I'd copied earlier from the book from 1883.

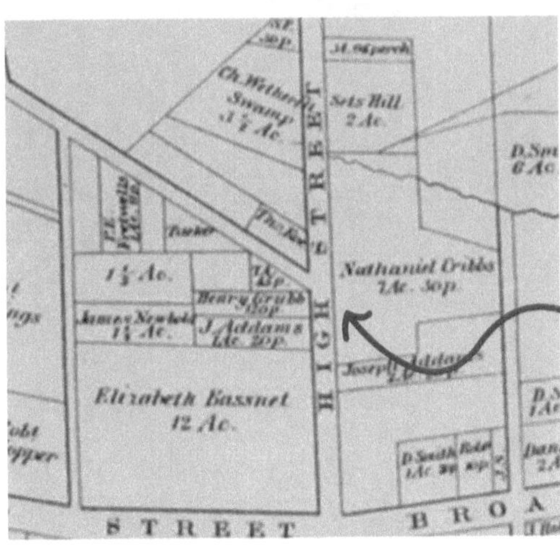

According to the map, my bus stop was positioned just to the right of the second "H" in High Street, smack in the middle of what once was Nathaniel Cribbs' property. I pulled out my phone and tried looking up "Cribbs" in the New Jersey Early Land Records database. Nothing came up. I tried "Cribs" and "Crib" too, but still got zero results.

I set aside the redrawn map and opened the photo I'd taken earlier of that old handwritten map, the one I'd snapped when I snuck upstairs at the library. Could it actually be an original Daniel Leeds map from 1696? Even a scanned copy would provide accurate details.

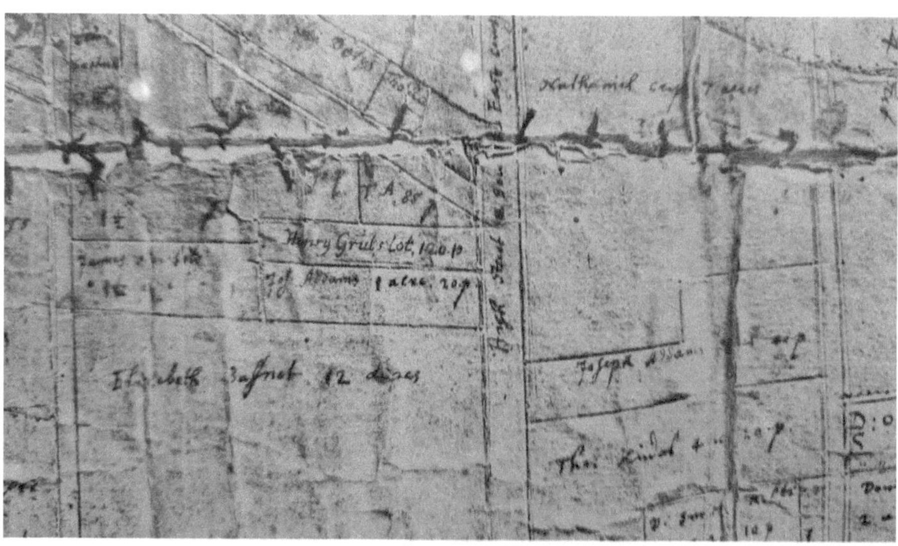

Where the redrawn map of 1883 showed "Nathaniel Cribbs," the original 1696 map clearly had "Nathaniel Crip" with a "p." The rest of the surname disappeared into what looked like a crease or tear that had claimed the final letters and then there were the number of acres.

I quickly searched "Crip" in the New Jersey Early Land Records Database. Bingo! Both John Cripps and Nathaniel Cripps appeared in the records as property owners in exactly that location. First, John the father owned property in that area, then Nathaniel his son started buying the land that abutted his fathers. When John Cripps died on on August 30, 1687, his land went to Nathaniel, who then owned it all. That was why Nathaniel, but not John, was listed on the 1696 map.

Sitting on the bus stop, the ground began to tremble beneath my feet. It started as just a tiny vibration, but it rose steadily up my ankles, through my calves, and throughout my entire body until it reached my head. I quickly stood up.

≈

The world around me started to shift and blur. The asphalt road dissolved into packed dirt, and most of the buildings simply vanished, replaced by a handful of structures that looked exactly like the colonial illustrations I'd seen in history books.

A smokehouse at the back of the property bellowed fragrant wood smoke that drifted far into the air. Wagons, horses, and goods crowded the narrow dirt road. People continued to stream in from all directions, many having left their horses and wagons at the town's edge because there was simply no more room. Their clothes were unmistakably colonial. Some in fine fabrics clearly imported from London, but most in rough homespun cloth. No one seemed to notice me at all. When I looked down at myself, I realized why. I couldn't even see my own body. I was just... presence. Essence without matter.

Suddenly, the chatter stopped. Every eye turned toward a wagon approaching from the direction of the river. There was a girl sitting in the back, her entire body shaking uncontrollably.

The wagon turned around and came to a stop just a few paces from where I stood. And then her eyes connected with mine. Did she just see me? In that instant, I felt her emotions wash over me like a wave. She carried such heavy shame, hanging like an anchor over her spirit. She was completely broken.

Her hair was pinned up, exposing her neck. Her nose and eyes were bright red from crying. Her face displayed a terrible mixture of deep despair, crushing humiliation, and something worse. A primal, animal fear of what was about to happen. I silently prayed that whatever was coming would somehow be stopped.

Another man spoke with the driver. The girl was instructed to prepare by exposing her back. Her hands shook too violently to manage on her own. A woman stepped forward to assist her, trying to preserve her dignity as much as possible under the circumstances. Tears streamed down the girl's face. When her hands were secured to the cart, maintaining any modesty became nearly impossible.

The driver was told when he began to proceed at an agonizingly slow pace. He would travel only half a mile over the course of an entire hour. The punishment would be methodically delivered, with a new stripe administered approximately every two minutes.

Her sentence was read aloud: "Mary Driver! The Bench have Considered of thy Lewdnesse in defyleing thy Mothers bed, of which thou hast beene found guilty: And for the same doe order that today betweene the howers of Eleaven and Twelve in the forenoone, thou shall be severely whipt on thy naked back at a Cart's Tayle from the house of John Cripps in this Towne to the River side and that thou shall have thirty Nyne stripes well laid on."

Oh Mary. No!!!!

I suddenly realized where I was and what I was witnessing. This was the actual punishment of Mary Driver. And I was standing right at the spot where it began, in front of John Cripps' house.

I looked around at the gathered crowd, sickened by what I saw. There were gawkers staring at Mary like she was nothing but trash. Voyeurs craned their necks, hoping for a glimpse of exposed skin. Even worse were the ones with that gleam in their eyes, sociopaths energized by witnessing another person's suffering.

Then there were those treating it like a social event, a day's entertainment. I spotted several men who had brought their wives and daughters specifically to witness what would happen if they dared stray from "the path of righteousness."

Among the crowd were several of the thirty-two men who had served as judges and jurors at Mary's trial. They stood tall, boasting about how they had protected the community and ensured justice was served. The well-dressed men with their superior attitudes made their message abundantly clear in every smug expression: "Don't cross the gentry landowners."

The man who had been speaking unfurled his whip and raised it high. When it came down across Mary's small, thin back, it sliced through her tender skin. Her scream pierced the air, a sound of pure agony that made my stomach turn. Blood began to trickle from the long, deep wound. The wagon driver nudged his horse, and the terrible procession began to move forward.

I turned away. I simply couldn't bear to watch anymore. The crowd shuffled slowly past me, following the gruesome parade as it continued down the street towards the river. The spectators' eager faces a testament to humanity's darkest impulses.

Couldn't they see it was their shame on display here, not hers? My heart ached so deeply for Mary, but nobody else seemed to care.

I heard the crack of the second lash, followed by another agonized scream that made me feel viscerally nauseous. Suddenly, my vision began to swim. The world around me blurred and wavered. The dirt road, the colonial buildings, the crowd ... all of it started to evaporate like morning mist. Then reality snapped back into place. A boy on a bicycle pedaled past me and I sat back down on the bus stop bench, tears streaming down my face that I hastily tried to wipe away.

I shook my head as the City of Burlington in 2022 materialized fully around me again.

———

The bats were fully swarming my belfry now, I thought. Two hallucinations in one day. Maybe I should ask Sara about medication.

I could already imagine her response: "It's probably just stress related to your worries about Parisol. This is normal."

I tried to pull myself together since the bus would arrive any minute. I was checking my tear-streaked face on my phone camera when I heard a car pull up alongside the curb.

"Hey, do you need a ride?"

Chapter 23

"D ad?" I turned my head and quickly whisked away the last tear.

The bus pulled up right behind his car. "Want to get in?" Dad asked.

I jumped into his car, immediately breaking into a sweat. *I am going to be grounded forever,* I thought.

We drove in complete silence until he turned right onto Route 130.

At the red light, he looked at me with a pained expression. "Your mom and I are extremely sorry we haven't been here for you these last two days. We got so focused on finding Parisol that we haven't been checking in with you enough," he said, wringing his hands. "We are so sorry, Sweetie."

"No, Dad, you've got this completely wrong. I want you to keep working to find Parisol. That's all that matters."

"When we got the text from school saying you weren't there, we panicked and immediately checked your phone's location. It makes sense that you'd go to the historical society. But how did you even get there?"

I bit my lip and whispered, "I took the bus," then braced myself for the inevitable lecture about safety and responsibility.

There was a long pause. Dad stared straight ahead into the traffic, nodding slowly in deep thought. Finally, he said, "I'm proud of you."

Not the response I expected. I hated it when they used techniques they'd read in some parenting psychology article.

Take the win, I told myself.

"Were the tears when I pulled up because you were afraid of taking the bus home?" Dad asked.

I couldn't tell him about witnessing Mary Driver's brutal whipping. He'd drive me straight to Sara's office and probably schedule an emergency psych eval. "No. I'm just missing Parisol."

"We're doing everything we can to get her back."

"I know."

Dad took the off-ramp for Bridgeboro Road toward Moorestown. That's when the familiar vibrations began creeping up my feet again, and the world around me started to shift and blur.

≋

Cars vanished. Paved roads dissolved into nothing. Modern street signs disappeared completely. Where South Bridgeboro Street should have passed directly in front of Delran Fire Company No. 1, there was now only a dirt path barely wide enough for a cart. A weathered wooden sign pointed back toward the creek: "John Buzby's Ferry at Rancocas Creek. Man & horse 3 pence."

Dense woods surrounded me, broken only by a handful of rustic buildings. As my essence drifted up the rough road, I spotted a painted sign on a two-story building: "William Allen's Tavern & Lodging."

I floated effortlessly through the wall into the tavern, where several patrons lingered over their morning meal. The tavern owner entered from the back room. His waistcoat hanging open over breeches smeared with ale.

"Ahh, the Jameses, eh? Still 'eeeere, rrrr ye?" the tavern owner said. "Begged charity for the first night. Besss now be movin' on."

The older James replied, his voice rough, "Twenty minutes, and we'll be gone."

The younger could have passed for a high school senior, but the lines on his face and the desperate look in his eyes came from a rough, weathered life. His coat was too big, his hands red and cracked. He tore a piece of bread with his teeth and spoke around the mouthful.

From the talk amongst the two, I gathered they had come east from the Pennsylvania and Virginia frontiers, meeting only recently in Philadelphia. Both had crossed the Delaware by way of Cooper's Ferry. But hen two Lenni Lenape women stepped into the tavern, their chatter quieted.

The women must have been well-known locals, since the regulars greeted them by name. The older one was called Hannah, though I heard someone refer to her as "Widow Hughes." The younger, Catherine, was heavy with child and looked to be due any day. Each carried a small bundle, one a clean shift, the other a piece of new linen.

Nobody seemed bothered by the women's presence except for the two men who'd recently arrived in New Jersey. Their agitation at the mere sight of these women quickly escalated into open anger as they began loudly calling them "heathens." When the men started hurling abusive words at them, the women took the high road and left.

At another table, a man was talking about rewards for catching runaways. The way he spoke, it was clear he wasn't picky. Free or not, anyone with dark skin would earn him a paycheck down South. He bragged about a man he'd caught not long ago, saying he'd returned him to an enslaver in "Senemenson." I presumed he meant Cinnaminson.

Once the women were gone, the two Jameses discussed following the women and ravishing them. They spoke casually that if the women didn't easily lie with them, the men agreed they'd put a hatchet in each of their heads. Their talk grew more vicious and repetitive. The older man repeated, "I want to lie with them. If they will not, I will knock their brains out." They downed their drinks and walked out the door.

With that, I felt my spirit pulled out of the building and down the dirt path.

The colonial scene dissolved around me, snapping back to the present day.

I glanced to my left. Dad was still driving, completely unaware of what I'd just witnessed.

"Please promise you won't take the bus anywhere again without telling Mom or me first?" Dad made a left at Ott's Tavern onto Hartford Road.

"I promise."

We continued in silence. My head was spinning from the scene with the Lenni Lenape women. *What the heck was that about?* I thought.

Dad made a right turn on Centerton Road and then another right onto Marne Highway, which was the Old Salem Road. I glanced right at the Lockheed Martin buildings, then left at the old Joshua Bispham home.

Not again. The vibrations crept up my feet and legs as the scenery began to shift.

≈

The paved driveway leading to Joshua Bispham's house became packed dirt. Several men and women stood in the driveway, staring toward a group of men about a hundred yards away, just inside the tree line. The men in the woods were holding handkerchiefs pressed over their faces.

As I was pulled closer to the men in the woods, a horrible stench slammed into me. It reminded me of the time Rex and I had walked past a dead raccoon at Medford's Freedom Park. We'd been in the section called Freedom Barks, with its twenty-six acres of open fields and cedar creeks where Rex always found other dogs to splash around with. The stink from that rotting raccoon carcass overwhelmed my nose from twenty feet away. The stench where these men stood was far worse.

What are those men staring at?

Oh NO! It was the two Lenni Lenape women from the tavern. They were lying motionless on the ground, covered in blood. I quickly turned away from the gruesome scene toward the dirt path, and the colonial world faded back to the paved driveway.

———

I stared out the car window in complete shock at what I'd just witnessed. I had never seen a dead human body before ...well, except for an elderly neighbor's funeral where the lighting and makeup made her look like she was peacefully sleeping.

Rage bubbled up inside me. My soul cried out for justice for these women whom those two men had murdered for no reason other than the color of their skin.

"Should we pick up food on our way home?" Dad asked.

"No thanks. I'm supposed to eat at La Vita's with Avalon and Wulf."

There was a pause before Dad responded. "Please keep us informed of where you're going. Stay safe and stick together!"

I couldn't stop thinking about those two women and how something as trivial as skin color could trigger such violent hatred. Those men saw the women as less than human, calling them savages, when they were the true savages.

Marne Highway turned into Main Street. The light was red at the intersection with Chester Avenue. The Moorestown Friends Quaker Meeting House sat on our left, and on the right was the Verizon building, site of the old Cox's Tavern.

Cox's Tavern before it was torn down

Even as a history lover, I'd never understood why people made such a big deal about this particular spot. So there used to be a bar here way back when. So what?

The familiar tingle of vibrations started in my feet.

≋

The paved road dissolved into dirt. *Ugh, am I ever going to get home?*

The tavern bustled with activity as men arrived and disappeared inside. Nobody re-emerged, except for John Cox himself, who was telling his enslaved to prepare for even more arrivals and to tend to all their horses. Something important was happening. My essence was drawn inside just as the Coroner's Inquest was beginning regarding the two murdered women. Witness after witness presented evidence and testimony to the assembled jury.

As it came to an end, I overheard a man say to his manservant that "the Court was adjourning to the Market House in Burlington, where the trial against the two men would surely be followed by their execution."

———

The scenery soon began to change back to current-day Moorestown.

Thankfully, we wouldn't be driving past Union Street in Burlington City. *I didn't need to see a hanging today. Or any day.*

I turned my head to the right and read the historical marker in front of Cox's Tavern. It had never occurred to me how crucial this spot was to our town's history.

"Where were you just now, Princess?" Dad asked.

"Just zoning out." *I wish.*

I texted Wulf and Avalon: "I'm almost home."

"I've got news," Avalon texted back.

Chapter 24

I turned on Netflix to find something to zone out to. Netflix's top suggestion for me was "The Jeffrey Dahmer Story." *Not today. Not ever.* I kept scrolling.

Rex jumped onto the couch to snuggle, and I moved my legs just in time. After several contortions, I settled with my legs draped over him.

Kami, the anti-Rex, perched regally on top of the China cabinet. She observed, stalked, and prowled from the sidelines, but never actually interacted with anyone.

Two quick butterfly knocks came from the front door, Avalon's unique way of announcing "I'm here." It was followed by Avalon and Wulf bursting in to commandeer the overstuffed comfortable couch.

"What did you find?" Wulf asked.

I told them about my research at the BCHS, then hesitantly filled them in on what I was calling my "hallucinations." 1) The auditory whipping at the mini park. 2) Witnessing Mary Driver's punishment on High Street. 3) The brutal murder of the two Lenni Lenape women in Moorestown.

I expected them to take a step back from me, but surprisingly, they didn't seem the least bit concerned about my sanity. Which, of course, made me question theirs.

"What's your news, Avalon?" I asked.

Avalon's demeanor shifted as she considered how to respond.

Oh no, I thought, bracing myself for awful news.

"The police just asked Galen to come into the station to answer a few questions." Her voice cracked, and she started to sob. Rex immediately trotted over and rested his head on her lap.

"What do the police have?" I pressed, desperate for any information about Parisol.

"I don't have any details. They just asked him to drop by the station later to answer a few questions." By now, she was falling apart and hyperventilating. I slid the tissue box across the coffee table.

"Pull it together, Avalon," Wulf said firmly. "We don't know why they asked him to come in. It could be anything. When you and Galen are actually a real couple, then you can have this... this drama. But until then, whatever this is needs to be zipped up and put away."

"But my inner child needs a moment."

"Tell your inner child, 'This is not the time.'"

"So Lottie can cry over seeing a hallucination of a whipping, but I can't cry over the guy I'm destined to be with, who is going through something traumatic right now?"

"Exactly."

Avalon slumped back and pouted. Her moods shifted so frequently that she'd be back to her usual bouncy self shortly. Until then, we'd talk around her while she rebooted.

"I seriously doubt Galen had anything to do with Parisol's disappearance," I said. He's put her on a pedestal and treated her with nothing but respect for over a decade.

"We keep talking about the Mary Driver whipping being a hallucination triggered because you read the court case. But what if it wasn't? What if it's somehow connected to your journal entries?" Wulf asked.

"But how would I even begin to prove that to myself? How would someone set up an experiment for something like that?"

"Maybe the situation has already been set up by today's events. Sort of like the RSVP and the confirmation at the swim club. I need to marinate on this."

Avalon fully rebooted, sat forward. "So while you were off playing detective in Burlington, I made this whole digital board with all our clues." She sent us the link.

Avalon always made everything beautiful, from the way she dressed to her breathtaking artwork. But this ...this was new. Avalon had created a gorgeous electronic corkboard for collaborating on Parisol's case, filled with the few clues we knew so far.

She had pinned up tidbits about Parisol's friends, Dax, Galen being called in for questioning, the limited timeline we knew, and my journal entries from Monday and Tuesday nights.

I added to the board what I'd learned about what a "Cart's Tayle" was. Avalon added a note about the audio hallucination from the mini park. Wulf added the Mary Driver case and my vision of her whipping. And we all started working on adding the three-part vision of the two Lenni Lenape women.

Avalon turned on the TV and cast the corkboard onto the screen. We all stared.

"Did time stop when you heard the whipping? Were the mother and children like statues at the mini park?" Wulf asked.

"No, they kept playing and reading."

"And when you were transported to different time periods, for example, with Mary Driver and at the tavern, when you returned to our time, had much time passed?"

"No. It was as if I'd never left."

"Interesting. So, just bear with me and let's imagine they weren't hallucinations. In that case, two different things are happening. When you heard something from the past while staying in the present, time kept moving normally here. But when your consciousness actually traveled to the past or more accurately you accessed history in Liber as if it was happening now, time stopped here completely. That's like quantum superposition, you existed in two states at once." Wulf said.

Please, not another quantum lecture, I thought.

"But it's for another day," Wulf said. He shook his head several times, as if physically tossing out the scientific thread he was pondering, then walked toward the large screen on the wall to examine each clue.

"How do we prove that the Mary Driver case was real and not a hallucination?" Wulf asked.

I shrugged. I had absolutely no idea.

Avalon piped up. "It's clear we just need to approach it in reverse."

Wulf and I exchanged glances, having no clue what Avalon was talking about.

"I don't understand," I said. "It's dreadfully confusing!"

"That's the effect of living backwards," Avalon replied.

"The Mary Driver case was documented in the court book. That's our evidence that it happened. Then you had the vision. So the question is, 'Did reading the case trigger a hallucination?' It seems obvious to me that we need to take a different event, maybe what happened in the mini park, and look for historical evidence of that. Since you had no prior knowledge of any event like that happening in this area, finding evidence would be confirmation."

We racked our brains. How does one find evidence of the whipping I heard in the mini park? Such evidence would prove I wasn't losing my mind. But we hit a wall.

"How do you determine whether something might have occurred 350 years ago?" Wulf asked himself.

"Sometimes you two are incredibly thick," said Avalon, smirking. "Initially, you found the whipping of Mary Driver in the Burlington Court Book, and then verified the address on the old map, and then you had the vision. Maybe the whipping that you heard in the mini park could have a property owner listed from the same time period on the map. If we find the owner's name, then we can look him up in the reference books and the historical online sites. Living backwards."

It was a long shot, but it was our only lead.

I pulled up a current map and located the mini park (P) and Quaker Meeting House (MH). Then I retrieved the redone 1696 map that I found in the book at the BCHS. Positioning them side by side, it appeared that the mini park (P) sat on what would have been James Wills' property. But eyeballing it wasn't precise, and there was a possibility the mini park actually fell on his next-door neighbor, T. Gladwin's property.

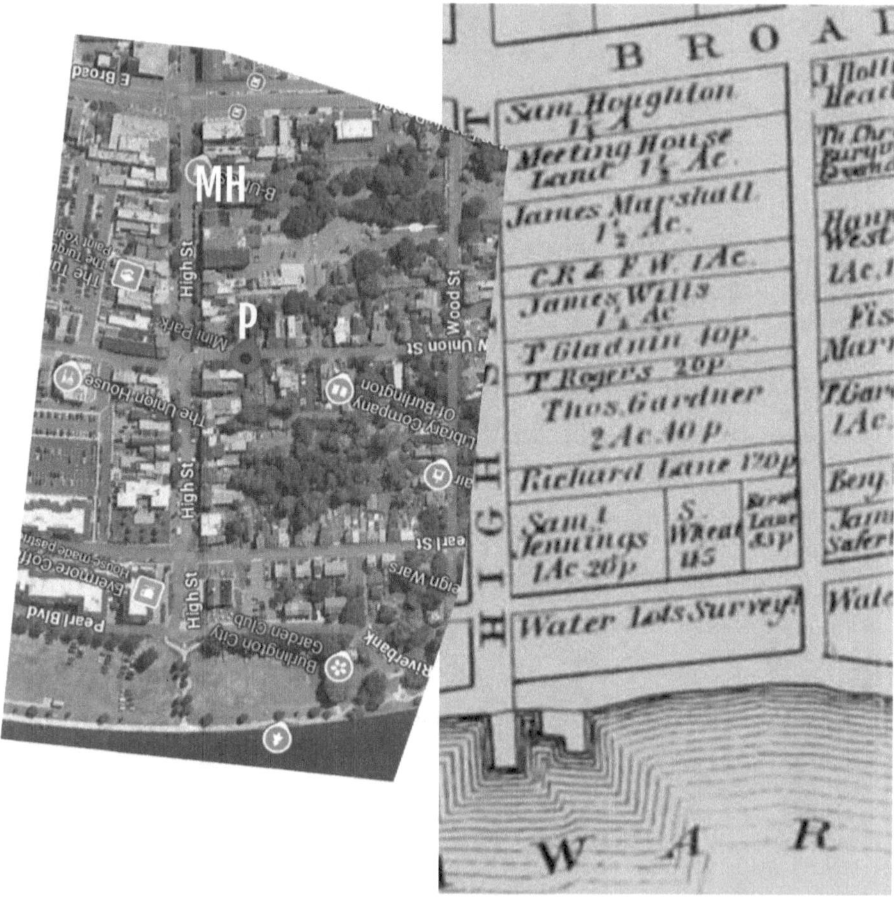

In 1696, Union Street, the street that now runs by the mini park and the Library Company of Burlington, did not yet exist. Properties were much deeper

136

back then and stretched straight through the large block from High Street to Wood Street.

"What about on the original map of Burlington that you took a picture of when upstairs in the old library?" Wulf asked. "Are the names spelled differently, like the Cribbs and Cripps were earlier?"

I pulled out the copy of the original map. "No, James Wills and T. Gladwin are spelled the same on both maps." A crease ran down the middle of their deep properties, but the names were still legible.

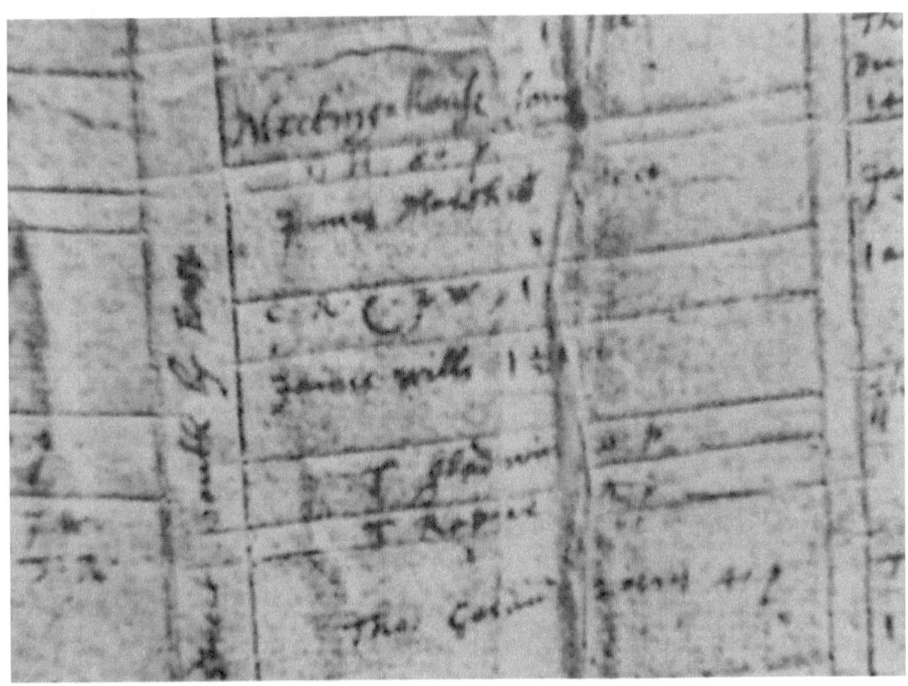

I pulled up the New Jersey Early Land Records Database and searched for James Wills in Burlington County in the late 1600s and found several records. He was a wealthy landowner.

Name	Descriptions and Location	Date	Reference
Wills, James (Grantee)	TO: James Wills FROM: SURVEY. 4 acres. Burlington Town; South Side of Burlington Island. For James Wills. [Caveat by Mr. William Burge: Oct. 2, 1712] OTHERS NAMED: William Burge LOCATIONS: West Jersey; Burlington; Burlington City; Burlington Island	Nov 1693	Basse A (Surveys, 1-206) (WJ) : Folio 76 (SSTSE023) View PDF
Wills, James (Grantee)	TO: James Wills FROM: SURVEY. 1.5 acres. Burlington Town; High Street and Wood Street. For James Wills. Bordering lands of Thomas Gladwin; and Charles Read. OTHERS NAMED: Thomas Gladwin; Charles Read LOCATIONS: West Jersey; Burlington; Burlington City; High Street; Wood Street	1694	Basse A (Surveys, 1-206) (WJ) : Folio 118 1/2 (SSTSE023) View PDF
Wills, James (Grantee)	TO: James Wills FROM: Anna Salter (Estate of) CONVEYANCE. Ferry Point, formerly Heulings Point. [Burlington County] OTHERS NAMED: LOCATIONS: West Jersey; Burlington; Ferry Point; Heulings Point	31 Oct 1690	D (WJ) : Folio 269 (SSTSE023)
Wills, James (Owner of adjoining land) (Named)	TO: John Chaffin FROM: SURVEY. 35 acres. In the Town Field. [Burlington County] OTHERS NAMED: Matthew Allen (Owner of adjoining land); Hannah Kimball (Owner of adjoining land); James Wills (Owner of adjoining land) LOCATIONS: West Jersey; Burlington; Town Field; Town Lots; House Lots	29 Apr 1682	Revels Surveys/Book A (WJ) : Folio 26 (SSTSE023) View PDF
Wills, James (Owner of adjoining land) (Named)	TO: John Chaffen FROM:	29 Apr 1682	Revels Surveys/Book A (WJ) : Folio 29

The second listing was for the property shown on the old map between High Street and Wood Street. In the description, it listed Thomas Gladwin as his neighbor.

"If you call your contact at the Burlington County Historical Society tomorrow, maybe he'll look up James Wills and Thomas Gladwin for you in that old Court Book," Avalon suggested.

"I can't wait that long. Every second counts," I said. "The Moorestown Library has a New Jersey Room dedicated to old books and historical documents. Maybe there's a copy of the Burlington Court Book there."

Wulf's stomach let out a loud growl.

"First, La Vita's," Wulf declared. "I'm hungry." La Vita's front door was on Main Street, and the back door exited to a parking lot just across the street from the library.

Avalon's phone vibrated. She looked at it and answered. "Yes, they are here with me. Okay," she switched the call to the speaker.

"I have something I need your help with, but you need to come to my house tonight to view it," whispered Sabielo over the phone. "It's about Parisol."

My mind raced, wondering what she needed our help with.

"My dad will be at a township meeting from six to eight. I can meet you and guide you around our security cameras, then help you in through our Christmas Tree Door."

"Your what?" Wulf asked.

"It's a hidden door that's about three feet up in the air on the outside of the house. There are no steps leading to it, and it doesn't look like a door. It's meant to blend in. We bring our Christmas tree into the parlor every year through that door, but it's actually a coffin door."

"I wish you had stuck with Christmas Tree Door," Avalon said. "I'm now going to be imagining ghosts in your house while we are there."

Welcome to my world, I thought.

"We should be done at the library, say by 5:45?" Avalon said, looking for my agreement. I nodded. Avalon continued, "Sab, you could meet us at the library and then show us the route to avoid the cameras. Wait, how many cameras do you have?"

"You don't want to know, trust me. But it was fun finding the holes in Dad's security."

Chapter 25

Avalon reached to close the door behind us, but I stuck my foot in the way and pointed to the sign. It read, "The Door must remain open when people are inside."

"This room has a book preservation system that activates when the door is closed. Turns out, what's healthy for old books isn't so healthy for people."

During our search for the old Court Book, I spotted a title on the shelves that started pulling me in, "A Study of Slavery in New Jersey (1896)." I was intrigued by a discussion of slavery written in 1896, just 30 years after slavery ended in New Jersey with the ratification of the 13th Amendment.

I pulled the book off the shelf. My inner critic thought, *What a geek*. But I couldn't help myself. The writer, at first glance, appeared against slavery and racism. Then I came to the bottom of page 55.

> "If a woman had children she was rendered less desirable as a slave. That laxness of morals ordinarily found among African slaves was present in New Jersey is sufficiently evident. Frequently slave women were offered for sale for no other reason than that they had children. They were, in some cases, sold without their child."

Wait what? "That laxness of morals ordinarily found among African slaves...." This author was a racist without realizing it. Did other white New Jersey residents share his views in 1896?

These enslaved women were raised knowing they didn't have a choice in saying no to male authorities. And this man writes of their lack of morals. I was stupefied.

Separating children from their mothers and their fathers... talk about a lack of morals. *Thankfully, I live in the United States, and it's 2022. At least racism is mostly gone for good here,* I thought. Nobody in their right mind would separate a child from either of its parents anymore, even if their skin color was a different shade. Would they?

"Found it," said Wulf. With that, I slid the book I was skimming back on the shelf and made a mental note to come back to it another day.

The librarian poked her head in. "Anything I can help you find?"

"I don't think so," I said.

"How about you, Wulf? Avalon?"

"We're on a top-secret mission," Avalon said with a grin. "Got to handle this one ourselves."

"I understand." She started to leave, then paused at the door. "Wulf, if your mission wraps up early, the new issue of Physics Phonon just came in." And with that, she was gone.

"What page was the Mary Driver case on in the Court Book?" asked Avalon.

I understood. Seeing it for oneself was completely different than hearing someone tell you about it. I opened up my phone and found the photo of the case I had taken earlier today. "Page 72."

I sat down across the table from Avalon. I had no reason to read it again.

Upon reading the case, Avalon sucked in a deep breath, closed the book, and slid it over to Wulf. "Here you look for James Wills. Specifically, any reference to owning a slave or slaves."

The first reference to James Wills that Wulf found, via skimming the book, was in 1683, when he was on a jury. Only male landowners were entitled to be jurors, so the jury pool was limited. James kept popping up on many juries over the years. But Wulf's cursory review didn't find any reference to a whipping on James' property.

He did find his own rabbit hole, though, the case of Phillis, Thomas Lambert's slave, that he read out loud to us.

"Att a Private Session held October 18th: 1693 Upon the Accompt of William Wardell. There Present Edward Hunloke Esqr. Deputy Governour. John Tatham, John Worlidge, Francis Davenport, Daniel Wills, Daniel Leeds Esqrs. Justices.

William Wardell (who was 16th October instant Comitted) being under indisposition of Body, requested to make his humble Submission and to Committ himselfe to the hearing and determination of a Private Session, which is this 18th October 1693 called at the House of Thomas Kendall in Burlington. Att the request of the above named Wardell, to make his Submission to the Justices: The Court called **William Wardell called And Confesses hee hath had Carnally to doe with Phillis, the Negro Woman, servant to Thomas Lambert:** And Committs himselfe to the Mercy of the Bench. The said Wardell (the Prisoner) by others on his behalf requests that he may have his punishment laid upon his estate. The Judgment of the Bench That the said Wardell shall be whipt at a Cart's Tayle tomorrow betwixt the howers of 10 and 12. from the Markett house to the River and shall receive Thirty Nyne Stripes well laid on: And pay all the Charges that hath been expended by Thomas Lambert in prosecuting him. And alsoe pay all Court Charges: or instead of the Thirty Nyne Lashes to pay the Summe of Five Pounds, And pay the Summe of Forty shillings over and above to Thomas Lambert for his losse of time in his Negro womans service: William Wardell called, And his Sentence above. Read: And the said Wardell chuses to pay five pounds instead of the Lashes, and to pay the other Costs and other Charges: Which Amounts in the whole to Nine Pounds, one shilling and Six pence."

When Wulf was done reading the case, he added, "This is crazy, the way the men talked of Phillis as property. There is so much here to unpack. Unlike with the white women, it wasn't the court's decision to whip Phillis. That would have been up to Thomas, her owner. Thomas was also paid for the loss of Phillis's work time due to the pregnancy and delivery."

I felt woozy under the weight of the day, the weight of the last few days. I needed to lie down. It had been a long day, and it wasn't nearly over. My head was overwhelmed and crying out, *Too much. Too much.*

Hearing the name Thomas Lambert made the history I knew bubble up in my mind. I needed to release it, but this wasn't the time. I lay down on the carpeted floor, just past the table, away from the view of anyone walking by our room's windows or open door.

It felt good to be horizontal for a minute and to close my eyes. Lying on my back, I allowed both hands to turn and touch the carpet. I could feel the threads and imagine their color. The air was slightly cooler at this level. I could breathe.

Within the confines of the peace, I allowed some of the pressure to release. The words quickly slid across my lips. "Thomas Lambert was one of the initial gentry. His town was originally named Lamberton, but later became the waterfront of Trenton, which was back when Burlington County went much farther north and much farther south than it does today."

"Sorry. I tried to keep it in." They ignored it and kept working. I lay thankful for friends who got me.

"It amazes me how you remember the original town names from hundreds of years ago. I still can't remember the name of Montana's state capital," said Avalon.

"Helena," Wulf and I said in unison.

From the floor, even with my eyes closed, I knew Avalon was rolling her eyes.

"Wulf, please pass me the court book," said Avalon. I heard it slide across the table above me.

After a minute, Avalon said sarcastically, "You two geniuses, you do realize there is an index in the back of this book."

"Let me see that," said Wulf. The book slid back across the table.

In the index, he found references to James Wills on close to two dozen pages. Wulf skimmed the mentioned pages. I could hear pages turning back and forth as he'd look at the index, and turn to each section, giving us a summary of each.

Then the whirlwind of turning pages stopped. But this time there was no summary. Just silence. Eerie silence. My anxiety started creeping back up again.

I could hear Wulf's fingers begin to rub together fast, back and forth, back and forth. Another of his tells. This one was obvious when an experiment showed signs of failure. He never noticed he was doing it.

Cutting through the silence, I heard from above the table, "I found it, Lottie. It's not good."

He read from page 56.

> "Att the Court held the 9th of the 6th Moneth 1686. The Governour present George Hutcheson present James Budd, Elias Farre, William Biddle, Thomas Gardner, Francis Davenport Justices. The Grand Jury Attested Symon Charles, John Shin senr., John Pancost, Joshua Humfreys, Thomas Butcher, William Budd, William Atkinson, John Crosby, John Day, Thomas Barton, Robert Young, Isaac Marriott, John Woolston senr. The Traverse Jury Godfrey Hancock, Richard Bassnett, William Hunt, Michael New-

bold, Henry Grubb, John Boarton, John Hollinshead, Bernard Devonish, Martin Holt, Daniell Leeds, William Brightwen, Daniel Bacon.

Attorney Generall for the King Christopher Snowden.

James Wills by Recognizance Bound over to appeare at this Court, and Indictment Fyled on the behalfe of our Lord the King called and appeares. The Evidence for the King Attested Katherine Greene, Thomas Greene, William Myers, George Lambert, Mary Grubb, William Peachee, James Hill, Thomas Gladwyn. The Grand Jury finde the Bill. The Prisoner Arraigned: And to the Indictment pleads not guilty as to giving the woman Negro any blowes that occasioned her death, but sayth hee caused her to be buryed, not knowing that the Lawe required there should have beene an Inquest touching the cause of her death.

And for Tryall referres himself to God and the Countrey. whereupon the Traverse Jury above is Attested, the Prisoner objecting against none of them.

Katharine Greene Attested. Deposeth, that the Negro woman Servant being by said James Wills sent to be a while at the house of the said Katharine, in regard the said negro had some distemper upon her, that shee might have conference with a Negro that belongs to the said Katharine: The said Katharine found that the Negro woman of the said James had her back very sore, and that the Negro woman told her it was with Fum, fum, which is (beating) and that further shee the said Katharine found a small Scarr upon her Belly which was sore, which the Negro told her came on the account aforesaid.

Avalon interrupted Wulf's reading. "So Katherine Greene had her own slave try to teach James Wills' slave to be more obedient? How many slaves were in the City of Burlington?"

"We don't know. Removing the whitewashing and the misconception of 'it didn't happen here' is a process," I said.

Avalon shuffled in her seat.

"Not something I thought about happening here either," said Wulf. He paused in deep thought before continuing to read from the case.

> "But sayth that shee did not perceive any blowes that in her judgment might be the cause of her death. Thomas Greene Attested, Deposeth the same in substance.
>
> William Myers Attested, deposeth that hee heard at a considerable distance many blowes or stripes and walking onward as hee thought hee heard a Negro Cry out many tymes, and, soe heard stripes or lashes continued till hee gott home, and then he supposed it to be James Wills beating his Negro woman, and heard still many Lashes more and Crying out, untill hee was greevd and went into his owne house and shut the dore, and said to his wife oh! yond cruell man, and sayth hee beleeves hee heard full a hundred stripes or lashes, but did not see James Wills beat his Negro.
>
> William Peachee Attested, sayth that hee with Thomas Gladwyn being in the Smithy of Thomas Gladwyn at worke and heareing severall stripes or lashings and one crying out, went forth, and sawe James Wills beat his Negro Servant and give her many stripes which greeved both him and Thomas Gladwyn, whereupon they went againe into the Smithy to worke.
>
> Thomas Gladwyn, Attested deposeth to the same effect. James Hill, Attested sayth hee sawe the said James Wills Beat his said Negro and tye her hands, and hang her up, but that her feet reached the ground and might sustaine the weight of her body, but hee beleeves it was painfull to her and that hee (this deponent, tooke her downe, but sayth the Negro was soe stubborne and willfull that might well provoke any Master to use her sharply:
>
> But sayth hee sawe nothing done to the Negro that in his Judgment might be the cause of her death; But that hee this Deponent beleeves she was unsound.

> The Jury bring in their verdict: And finde the said James Wills not guilty. But in regard it appears the said Negro was unsound, it was a fault, that hee did not therefore be the more spareing; And for that hee buryed her without a Jury or Inquest: Therefore they appoint (with the approbation of the Bench) that hee pay all Court charges, which is assented to by the Bench.
>
> James Wills cleared by Proclamation, paying the same."

"Oh my Lottie, he did beat her to death. You weren't hallucinating," said Avalon as she lay down on the floor next to me and reached out and grabbed my hand.

I kept my eyes closed to hold back the tears. I tried not to hyperventilate. James Wills beat his slave to death on his own property. People heard it going on. She was crying out. They believed he was going to kill her, and yet nobody did anything. Instead, they shut their doors and called her desire to be free and do what she wanted mental problems. Then when she died, he just happened to forget he should notify the government for an inquest, and instead immediately buried her. Then his friends found him not guilty.

So unjust. Tears were pooling around my eyes. After a few minutes, I sat up.

"That park should be dedicated to her and the other enslaved in Burlington County who were stolen from their families, stolen from their freedom, stolen from their futures. Stolen." I took a breath. "Would you two go with me sometime soon and bring flowers to her park where she was whipped?"

"Of course."

I lay back down on the library's carpeted floor and let go of Avalon's hand. Avalon stood back up and started pacing. "Why do you think there is no mention of the enslaved at that park?"

"They probably don't know," said Wulf.

I could hear Wulf open his notebook and begin to scribble furiously.

"More quantum formulas?" asked Avalon.

"Not quite. A formula for learning from the past. All wisdom comes down to formulas."

"Tap, tap, tap." The sound of a fingernail tapping on glass.

"Come on in. We're just finishing up," said Avalon.

I could see Sabie's black boots step into the room.

"Where's Lottie?" She asked.

"Down there," whispered Wulf.

Sabielo peeked over the table. I awkwardly gave a little wave.

"What are you working on?" she asked our group.

"Just a research project for school," said Wulf.

Usually, I'd jump up from embarrassment at being found lying on a public floor, but Sabielo was safer than most, and it felt good down here.

While Avalon and Wulf were finishing up, Sabielo roamed around the room. I heard her footsteps, the sound of books being pulled out and put back. Then I heard her place one on the table and the sound of pages being turned.

While Sabielo was preoccupied, Avalon's chair pushed back from the table, and she walked over to the shelves. I opened my eyes to see her sliding the Court Book back onto its shelf.

"I'm sure you've all heard of the case of Carolyn Majane," said Sabielo.

Nobody said a word.

"Seriously? Not one of you?" She shook her head. "Well, back in August 1975, about to enter her junior year at MHS, she disappeared one night after leaving her friends at Friendly's on Main Street. Friendly's was where the bank is now located, next to Wawa. She never reached the party she was headed to. Here is her class photo from the MHS 1975 yearbook."

I opened my eyes and got up to take a look at the picture of Carolyn Majane.

"She had an amazing smile," said Wulf.

"She was beautiful," added Avalon.

"She would have graduated with the class of 1977."

Sabielo turned a few more pages. "I know there is another picture of her in here somewhere."

After not finding the other picture, she shut the book. "The police didn't investigate right away, ignoring her parents' pleas. The police presumed she was a runaway, as they presumed regarding most teen girls who vanished back then."

"In 1985, they found Carolyn's remains just across the Moorestown border in Mt Laurel, when kids were playing where a new development was going in. It's past Laurel Creek. a little

Back in 1975, when she disappeared, the place where her remains were found was referred to as the Texas Pond, a leftover pond from the old sulfur match factory in the woods next to the Rancocas Creek. Teens used to party back there in the 70s."

"Somebody dropped the ball on that case," continued Sabielo. "Her classmates are now in their 60s. Her family and her friends deserve answers, and I'm going to find them."

"I wish you'd find Parisol first," I whispered.

Sabielo nodded. "Let's get moving before my Dad gets home."

Chapter 26

Sabielo's house wasn't far. Maybe a 15 minute walk from the library. It was romantic, stately, historic ... pure perfection. The kind of home that appeared on old postcards with illustrations of Moorestown's historical homes.

It wasn't Moorestown's largest home, not by far. That honor went to Villa Collina, the largest home in New Jersey at 46,000 square feet. It wasn't Moorestown's oldest standing home either. That title belonged to the French-Hollinshead House, which originated around 1695. But Sabielo's home was perfect nonetheless.

I first fell in love with Sabielo's home when we used to pass by it every Sunday when leaving church to have lunch at grandma's. As we drove by, I imagined holding parties inside the grand ballroom, enjoying picnics on the lush lawn under the massive oak trees, and throwing pennies in the old grey stone wishing well.

Sabielo's grandmother left the house to her mother. *Hmmm.* "Sabielo, won't your mother be home?" I asked.

"No, she's in Virginia on a business trip."

Sabielo's brother was a freshman at Yale, studying for a double major in economics and political science. He's much more like their mom, who is a Constitutional Lawyer. But then again, I could see Sabielo going that direction, too.

Once, when we were working on a school project in Sabielo's bedroom, she showed me a hidden stairwell that went from the back of her closet on the third floor down to the basement. It actually wasn't a staircase, not something anyone would use regularly at least. It was more of an emergency escape route with footings here and there, located between the walls. This house had stories to tell. If only I had time to investigate.

As we approached Sabielo's block, she had us duck into the bushes in the neighbor's yard and navigate through the thicket for about a hundred feet until we came out behind an old barn. She turned to the three of us and held up her palm, indicating she wanted us to stay. She turned to Avalon and put her finger to her lips. Avalon nodded, and Sabielo left us.

The free moment gave me time to explore the old structure with my eyes. Through gaps in the rough boards, I could see what looked like an old horse barn with space for maybe three horses and a carriage. A hole in the roof illuminated a dirt floor. Another gem that would soon be taken by time.

I felt a tap on my shoulder and jumped a foot off the ground. It was Sabielo. All three of them silently laughed. She then steered us around the barn and through several forsythia bushes, where we came upon an old brick outbuilding. It might have been a smokehouse.

We were now deep in the neighbor's backyard, far from the house and anyone who would hear us. Wulf sped up his pace with determined purpose, navigating around me and catching up with Sabielo.

"How did you figure out the route not covered by the cameras?" he whispered.

Sabielo began filling him in on her multi-step method while continuing to navigate the path.

She told him about her initial visual walk-through, scanning the Wi-Fi network for devices, using an RF detector, and using a flashlight to look for reflections. "But do you see that camera hidden in the crabapple tree up there?" she asked.

"Where? I don't see it."

She pointed, "On the branch with the bird feeder."

He leaned in close to her and followed the path from her arm up to her fingertip and out to the tree.

"Yes, I see it now."

She stepped back, moved her hair behind her ear, and looked at the ground. "That one was trickier. I used my phone camera at night in all the spots where I would've placed surveillance. That one showed up as a bright dot from the..."

"The infrared light," he nodded with a grin at completing her sentence.

The thought occurred that I should get between the two of them.

What the heck Lottie? I thought. I wasn't interested in Wulf that way.

As her house came into view, my worry about the two of them relaxed. I caught my breath at the gorgeous Victorian with three staircases, service bells, a wraparound porch, and the carriage house with the old servants' quarters above.

Not that the Huertas lived an extravagant life. The house was in need of some heavy-duty repairs. But that wouldn't stop me from getting lost in her house, just as I got lost in special books. Every nook and cranny deserved to be investigated.

As we approached the property line, Sabielo turned and said, "From here, we need to crawl about twenty feet over to that shed. Be sure to be fully behind the shed before standing up."

As we crawled along, the two of them started discussing self-defense tactics. It seemed flirtatious, but I didn't know why. They continued to chat as we crawled past the old wishing well, which was now hidden by thick brush.

I turned to look at Avalon to see if she also noticed Wulf and Sabielo's interaction, but she was too busy nursing a broken nail.

Behind the shed, Sabielo asked us to follow exactly in her footsteps. As we continued, I was nearly put to sleep as they discussed lock-picking techniques and Wulf filled her in on his competition results. This was old news.

"So far, there is only one lock I can't pick. My grandfather's old lock," said Wulf.

"I'd love to try my hand at it," she said.

I wanted to unfurl my claws. Not that I had claws, but some inherent animal instinct was trying to kick in.

Cut that out! I told myself.

"You should come over and try it after we're done here," Wulf said.

"What? I yelled in my head as I felt my shoe slide into something mushy. I looked down. "Crap," I said, grabbing a stick. The three of them laughed.

As I dug at my shoe to get the poop off, Sabielo looked up at Wulf and said, "Okay. I'll come."

Chapter 27

Everyone but me was through the Christmas tree door. "Hand me your backpack," said Wulf, "and we'll hoist you up."

I shook my head vehemently side to side and scrunched my face. *Nobody touches my backpack!* He knew better.

"What's the WiFi password?" Avalon asked Sabielo.

"I turned off the WiFi as part of dismantling the security system."

Before Avalon could whine, Wulf turned to me and said, "Option two is we hurt our backs."

"Option two it is," I smiled.

Wulf and Sabielo each stood with one foot braced behind a doorway and reached out a hand. It took a few tries, but eventually, swinging one foot up combined with them pulling with a hand under each of my armpits, they got me and my backpack up inside and onto my knees.

Before I could stand, Sabielo said, "Lottie, shoes off." I pulled off my shoes and stood. The hidden door swung closed behind me, muffling the birds' tweets.

I held my shoes out twelve inches from my body, unsure where to put them. The majestic room, with its mahogany walls, paintings from centuries past, large fireplace, and exquisite pieces of furniture, was made more homey by the worn wooden floors and oriental rug. A grand house, yet not photoshoot-perfect. Albeit warmer and more inviting because of the lack of effort to keep up with the Asters.

"I just need to grab something from my room, and then we'll head to Dad's office," said Sabielo. She guided us up the less grand of the two family staircases, which twirled its way upwards. The grand staircase was in the foyer by the front hall. The servants' staircase was along the inner wall near the kitchen. All three were family staircases with this generation, having only four family members. Well, actually, three with Jessie away at college.

As we climbed past the second floor and up to the third, the maze of rooms, nooks, hiding spots, and sharp angles common in Victorian architecture was fully on display. From no point in the house did I feel I could view a central path within the home. There was no symmetry. Instead, it was a puzzle that needed solving, like a complex map that required more time to get straight in my head.

As we entered Sabielo's room, memories of past school projects flooded in. I remembered her bedroom as having a personality of its own, as if it were designed for a royal eccentric spirit still lingering around the edges. The furniture, reupholstered and repaired, had been passed down for several generations.

As Sabielo gathered notebooks and papers that were scattered around her room, Avalon spotted the Victorian chaise lounge, "Oh my god, it's giving Bridgerton!" Dramatically, she approached and collapsed onto the chaise with the back of her hand clutched to her forehead. "Tell my followers, I died ... from a WiFi outage."

The fact that women from the Victorian period never called it a fainting couch would never hold back Avalon from a good dramatic scene.

Performance over, Avalon started taking selfies. I walked over to the two windows that looked out from the center of the house. Underneath them was an antique desk. I'm not sure I would get anything done at this desk. Sabielo had the best view of the front grounds and gardens of any room on the third floor.

My eyes dropped to her desk. On it were various books on criminology. The book on top was open to a chapter on Repeat Victimization. "Research consistently demonstrates that victims of crimes face significantly elevated risks of being the victim of subsequent crimes compared to the general population. This increased rate of 'repeat victimization' occurs for two reasons. First, victims who are left physically or emotionally weakened are more vulnerable to experiencing another crime. Second, the victims who had a higher risk due to lifestyle (work or social activities) or a higher risk due to living in a neighborhood with a higher crime rate, and who remained with the higher risk after experiencing the first crime, are more vulnerable to experiencing another crime."

Bored, my eyes darted around the room. Wulf was looking up at the ladder fastened to the wall next to the front windows. It traversed through the high ceiling. He glanced at Sabielo and pointed up with a quizzical look.

"Knock yourself out. You're welcome to climb into my tower," said Sabielo.

I climbed it a few years ago. All that was up there was a wide, comfortable chair, a lamp, and a telescope. Great for a cozy read. But it's exhausting climbing straight up for twenty feet, just to take a peek. Let alone with my backpack that grows heavier every year. It's also unbearable in the tower on hot days.

With Avalon, Sabielo, and Wulf busy, I used the break to visit Sabielo's bathroom. Not that I needed to go, but her bathroom was a sight to behold for anyone who loved historical buildings. An advertisement from the Mott's Plumbing Catalog from 1907 was framed on the wall. Her great-grandmother once told her the story that Mott's installed the bathroom and liked the design so much that they put it in their ad.

While Sabielo's chair and scale were different than those in the illustration, everything else, including the layout, was identical.

Sabielo's mom was one of the last in the Beaumarchais line. Pierre-Augustin Caron de Beaumarchais was famous for being a playwright in his own time, spying on the English Court for the French, supporting the American Colonists, providing them with arms against the British, being friends with Thomas Jefferson, and being stiffed for payment by the American government.

From watching the cases that Sabielo's mom's practice accepted over the years, it's clear Pierre's descendants still strongly supported the rights contained in the Constitution. Yet, they were better at cloaking their wins in humility and not feeding their egos.

"Let's head down to Dad's office," said Sabielo. This time, she took us down the grand staircase, across the foyer, and through the double doors into the game room. There were three sections to the room. The first section we walked into had the card table, the pool table, and a game in progress on the chess table. The center section of the room had three couches in a U-shape, facing a luxurious fireplace.

The final section contained four 360-degree swivel gaming recliners and a massive TV. The floor-to-ceiling built-in bookshelf contained various gaming consoles and accessories, including virtual reality gear. Wulf salivated as we passed.

From here, she led us to a hall that went past the kitchen. It was designed over a century ago for a staff with a live-in cook. Sabielo popped into the kitchen, opened a drawer, and grabbed a bag. She tossed it to me. "For your shoes."

I sniffed the air. So captivated by the house, I hadn't noticed the rank odor that had followed me from room to room.

The next door was familiar to me. It opened to a large walk-in pantry, where snickerdoodles were kept on the top left shelf. Sadly, we passed by that door.

We came to a stop in front of a small, unassuming door. Sabielo looked at Avalon and said, "Listen carefully. You cannot touch anything. ¿Entendido? This is an active investigation. You must promise."

"Of course," I said. Wulf and Avalon nodded.

"Turn off your phones and leave them in this bag here on the table."

What???

Chapter 28

Walking into his office, I was struck by how small and barren it was compared to the rest of the house. A folding table, an office chair, and two white plastic outdoor chairs were crammed into an area the size of a full-sized bed. The servants' staircase took a chunk out of the ceiling, requiring anyone headed towards the visitors' chairs to duck before sitting.

Sabielo sat down gingerly in her dad's chair and invited us to, "Take a seat."

Avalon, Wulf, and I scrambled for the two empty seats like we were playing musical chairs. Wulf reached the one farthest against the wall and was punished for his win by smacking his head on the low ceiling. I slipped in my socks and ended up on the floor.

Avalon reached down a hand to help me up, while snickering at Wulf and me. But ultimately, she shared half her chair. The clown show over, I put my bag of shoes on the floor to my left and set my backpack on my left foot. I didn't want to forget it.

"What's with your dad's office?" asked Avalon.

"He uses the old butler's office when he brings work home. But that only happens when there's a case that really matters to him. Mom wanted to make it nicer, but he said no. Keeps him focused, knowing the criminals are out there."

Sabielo pulled folders from the third section of the file sorter and spread them on the table. She opened the first folder and turned to me. "Can I ask you a few questions since you know Parisol mejor que nadie, better than anyone?"

I nodded yes, feeling like I was about to be interrogated.

Avalon fidgeted in her seat, elbowed me, and started hiccupping. I shot her a look.

"I have phone withdrawal yips. Deal with it," she shrugged.

"Eris and Dax both mentioned that Parisol was in a lyric-writing mood on Monday after school. Was that normal for her?"

"Yes, she writes often. It's non-stop when her emotions are high."

Sabielo nodded and wrote something in her small notebook. 'When was the last time you saw her?

"In school on Monday."

"And her mood?"

"Normal, happy, bouncy Parisol. She was with Dax, and nothing was out of the norm."

"How about you guys?"

"Same. Seemed normal," said Avalon.

"I might have seen them in the halls, but if I did, I didn't take notice," said Wulf.

Sabielo flipped through a few more pages in the open folder. "Lottie, Eris said she called you the night Parisol went missing to see if you knew where Parisol was. Did you receive a call from her?"

Stunned, I bent over and felt around in my backpack. There it was. I hit the record button on VAR, my voice-activated recorder, and came up with my water bottle. Not that I was thirsty. "No, there weren't any calls from Eris. I could check missed calls, but I'd need to get my phone and turn it on."

"No, that's unnecessary. The history of calls on Eris' phone doesn't show any calls to you. I just wanted to confirm that fact. But don't you find it surprising that Eris would feel the need to lie about that?"

The question made me uneasy. I wanted to fly home. "Sh-shee can't stand me, so maybe sh-shee was trying to protect her fake reputation of being nice."

"I can attest to that. Eris strongly dislikes Lottie," said Wulf. "Has for years."

"Do you know why?" Sabielo asked, turning to me.

I shook my head 'no'. *Just unlikeable*, spouted my inner critic.

The next folder contained the timeline that the police created from the evidence. Sabielo handed me the timeline from across the desk. Avalon and Wulf leaned in ....

Chapter 29

I counted the pages in the timeline. Just five. *I can do this.*

As they squeezed in to read along, I felt Avalon's breath on my right hand and Wulf's breath on my left. Sirens were going off in my head; my personal bubble was pierced.

Wanting to focus and actually focusing were two separate things with my ADHD brain. Mine decided to hippity-hop all over the page. I re-read several sentences on the first page. *Dammit, my brain was turned off.* I wasn't retaining much.

I knew they had finished reading the first page, as they both leaned back slightly. I decided to just skim it, dejected that I couldn't push through to focused reading... even for Parisol.

Missing Person Case - Parisol Bonneville - Timeline Monday, September 19, 2022

3:00 Parisol Bonneville attended the Boys Varsity Rugby Game with Eris Scharf to watch Dax Caflisch, her boyfriend. Parisol discovered Dax was cheating on her by viewing his texts. Parisol (upset) and Eris left the game together early. (Confirmed by Eris and Dax)

5:33 Dax called Parisol, no answer. (Confirmed on Dax's and Parisol's phones under Recent Calls)

5:34 Dax texted Parisol, "Heading to get mom. Around later?" (Confirmed on Dax's and Parisol's phones via Txtiq app)

6:52 Dax called Parisol, no answer. (Confirmed on Dax's and Parisol's phones under Recent Calls)

6:55:58 Parisol was recorded walking on the path at Strawbridge Lake by homeowner A's security camera. (Video PB22B19)

6:56:01 Parisol went out of the camera's range.

6:58:06 Parisol was recorded veering off the path and through the grass towards where she goes past the green pond by homeowner B's security camera. The heavy brush blocked the view of Parisol before she reached the little peninsula and the bench. (Video PB22B22)

6:58:18 Parisol went out of the camera's range.

7:02 Parisol texted Eris. "At SL. 9:00 still work?" (Confirmed via Parisol's and Eris' phones via Txtiq app)

7:02 Eris texted Parisol. "Yep. Did you hear from donkey emoji?" (Confirmed via Parisol's and Eris' phones via Txtiq app)

7:03 Parisol texted Eris. "I've ignored his calls/txts." (Confirmed via Parisol's and Eris' phones via Txtiq app)

7:04 The lyric writing app Lyroopin was opened on Parisol's phone. (Confirmed via Lyroopin app history)

7:18 Dax texted Parisol, "Are you mad at me?" (Confirmed on Dax's and Parisol's phones via Txtiq app)

7:19 Parisol texted, "We need to talk. I'm at SL. Regular spot." (Confirmed on Dax's and Parisol's phones via Txtiq app)

7:19 Dax texted, "See you soon. Heart emoji." (Confirmed on Dax's and Parisol's phones via Txtiq app)

7:20 Parisol called Eris. The call lasted 3 minutes. (Confirmed on Eris' and Parisol's phones under Recent Calls).

7:25 Eris texted "Stay strong. Arm muscle emoji." (Confirmed via Parisol's and Eris' phones via Txtiq app)

7:32:55 Dax was recorded parking his car at Strawbridge Lake, walking off the path by the green pond, and going out of view at 7:33:20 by homeowner B's video camera (Video PB22B26)

7:33 The lyric writing app was closed. It was not reopened. (Confirmed via Lyroopin app history)

7:52:32 Dax was recorded on homeowner B's camera walking away from the bench area, getting into his car, and driving off. Parisol was not seen. It was much darker than in the earlier videos. 7:53:55 Dax drove off. (Video PB22B36)

7:59:47 Dax was recorded by his home's security camera, driving up his driveway at 7:59 pm. Dax's neighbor, holding a basketball, was just about to get into his own car when Dax pulled up. A thin grassy area separated their two driveways. The two of them chatted and played one-on-one for a minute. Dax went inside at 8:03, and the neighbor got in his car and left. (Video PB22B48)

7:59 Dax's Car's GPS showed he arrived home. (Confirmed via Snitchy app)

7:59 Dax's Phone GPS showed he arrived home. (Confirmed via app on phone)

8:04 The internal security camera at the Caflisch house recorded the kitchen. Dax arrived at 8:04 in the kitchen, grabbed a snack, and went into another room through a door at the back of the kitchen at 8:05. (Video PB22B51)

8:09 Parisol's phone texted Dax. "Did you get home safe? Heart emoji. (Confirmed on Dax's and Parisol's phones via Txtiq app)

8:09 Dax texted Parisol. "Yep. Heart bouquet emoji. (Confirmed on Dax's and Parisol's phones via Txtiq app)

8:11 June texted her daughter Parisol, "ETA?" (Confirmed on June's and Parisol's phone via Txtiq app)

8:12 Galen got gas for his car at the corner of Lenola and Kings Highway. (Confirmed via gas receipt timed 8:15.)

8:12-9:30 Galen had no phone activity between 8:12 and 9:30. (Confirmed via his phone's call log and Txtiq)

8:18 Eris' phone texted Parisol, "How did it go?" (Confirmed on Eris' and Parisol's phones via Txtiq app)

8:30 Galen had no GPS on his phone, nor on his car, to confirm his whereabouts. Galen played basketball at the Maple Dawson Park from 8:30-9:30. (Confirmed by Dale & Joules Greenbell.)

8:25 Parisol's phone texted Dax, "Movies this weekend? The Woman King? (Confirmed on Dax's and Parisol's phones via Txtiq app)

8:26 Parisol's phone texted her mom back. "9:20ish." (Confirmed on Parisol's and June's phones via Txtiq app)

8:27 Dax's phone responded to a text from Parisol, "Sure." (Confirmed on Dax's and Parisol's phones via Txtiq app)

8:31 Parisol's phone responded to a text from Eris, "He's so sorry. It won't happen again. I'm giving him a 2nd chance." (Confirmed on Eris' and Parisol's phones via Txtiq app)

8:31 Eris' phone called Parisol, but there was no answer. (Confirmed on Eris' and Parisol's phones under Recent Calls)

8:31 Parisol's phone texted Eris, "Still lyric writing. I'll update u at 9." (Confirmed on Eris' and Parisol's phones via Txtiq app)

8:49 Parisol's phone texted Dax, "Heading out soon. Heart emoji." (Confirmed on Dax's phone via Txtiq app)

8:50 Eris' car left her home. (Confirmed on Eris' car's GPS)

8:54 Dax's phone texted Parisol, "Have fun. Can't wait. Heart emoji." (Confirmed on Parisol's phone via Txtiq app)

8:55 Dax walked into his kitchen in a towel, grabbed an apple, and went into the back room and closed the door. (Video PB22B70.)

8:58:46 Eris is recorded parking her car at Strawbridge Lake by homeowner B's video camera. Eris parked in the spot to the right of where Dax parked earlier (Video PB22B72)

8:58 Eris texted "I'm here." (Confirmed on Eris' and Parisol's phones via Txtiq app)

9:00 Time set for Eris to pick up Parisol at Strawbridge Lake. (Confirmed via earlier texts between Parisol and Eris at 7:02 and also at 8:31 via Txtiq app)

9:00 Eris' phone called Parisol. No answer. (Confirmed on Eris' and Parisol's phones under Recent Calls)

9:01 text from Eris, "Where are you?" (Confirmed on Eris' and Parisol's phones via Txtiq app)

9:01, 9:01, 9:02, 9:02, 9:03. Eris' phone called Parisol multiple times. No answer. (Confirmed on Eris' and Parisol's phones under Recent Calls)

9:04, Eris texted Dax. "Is Parisol with you?" (Confirmed on Eris' and Dax's phones via Txtiq app)

9:05 Dax texted Eris. "Nope. She stuck around to write lyrics. I left SL a little before 8:00." (Confirmed on Eris' and Dax's phones via Txtiq app)

9:05 Eris' phone called Parisol. (Confirmed on Eris' and Parisol's phones under Recent Calls)

9:06 Eris called Parisol's mom and asked if she knew where Parisol was. (Confirmed on Statements from Eris and June)

9:08-9:14 June is recorded parking her car at Strawbridge Lake next to Eris's car by homeowner B's video camera. June and Eris speak and then search the area together. They go in and out of view as they walk quickly around using phone lights.   (Video PB22B75)

9:09 June called Dax. He told her he left Parisol at the lake around 8:00. (Confirmed on June's and Dax phones under Recent Calls) (Confirmed in June's and Dax's statements)

9:12 June called the police.

9:14 First police car arrived.

Chapter 30

"Does anything stand out to you?" Sabielo asked me.

"Without time to study it, I can't think of anything."

Wulf chimed in. "Parisol's lyric writing app was opened at 7:04 and closed at 7:33. There was no other mention of the app being reopened. Then at 8:31, Parisol's phone texted Eris, 'Still lyric writing.' At 9:05, Dax texted Eris 'Nope. She stuck around to write lyrics,' referring to 7:52 p.m. when he left Parisol at the lake."

Avalon's mouth dropped open. "That was sick. You're like a robotic detective in a baseball cap."

"That's me. Sick," Wulf said sarcastically. He looked at me, "Would Parisol write outside the app?"

The implication sent an electric shock up my spine. "Ever since she got the app two years ago, she has only written in the app. The only time I've seen Parisol write outside the app has been when a line of inspiration came to her while she was at a location where she couldn't open the app, like a class or a restaurant."

Sabielo reached out her hand for the timeline, and I hesitantly gave it back. "Come around and tell me if you see anything that stands out in these videos."

We squeezed in tight behind her and watched her pull up the police login page. She entered a password, was asked for a number that was emailed to her dad, opened a new screen, opened her dad's email, copied the number, deleted the email, and entered the number into the police login system. Sabielo glided through, breaking into their server like a swan with a PhD in subterfuge.

A few clicks later, she played Video PB22B19. The camera was focused on a section of the western end of Strawbridge Lake, close to Kings Highway. Parisol entered the frame, walking on the paved path, and continued until out of the camera's view. Seeing her hit me harder than I expected.

"Any thoughts on this video?" asked Sabielo.

A tear formed in my eye. "Her happy demeanor is missing. It's been replaced by a huge wet cloud of sorrow." I swallowed. "She's not herself. She looks weighed down." I bit my bottom lip. *Parisol, why didn't you call me?*

Sabielo nodded. "Makes sense since she was planning on breaking up with Dax."

She hit a few more keys. Next up, Video PB22B22. Parisol entered the frame, walking on the path. Empty parking spots were coming up on her left just as she passed the thick brush on her right and turned right towards the lake. She walked until she hit the dense brush running along the lake. She turned right, heading west towards the bench under the old tree. Essentially, she had made a U. But the backside of the U was not viewable to the camera because of the thick brush around the green pond at this time of year.

As Parisol exited from view, I made an effort to ground my feet with the floor and take in a breath. *Be safe, Parisol. Be safe!* I pleaded.

"Your thoughts on this video?" asked Sabielo.

"Nothing stood out. Parisol continued to look sad. But at the end, when she turned right towards the bench, she picked up her chin, enjoying the view."

A natural silence ensued for a minute.

After we finished analyzing that one, she queued up Video PB22B26. Dax was recorded pulling into a parking spot at 7:32, walking past the green pond, and turning towards where the bench was. He looked arrogant and smug. His normal.

Sabielo clicked on the keyboard. "There is just one more video at the lake, I want you to take a look at." Video PB22B36. At 7:52, the recording showed Dax leaving the area. As he got closer to his car, he turned, waved, blew a kiss, and gave an air hug in the direction of the bench.

"Hold it right there," I said, pausing to collect my thoughts. "That blown kiss and air hug.... it just seems out of character for Dax. Then again, maybe that's what he's like when he's alone with Parisol," I shrugged.

"How many more videos are we going to go through? .... Not that it matters," said Avalon. She was being a trooper, having a scrolling addiction like hers. This might be the longest she'd been separated from her phone in years.

Video PB22B48 was just as described in the police timeline, except the neighbor holding the basketball ... that was Galen. "Why didn't anyone tell me Dax lived next door to Galen?" I asked.

"Just figured you knew," said Avalon.

"It's new to me," said Wulf.

Dax drove up his driveway, just as Galen, holding a basketball, was about to get in his own car. The two chatted for a minute and started to play a short-lived one-on-one game. Galen's dunk shot must have come down directly on Dax's toes. It must have been very painful, with the reaction he had. After rubbing his piggies, Dax headed inside, and Galen headed out in his car.

"Maybe this is why Galen was asked to come into the police station," said Wulf, "to confirm the time."

Video PB22B51 was just as described. Dax had a snack in the kitchen and then went through the door in the back and closed it behind himself. "Is there a way we can find out what room is behind that door?" Wulf asked Sabielo.

"It's Dax's bedroom," said Avalon.

We all turned our heads towards Avalon. I knit my brows together. "Do we need to talk?"

"Pishaw. It just happened that I was in the area. Pure coincidence that Dax had that party."

I rolled my eyes. *Surveilling Galen's house and taking advantage of the party was the more likely scenario.*

Sabielo closed the Timeline folder, flipped past some interview folders, flipped past other folders I didn't catch, and opened a folder titled Strawbridge Lake Maps.

Sabielo was going too fast for me to keep up. I knew we were in a time crunch with her dad, but I also needed this information. I needed to help. I needed to do something.

The first map in the folder was the west end of the lake, as drawn by an officer. Asterisks marked the locations on the map where Parisol was recorded by the cameras.

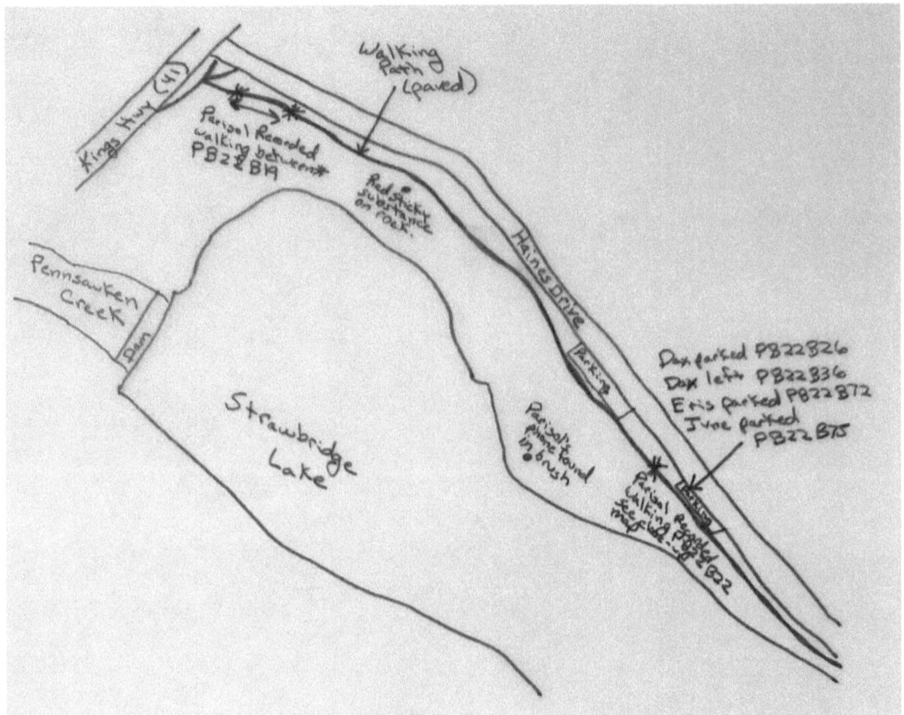

173

The second map was similar, but it narrowed in on the location where Parisol was last seen.

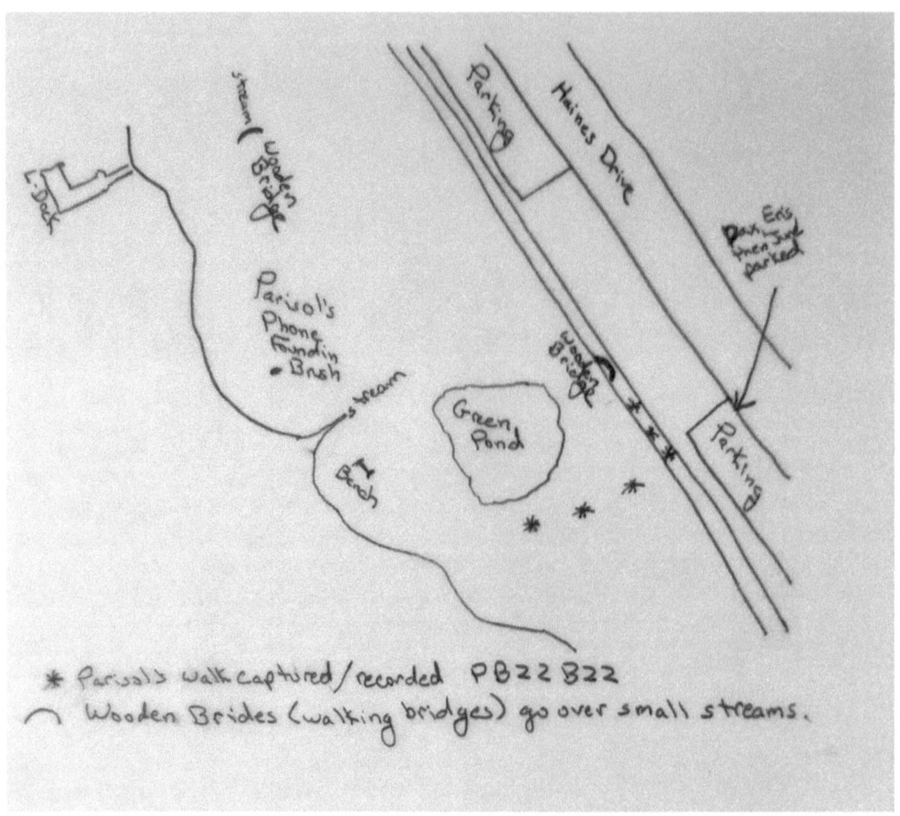

The third was a Google Maps Satellite View of the area.

Sabielo opened the last folder. It contained a list of the seven cars that drove on Haines Drive between 7:52 and 9:00 p.m.

"Bzzzt-bzzzt," echoed from Sabielo's pocket." She pulled out her phone and put her finger to her lips. She answered it as she stepped out the door. "Hi Mom......" The door clicked closed.

This was my chance. I dropped down to my backpack and pulled out my little camera.

"How come you got to keep your ph...?" Avalon began to ask, when she realized it was just a camera.

I ignored her. Flip and click, flip and click.

"You can't do that," Avalon whispered. "You promised not to touch anything. We all did."

"No time to argue, Avalon. This is for Parisol."

"But you lied to Sabielo. By not speaking up, you're making me a liar, too." Avalon paced back and forth over a two-foot area in the cramped office.

I kept flipping and clicking, while Avalon freaked out. There was a folder here with interview notes from the girl nicknamed Whisp. I clicked away. I clicked and clicked, as Avalon paced faster and faster.

"You are endangering me. You know I don't want to turn into my mom," said Avalon.

This was terrible timing. I had avoided having this conversation with Avalon for a year, and now I was forced to have it.

I kept clicking away. "Your mom's lies didn't cause her Borderline Personality Disorder. When she's off her meds and has a BPD episode, she lies."

"You're not there," said Avalon. "She starts lying. She gets more emotional. And then she oscillates between loving intensely and hating intensely, and gets possessive and manipulative. And our first sign every time is when we catch her telling a lie."

Wulf chimed in. "Lottie is right that lying is a symptom of BPD, not what causes it. Avalon is right, you shouldn't be doing this to Sabielo. You promised. You need to stop."

From the hall, we heard "Mom, I've gotta go. Lots of homework." My cue to close the files and put away my camera. But I'd just gotten to the three-page list of the seven cars & owner background checks. I kept clicking, 3, 2, 1.

Avalon's pacing was more like a tennis player jumping from foot to foot watching for the next serve.

I flipped the pages to where Sabielo left off, reached down .... Sabielo walked in. I came back up with my water bottle and took another sip.

Sabielo looked around. Everyone was flushed. "What's going on in here?" she asked.

"It's rather warm in here. Can you leave the door open?" asked Wulf.

Just then, we heard the light rumble of "snap crackle." We all stood still and listened. It was growing closer. Tires traveled up the pea gravel driveway.

"¡Ay, caramba! Dad's home," Sabielo said.

I grabbed my shoe bag and my backpack. Sabielo tapped the folders and put them in section two of the file sorter. As she turned off the computer and straightened the chair, Wulf reached across and moved the folders to section three. Their eyes met and held for a second too long.

I wasn't wanting to watch them interact, but I couldn't stop myself. Deep inside, I wanted to growl.

As we followed Sabielo down the hall, she grabbed the bag of phones. "Hope nobody's afraid of cobwebs or arañas."

Chapter 31

Sabielo turned down a hall, just behind her dad's office. At the end of the hall were several doors. Upon opening the door on the right, we entered a room filled to the brim with old furniture, boxes, paintings, a dollhouse, and all sorts of other things. She hastened us into the room and closed the door behind us, navigating us through the maze of antiques. At the other end of the room was another door. We passed through it, and she gingerly closed it behind us.

Looking around, we were in a grand bathroom. But unlike Sabielo's crisp white bathroom, this one was darker and more foreboding. On the wall hung another framed illustration from the Mott's Plumbing Catalog. The ad looked like the bathroom we were in, with its mahogany hooded tub with a steel basin and a rounded backrest.

J.L. Mott Catalog

Sabielo pressed on the mahogany hood panel right next to the bathroom door. She tried various spots, but nothing happened.

"Sabielo, are you home?" We heard from the hall. My heart paused…waiting.

She sped up her hunt, pushing on more spots. Finally, she pushed on a spot about nose height, and the panel popped open.

The opening looked too small to allow a person through. I guess that was the idea.

Sabielo stepped over the horizontal paneling that ran the length of the tub and then contorted herself around the back of the rounded tub. Maneuvering past that, she then shuffled along the wall … within the wall, until she disappeared. Avalon went next. Followed by Wulf.

As Wulf stepped over the wooden side and started angling himself just right, I realized my backpack wasn't going to fit through the tight opening while wearing it. Crap.

My brain ran through the options. Either let one of my best friends, whom I trusted, hold my backpack, or run into Detective Huerta. It seemed like it should be a no-brainer. It was a no-brainer, and yet nobody would ever get why my backpack was the one thing that made me feel like I could be safe in the world. The idea of letting Wulf touch my backpack tied my stomach into knots.

I whispered to Wulf, "When you're past, I will hand you my backpack."

He nodded.

Once he'd maneuvered past the tight spot, he held out his arms. I placed the backpack into his hands, and the two of us twisted it until it slid through.

That's when I did it. I let go, grasping my shoe bag close to my chest for comfort. I had a fleeting thought about opening the bag and putting on my shoes, but I didn't want the smell to give us away.

The wood floor outside the bathroom door creaked as I stepped over the wooden side in my socked feet and onto the rough, dusty wood with cobwebs … and who knows what else. *Best not to think about that.*

Once I squeezed by, I eased the hidden panel closed. Immediately, it was pitch black. A second later, Sabielo's cell phone's light turned on.

"Can I have my phone back?" Avalon whispered.

"Does it make a sound when you reboot?"

Avalon wrinkled her face.

We followed Sabielo's lead. We shimmied through the tight wall, around posts and nails, barely fitting. The next step was climbing down the hidden footholds in the wall. They were similar to the ones leading from her bedroom closet to the basement. It took me a long time to find the footholds. Sabielo's light was too far away to be of much help.

"Wulf," I whispered. "Stop for a second."

I reached into my backpack and felt around for the 2nd zip pocket on the left side. I unzipped the pocket, and there it was, my indestructible flashlight.

I shined it on the wall to my left, and jumped a foot upon seeing a skeleton. Returning my light to it, I breathed easier when I realized some past jokester had left a plastic skeleton sitting on the beam with a bag of candy in its hands.

"That's Cliff", whispered Sabielo from below. "Jessie left him for future residents to find.

Sabielo continued to spot the footings, and we followed. Down, down, down, until we came to a dirt floor, the basement level. We rested for a minute. I figured we'd soon be entering the main basement area from a hidden door.

"Avalon, if you crouch down real low, you'll find the little door that leads out," said Sabielo.

Avalon borrowed my flashlight, bent down, and looked for a little door. Finding none. However, on the second time round, she came upon a low curtain she had not noticed before, and behind it was a little door about fifteen inches high. The door was wider than it was tall, maybe twenty-five inches wide.

Giving up on keeping her knees clean, Avalon begrudgingly knelt and shined the flashlight on a padlock holding the little door closed. She turned it over in her hand. "Sabielo, please tell me you have the key."

"What?" said Sabielo as she shimmied by me. She knelt down and examined the lock. "That's new."

"I wish I had brought my tools," said Wulf.

"This stinks," said Sabielo, as she resigned herself to turning back, thinking of how she was going to sneak us past her dad.

Sabielo needed me to move to the side to get by, but I just stood there blocking the way. Looking at the ground, I whispered to Wulf, "Can I have my backpack, please?"

Wulf took off my backpack and handed it over. I reached inside, feeling around for the pouch with the Velcro closure. It took a minute to find. I handed it to Wulf as he knitted his eyebrows together.

"I may have been practicing a little here and there since our lock bumping days," I said.

Wulf took the lock picks. And slowly slid past Avalon, which looked awkward in the tight area between the walls. But when attempting to slide past Sabielo, there was no room to do it without touching. Every inch of motion was slow, deliberate, and way too close. And through the silence ... sparks flew.

Wulf took in a deep breath and pretended that that didn't just affect him. But the heat in his cheeks and his deeper breathing said otherwise.

He dropped to his knees and then his stomach in order to have the lock picks at the right angle. Once we corrected the lights to focus on the picks, he went to work.

Sabielo kneeled next to him and leaned closer to watch, her breath warm against his neck. When he succeeded, she placed her hand on his shoulder, her fingers lingering just a moment longer than necessary.

'Impressive,' she whispered, close enough that her lips brushed his ear." Not that I was watching.

Wulf hung the lock on a nail to the right of the door and pulled the door open. He then squeezed to the side to let Sabielo in front to take the lead. I turned my head to avoid watching the stoking of the fire as they slid by each other.

When Wulf was near, I held out my hand for the return of my lock picks. My backpack wasn't complete until everything was in its spot. I held out my hand to Avalon for my flashlight.

Sabielo lay on the floor and shimmied her way through the little door and into the tunnel. Avalon and Wulf were next.

When it was my turn to pass through the door, as I peeked my head through, I noticed the change from dirt floor to rounded pipe. The pipe was much larger than the door. I pushed my backpack through the door. The old pipe was hard on my knees and hair, which was now fully fluffed, standing at attention, and catching on the top of the tunnel. We crawled and crawled, I'm not sure how far. But my crawling, bending over muscles were starting to ache.

It felt like we had crawled maybe twenty or thirty feet when Avalon entered a section where she could stand. When I caught up to them, Wulf reached out a hand and helped me up in the four-foot round room. There was nothing in the room besides an old wooden ladder and a round hatch at the center of the ceiling.

Sabielo climbed the ladder and held up her light, where she discovered another lock at the top. "Dad's been busy," she mumbled.

I reached back into my backpack to grab the lockpicks, but before I could unzip the pocket, Sabielo said, "This one is a six-digit combination lock. No hole for a key."

"If it doesn't have a key, then I don't know how to pick it," Wulf said.

Sabielo tried birthdays and various combinations. After five minutes, she came back down, disgusted. "Anyone else want to give it a try?" She asked.

Wulf went up and tried, to no avail. As everyone realized that we'd need to turn back, I looked up at the ceiling above and bit my lip. Sabielo dropped back to her knees, disgusted with the situation, and started to crawl into the tunnel.

"Never mind that," I said. Sheepishly, I dug into my backpack as Wulf helped Sabielo back up. My hand found what I was looking for, but I didn't want to pull it out. I didn't want to let them into my backpack secret. It said too much.

With a resigned breath, I pulled out my mini-bolt cutter and handed it to Sabielo. As she climbed back up the ladder, Avalon leaned back to me and whispered, "When we get out of here, we are discussing your backpack."

"Remember, you can't for a month," I said.

"In twenty-eight days, we are discussing your backpack," said Avalon.

"What else do you have in your backpack?" Wulf asked.

"Just a combination seatbelt cutter and window breaker," I lied. I wasn't ready for the questions that peeking in my backpack would lead to.

Sabielo cut off the lock, handed the bolt cutter down to me, and stuck the cut lock in her pocket. She shoved the hatch door open.

Wet, decaying leaves poured down on her. Undisturbed, she shook her head and stepped through the hatch. Wulf and Avalon soon followed.

I, on the other hand, was gasping for air as I climbed the ladder with my backpack on. One step at a time on the ladder required a pause to catch my breath. Coming down the walls without my backpack on was much easier than up this ladder with it on.

Finally, reaching the top, I stepped into the fresh air and looked around, trying to catch my breath and regain my bearings. We were inside a round, grey stone and mortar structure, maybe five feet in diameter.

Chapter 32

I looked up into the trees, trying to figure out where we were. With all the twists and turns in the hidden passage, I didn't know where in the yard, or even within whose yard, we came up.

I tilted my head straight up and recognized the bucket overhead. *Sheesh. I hadn't expected to come up in her wishing well.* I longed to go back in time to easier days, when I used to laugh and play without a worry, back when I longed to toss a penny into this well and make a wish. Now overgrown with bushes, it held less of a pull. It wasn't even a real well. Another childhood dream squashed.

Sabielo closed the hatch and covered it with leaves and dirt. Some of it landed on my sock. *Frk. I need to put my shoes back on.*

I held my breath as I opened the bag and grabbed a stick, digging into the crevices of my sole once again trying to remove the brown mush. I traced each row of the tread, but it took too long, and "Woosh," the air rushed out of my lungs.

I braced as my nose took in a deep, cool, and utterly grotesque lungful while still picking away. *Good enough.* Maybe the walk would remove the rest.

As we all dusted ourselves off, I felt itchy all over. Whether actual or imagined bugs, I didn't know. I didn't want to know.

I tried to tame my hair, but failed. Not my best look. But then again, not my worst. While everyone else just looked like they had been having fun, I always looked like that one disheveled bear cub that crawls out of a trash can with pine needles stuck to its body, a streak of dirt on its face, and tufts of fur sticking together at sharp angles.

I looked up at the sky. *Just a little invisibility, please?* But such requests were never granted.

We hopped out from behind the bush and trailed after Sabielo, weaving left and right like children trying to keep up with a shadow.

When we reached the sidewalk and were several houses away, Sabielo handed back our cell phones.

"Finally," Avalon sighed as she cradled her phone to her chest. "Baby, I missed you," she said, giving it a kiss.

"Ding, Brrr, Trrrng," a cacophony of notifications went off as we turned on our phones.

My most pressing message was from my mom. She'd noticed my disappearance from GPS and had given me ten minutes to respond before she'd start freaking out. I had a minute left. I pushed dial just in time. She just needed reassurance that I was safe and with good people.

Over my shoulder, I heard Wulf having a similar conversation with his mother.

After my mom calmed down, she got around to the original point of her earlier call. "Lot, I wanted to give you a heads up. The community is planning a Candlelight Vigil tomorrow night for Parisol. Please don't feel pressured to go."

She knew me well. Yesterday, I would have eaten myself alive over making such a decision about attending a large gathering of any type, but that was a lifetime ago. Today, bigger worries loomed.

As we walked along Chester Ave, I couldn't help but stop while passing Harmony Hall, taking in its grandeur. The Georgian mansion built by Samuel Stokes Sr. in 1753 was, hands down, the prettiest in Moorestown.

I could get lost in its charm. Yet, the historic mansion was marred by slavery. That is, until other Quakers persuaded Samuel Stokes to manumit his enslaved in 1777.

At some point, Sabielo must have realized I was enchanted by Harmony Hall and made her way back to me. Slowly, she slid her hand into mine, intertwining our fingers. "Did you know one of the Stokes women was the first to vote in an American Election?"

I shook my head "no."

"Brrring-brrring. Brrring-brrring." The bright little chime of a bike bell carried down the street.

We turned to see two girls pedaling toward us, one on a pink bike, the other on a purple one. Their helmets perfectly color-matched. Streamers fluttered from the handlebars as their training wheels clattered against the sidewalk. Behind them, their moms strolled along, one casually holding the leash of a golden retriever who padded happily beside them.

We stepped aside to let them pass, and the women smiled their thanks.

"Mary Stokes voted in the 1807 election when New Jersey's Constitution allowed all inhabitants of age who were worth fifty pounds to vote. Since men owned their wives' property, Mary must have been single or a widow at the time."

"But I thought women didn't get the vote until 1920," said Avalon.

"It's a lesson in not becoming complacent," said Sabielo.

"A republic, if you can keep it," added Wulf.

Sabielo let go of my hand and returned to Wulf's side. "I'm impressed. Quoting Benjamin Franklin. I may have to rethink the box I put you in." They started walking again.

I rolled my eyes. Nauseous. I tried to ignore them and looked around to ground myself.

As we continued walking past homes, I was thankful we were on the west side of the street. Passing near places where murders had occurred always felt like I was walking through the threads of the emotions that lingered.

Glancing up at the Tudor house, I saw a shadow resembling a man on the roof heading towards an open window. It was just my imagination. When there was dark history surrounding a location, shadows could put me on edge.

I tried to ground myself by focusing on the sidewalk ahead of me. But my mind was already tracing the heavy ache contained within the thread from that first Saturday in June 1929. That day, Ruth Wilson, Horace Roberts Jr., and two other friends, all in their early 20s, drove to Ocean City, New Jersey, to visit the beach and boardwalk.

I blinked hard, trying to stop my brain from pulling up the history, but the harder I tried not to think about what happened here, the deeper it pulled me in.

They were all from wealthy families. Both boys owned cars. Ruth had recently graduated from college. Her father was a well-known banker and attorney who believed in equal education for women. Horace came from the prominent family at Hootan Hall.

Ruth had broken off her engagement with Horace two months prior. Ever since, he refused food, appeared irrational, and threatened her life and his. Her parents had made her promise the day before the Ocean City trip that she would tell him that he must abandon hope of their marriage ... that she liked him, but could never love him.

No, no, no. I don't want to think about the rest. My hands started to tremble.

When her parents came home that evening, they found light coming from underneath her door. They knocked, but she didn't answer. They tried the knob, but it was locked.

Her poor father crawled out on the porch roof and into her bedroom window, where he found her and Horace both shot. She was barely alive. He called in four physicians to try and save her. But she died within an hour. The inquest found it was a murder/suicide.

Brutal. Just brutal.

Finally, I was free from my mind replaying that event. It wasn't a vision like with Mary Driver or the two Lenni Lenape women entering the tavern. Rather, it reminded me of something we were taught in science. "Don't picture the Statue of Liberty," our teacher said. Of course, my mind pictured the Statue of Liberty. It was impossible to avoid.

The same thing happened whenever I was near a historic site. My brain pulled out the history that I already knew, whether I wanted to think about it or not.

Wulf and Sabielo started giggling like young mischievous children. He then leaned in and wiped an imaginary dust smear from her cheek.

Stop that!

Avalon leaned in and whispered, "What's up with them?"

"Nothing, I'm sure."

With that, Wulf's hand brushed past the back of Sabielo's hand. They looked at each other, locked eyes, and smiled.

I'm going to puke.

Avalon shot me a glance of, 'Did you just see that?'

I ignored her. After a few more steps, Avalon put her arm through mine and whispered, "I do know in my mind that lying doesn't cause BPD," she said, pulling me in closer. "But inside somewhere, there is some superstition that I can't get past, where I feel like something bad is going to happen if I tell a lie.

"Sarah says when my mind and emotions are at odds, look to the inner child."

Avalon didn't say anything for a minute. As we came to the railroad tracks, Avalon slowed down, putting more distance between us and Sabielo & Wulf. "Are you having any visions of the headless man who smells like gasoline and wanders the tracks?"

"No. And please don't put those things in my mind." I let go of her arm and made a cross with my fingers and held it up to her.

"Look who's being superstitious now," said Avalon.

Sabielo stopped and turned to face us. "Have you ever heard of the case of Matilda Russo?"

We all shook our heads "No."

She pointed east up 2nd Street. "Just there, she was playing out front of her home on the first Saturday in June 1921. When her parents noticed their seven-year-old daughter missing, they searched for 30 minutes before her father knocked on their next-door neighbor's door. Mrs. Lively and their child were away for the week, but Mr. Lively said he hadn't seen Matilda. Six days later, the police found Matilda's mutilated body buried in Mr. Lively's dirt basement."

I looked at the ground. *Please Parisol, hold on. You're strong. Hold on.*

I heard Wulf whisper to Sabielo. "Read the room."

I took a breath and started walking at a faster pace, trying to outrun my thoughts.

We passed the Friends Cemetery on our right and crossed over Main Street. Avalon had something to drop off at the Moorestown Friends Meeting House. We sat in the grass near the sidewalk, waiting for her.

As Avalon walked down the hill, she turned and asked if anyone wanted to join her.

"Can I use the bathroom?" asked Sabielo.

"Yep."

I couldn't deal with seeing any more visions today, or for that matter, just remembering the history I already knew. The Meeting House was thick with historical emotions, both good and bad, a woven blanket of lives with strings that led all over town.

I could feel the emotional strings from the British forces taking over the Meeting House during the Revolutionary War. There were strings from the heated discussions regarding slavery that took place here. There were the strings of Members putting pressure on other Members to manumit their enslaved. There were the strings of emotions of some members who were secretly assisting runaways, and the related fears of being caught and questioning their decisions that put their own family members in danger. Let alone the strings of Alice Paul's education within these walls that led to her becoming a leader in the women's suffrage movement. Yet, other strings that rooted her in entitlement and discrimination.

STOP THINKING! I tapped on my head. As more historical thoughts tried to creep in, I yelled, "ATCHAFALAYA."

"Did you just swear in... Louisiana geography?" Wulf asked with raised eyebrows.

"Just overwhelmed. Too many things floating around in my head." From our perch, we could see the lush green sports fields behind the school below, surrounded by homes and a little forest at the bottom of the hill.

"Any hijacks to times past, since the earlier transport at Cox's Tavern?" asked Wulf as he motioned to the historic spot just behind us. I didn't dare turn around to look.

"No. Thank God."

Avalon and Sabielo rejoined us. A moment of peace. Avalon pointed at a house. "That's where Galen lives," she said.

"Slightly obsessed?" I asked.

"Not at all. He just doesn't know we're meant to be yet. It's only an obsession if it doesn't work out. Otherwise, it's just reading the tea leaves."

"¡Madre mía!" exclaimed Sabielo as she put her palm to her forehead. I could see Sabielo becoming part of our group.

Wulf's stomach growled loudly. "Anyone else hungry?" he asked. "I'm going to head across the street to Carollo's for dessert."

"Who wants to split a piece of tiramisu with me?" asked Avalon as she jumped up.

"That works for me," said Wulf.

Sabielo looked at me, "Want to split a cheesecake?"

"Sure," I said.

As we walked back across Main Street, tiny vibrations began to tickle my toes and rose up through my feet to my ankles. "CRAACK." *Not here. Not here.*

Chapter 33

The world around me blurred and shifted once again. The fence around the Quaker cemetery in front of me disappeared. The Wells Fargo Bank was replaced by a tavern. Just to the right of the tavern was a large buttonwood tree, known by some as an American sycamore.

Four photos I'd seen of the buttonwood/sycamore tree standing tall next to the Coles Hotel popped into my head. In the first photo, the buttonwood was to the right of the Coles Hotel.

Sycamore Tree Planted 1740, Moorestown, N. J.

In the second, the hotel had been extended deeper into the lot.

In the third, the buttonwood was to the right of the Coles Hotel, half in and half out of the frame.

In the fourth photo, the buttonwood trunk was in the distance behind the man.

But looking around at my changed view, the time I was transported to was earlier than any of the photos. This was before it was the Coles Hotel. Before it was the William Penn Hotel. Back when it was a tavern.

I remembered from local history that people attending the Quaker Meetings early on fastened their horses to this gentle giant of a buttonwood tree. But as my essence floated closer and saw the crowd surrounding the tree, I realized that wasn't a horse tied to the tree.

"CRAACK."

A young black man with blood dripping down his back was tied to the tree, as the local Chester Township Constable whipped him. It was a despicable sight.

"CRAACK." The young man screamed with the next lash, his body seizing from the pain. The cruel whipping lacked all traces of humanity.

With that, I floated west down Main Street and Kings Highway, past the Cowperthwaite house, to a little brick schoolhouse on a dirt road just over the border between Moorestown and Maple Shade. Back then, it was all part of Chester Township.

It was located on what is now known as Schoolhouse Lane, near Holman Enterprises.

I was glad to be away from the scene where the young black man was being whipped, but I had no idea what I was meant to see at this school.

"Swish." The door swung open, and children ran out, happy to be free. As one boy ran through the door, a large hand grabbed him by his collar and stopped his escape.

I followed them back into the schoolhouse. The boy shook and cried as the teacher, still holding him by the collar, gave him a speech, while firmly holding a whip in his other hand. He then administered such a beating that the boy's shoes had blood in them when he finally started walking home.

"What kind of world was this?" I cried out. The corporal punishments of that time drew sadists and sociopaths to positions where they gained pleasure, all while being paid to hurt those who were in a weaker position.

As my essence was pulled towards a house where a woman was beating her slave, I cried "Enough. Enough," out into the ether.

I flew back up the road towards the whipping tree. As I traveled, the scene got fuzzy, and I was back in 2022, still crossing Main Street.

"Wulf," I said. "Later, can we chat about quantum? I need some answers." What I really needed was a way to figure out how to help Parisol without losing my mind and going on these side trips. It was enough when my memories ruminated on negative history, but the addition of being transported to such cruel events was more than I could take.

He looked me in the eyes and nodded, "Of course."

Avalon opened the door to Carollo's. The smell of Italian cuisine drifted under my nose, lighting up my brain. We followed the server, but stopped when Wulf recognized someone.

"Hey, Dad. What are you doing here?"

Wulf's dad didn't say a word, but instead glanced up hesitantly.

"Let's join my dad," Wulf said, sliding into the booth next to his dad with a glimmer in his eyes. Avalon, Sabielo, and I slid in the other side.

Mr. Biko side-eyed Wulf. "Your mother made Vegan Wheatgerm Ratatouille for dinner."

"Enough said," Wulf replied, carefully arranging his napkin in a perfect square.

The server approached with Mr. Biko's Crab Cake alla Carollo, featuring spinach and shrimp over cheese ravioli in a vodka-blush sauce. It smelled delicious. She took one look at Wulf and asked, "Tiramisu?"

"You know me well," he laughed.

"So, where were you four? It looks like you've been cleaning out an old attic," said Mr. Biko.

"They were just helping me with some things," said Sabielo.

My plate with a half-slice of cheesecake arrived. I played with a corner of it while everyone around me chatted and ate.

"CRASH."

In a split second, my body responded to the startling sound with an adrenaline shot, my heart sped up, and my body ducked under the table ... all before my friends had a chance to blink.

Less than half a second later, my mind realized the sound was just a dropped glass from the kitchen, and I popped up from under the table, pretending nothing happened. While I knew people at other tables were likely gawking, everyone at my table was used to me. They didn't even look over, just continued to eat and chat.

Frig. I thought that was gone. Utter humiliation. My hyper-reactive flight response hadn't embarrassed me with a response like that in a long time.

Everyone at our table continued chatting. If anything, they were trying to normalize what just happened by increasing the volume of their conversations and being more animated in their gestures. They indicated they weren't bothered, so neither should anyone else.

Wulf glanced at my cheesecake, the last piece of food on the table. And then he glanced again. Without thinking, he put his fork into my cheesecake mid-sentence and raised it to his lips. Just before his fork entered his mouth, he stopped. Realizing what he was about to do, he shook the fork gently and asked me, "Yes?"

"Go ahead," I said.

Within seconds, the cheesecake on my plate was devoured.

Mr. Biko rolled his eyes. "Teen boy. Need I say more?" He grabbed the check and nudged Wulf with his elbow, who slid out. "I was never here."

Back on the sidewalk, it was a beautiful evening to walk. The lights flickered on, and there was a spirit of daring and excitement in the air. Walking past the shop that gave off cozy vibes, Avalon said, "I just need to jump in here for a second." She disappeared before anyone could rein her in.

Wulf and Sabielo were deep in conversation, the physical space between them grew smaller and smaller. Annoyed, I slowly placed myself between them, pouring water on the flames. *I wish Avalon would get her butt back here.*

I glanced at the store windows, hoping to see Avalon approaching the exit. But she wasn't. I turned around. and spotted Dax and Oscar coming our way.

Panic set in; I hadn't seen them since the Tuck locker incident.

They started walking towards us. *Oh Sh…*

Chapter 34

My brain ran through the options ... fight, flight, freeze, or fawn.

Flight won. "I'm going to go see what's taking Avalon sooo long," I said, racing towards the store door. I didn't want to face off with the evil duo.

Safely inside, I went to stand next to Avalon, pretending to read the birthday cards while watching for Dax and Oscar to walk by. I spotted them, but instead of continuing down the street, they were coming in. *Crap.*

I dashed to the back of the store, turning my back towards them, and picked up a candle. I took off the lid and breathed in vanilla and raspberries. I put the candle down and reached for the honeysuckle one.

"I'm here collecting for tomorrow night's Candlelight Vigil," said Dax. "Who do I speak with about donations?"

I turned my right ear toward the front of the store to hear better and nearly jumped out of my skin. Oscar was right there, staring. Just inches away.

I sucked in a sharp breath of honeysuckle as he loomed over me.

"Hi, Lottie. I'm Oscar. I'm friends with Parisol. I just wanted to come over and tell you how sorry I am that she is missing. I'm sure she'll be home safe and sound soon."

Frozen, I fidgeted as he continued. "She spoke about her little sister all the time. I can't wait for her to be back, too," he said with a tear sliding down his cheek and biting his lip to hold back more tears. He reached out and hugged my paralyzed body. I couldn't move.

"OSCAR," Dax demanded.

Oscar released his bear hug, smiled at me, and bolted back to Dax's side. I slowly tried to move, but I needed to thaw out first.

Could I have been wrong all these years? Maybe Dax was pulling Oscar's strings. Not an excuse. But a different view. Oscar might not be the complete sociopath I thought he was.

With that, the two of them walked out the door.

Avalon came to my side. "What was that about?" she whispered.

"I... I'm not sure," I said as I put the candle back. "A trace of humanity, I believe."

As we continued walking home, I was dumbfounded. The world was more confusing than ever. I longed to return to hibernation. I longed to go back in time when Parisol was home.

"You know I could take you down in ten seconds," said Sabielo.

Wulf laughed, "Sure, if I let you win. Which I might, for science."

"Krav Maga doesn't need your charity."

"Yet, Brazilian Jiu-Jitsu might just topple you in close quarters."

"Adorable that you think that," she laughed.

As we came to High Street, I stopped to put some distance between myself and Flirt Fest. I pretended to be looking at the Smith-Cadbury Mansion up the hill, where the Moorestown Historical Society was located. Avalon stopped and said, "I haven't been back there since the Ghost Tour."

Sabielo stopped too. "Do you know what the Ghost Tour is missing?" she asked. "The ghosts of the women and girls who were ravished by the British & Hessian troops that came through Moorestown. But the tour would need to change its name to the Horror Tour."

Avalon drew closer.

"The orders for rape came down from high-ranking British officers. There were even enemy newspaper articles and cartoons that joked about the rapes going on here. Thomas Jefferson received a letter from a friend stating, "The Enemy like locusts Sweep the Jerseys with the Besom of destruction. They to the disgrace of a Civilisd Nation Ravish the fair Sex, from the Age of Ten to Seventy." Another wrote Jefferson that, "They play the very devil with the girls and even old women to satisfy their libidinous appetites. There is scarcely a virgin to be found in the part of the country they have pass'd thro'.""

"In town after town where the British Army and Hessian troops stopped along the way, taking over houses and fields, setting up camp, there are stories of mass rapes. A common cry was that family members were forced to watch the rape of their daughters. Many of the girls were then taken back to the camps, where the torture continued.""

"As the soldiers approached Hopewell, NJ, sixteen brave young women attempted to save themselves by running to a nearby mountain. They were captured and dragged to a temporary camp where they were raped for days until the troops moved onto another town.""

In one New Jersey town, "An American officer who arrived shortly after the British withdrew came across a young girl who told him she had been raped by seven or eight different English officers. She could speak only "in broken accents of the most excessive grief' saying "that she was ruined and wished never again to be spoken to.""

"And yet, here in Moorestown, where the British and Hessian troops stayed overnight, we are to believe it incredulously didn't happen here? In a town with a population of a few hundred at the time, and 8000 soldiers with 1500 carts rolled into town, taking over the homes, Quaker Meeting House, and all available fields, all of a sudden, those soldiers changed their ways? Our girls were spared?"

I remembered from history class the map from 1777 of Hessian locations in Moorfield (Moorestown), near Moorfield Creek (Pennsauken Creek). The map showed three camps where the soldiers who couldn't cram into homes spilled into the three fields. A large camp was close to where Lenola Road is today. There was another large camp at the Quaker Meeting House field. And a third camp near Bridgeboro Road.

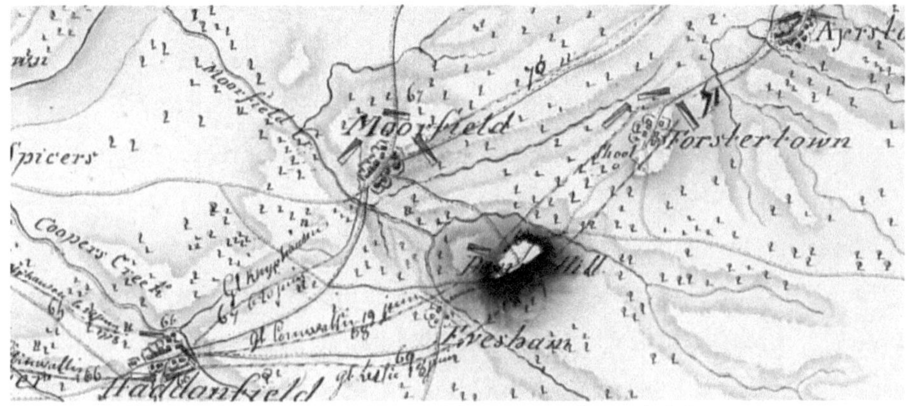

Hessian Map - 1777 - Troop Movements through Moorestown

I remembered faintly a second map showing the British and Hessian Troops being stationed in Moorestown (Moorfields).

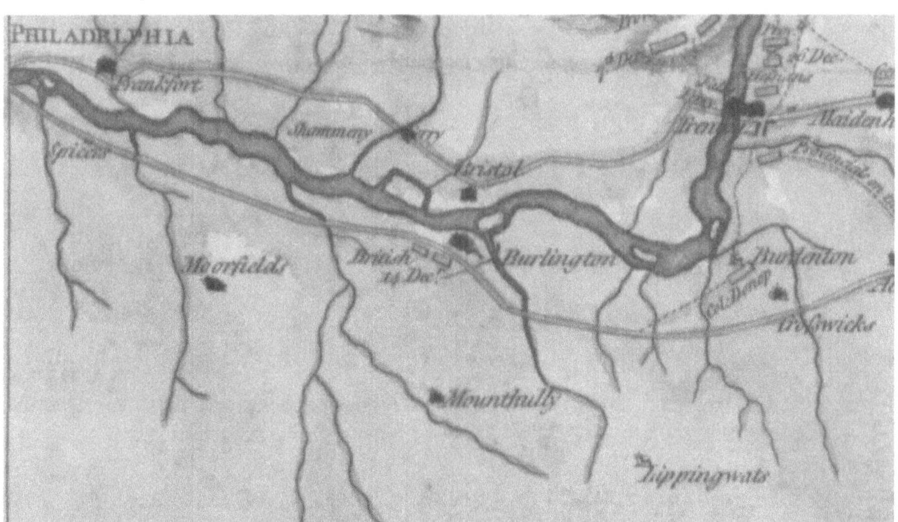

"The everywhere but here attitude...is highly sus," agreed Avalon.

When the British took over the Smith-Cadbury Mansion, the women and girls were warned to stay in their rooms. A cleaned-up story is told that fourteen-year-old Miss Elizabeth Murrell, a niece of Smith, tried to visit another room. A Hessian soldier caught her and tried to kiss her, but her screams were so loud that they alerted the commanding officer, who put a stop to it.

"Yeah, he tried to kiss her," said Avalon with disbelief.

She leaned in closer. "Nobody remembers the ghosts of these girls. But I do. And now you will too."

Hmmmm. I wondered.

Our little group walked silently for several minutes. The lack of humanity and a moral compass in those who chose to be blind was crushing. *This night couldn't get any more bleak*, I thought. Then I knocked on a tree, thinking I'd better not put a challenge in the air.

The second Avalon spotted Galen across the street, her hand shot up in an over-enthusiastic wave, shouting "Hi" too loudly for the distance. *So much for chill.*

Galen was walking with several other juniors, including Eris. Upon seeing our group, Eris ran across the street towards us, cars screeching to a halt as she made her dash. Galen, Rhize, and others slowly followed.

I braced for Eris' evil eye and tried to ground myself. She bee-lined towards Avalon. No, she was headed directly towards me, focused on me. Fruitcake. I geared up for her bullying.

"Oh my God, Lottie, you must be so devastated," she said as she leaned in and forced a fake hug upon me. The rest of the juniors with her caught up. She continued at a highly caffeinated speed. "We're collecting on the other side of the street for the vigil. Dax and other seniors are taking this side. You heard about the vigil, right?" she asked without waiting for an answer. "Well, you must come and speak. It wouldn't be right if you didn't speak. 8 p.m. Call me if you need anything. Stay in touch in your time of need." And with that, she was gone, being followed by her entourage. Well, except for Galen, who stuck around for a minute.

Thankfully, Galen was standing next to Avalon and couldn't see her face. She wasn't doing a good job of hiding her fangirl gaze.

"You know I'm here for you, Lottie, and for Mrs. Bonneville too," said Galen. "If there is anything I can do, no matter how small, please let me know. What's your number so I can text you my info?"

Between Oscar being nice, Dax remaining a jerk, Eris feigning friendship, and Galen being the ever gentleman, I felt like I had walked into a Picasso painting, where some things made sense, but a lot of things didn't.

My phone dinged. I glanced at my phone and looked up at Galen. "Got it. Thanks."

Galen nodded and walked away to rejoin the juniors.

Main Street was lively tonight; everyone seemed to be out walking. A shiny new coupe from 2022 slid into a spot at the curb, the kind of car that turned a few heads. A couple climbed out, still laughing about something between them. She carried a bottle of wine, and together they crossed the sidewalk and headed up the walkway toward a friend's house, their voices light as the door swung open to greet them.

Passing Wawa, I thought about the old Friendly's that used to sit next door and the times Parisol and I went there as kids. Then, like a punch, I remembered that it was also the spot where Carolyn Majane had her last ice cream with friends before she was murdered.

I told myself I should probably ask Sarah to remind me what I'm supposed to do when my brain gets stuck on dark stories instead of staying in the moment. Not that I'd ever told her anything truly bad from my own life. She just dropped those things into our talks like she knew I needed to hear them.

I did remember one thing she said, though: "Kids who go through significant trauma sometimes have brains that get rewired." They scan for danger without even trying. It can be a gift, like noticing stuff other people miss. But it's also a curse, because the brain won't shut up about possible threats, and it leaves barely any space to notice the good things right in front of you.

Wulf nudged Sabielo. "Your house was built in the late 1800s or early 1900s, right?"

"Yes."

"Why then did your family feel it necessary to build the hidden passages? The Revolutionary War was already over, and people no longer needed to hide from enemy soldiers. Slavery was already outlawed, and freedom seekers no longer needed to hide along the Underground Railroad. So why build secret passages?"

"Lincoln said it best, 'Human nature will not change. In any future great national trial, compared with the men of this, we shall have as weak, and as strong; as silly and as wise; as bad and good. Let us, therefore, study the incidents of this, as philosophy to learn wisdom from, and none of them as wrongs to be revenged.'"

She continued, "My forefathers took the position in designing and building our home that in the future there will be a time when hidden staircases will again be needed."

They continued to discuss politics while I zoned out. Not that I wasn't interested, but the day was catching up with me. "This feels like the longest day in history," I said. "It reminds me of Frodo and Sam's quest to reach Mount Doom."

"Same," said Avalon. "But it's more like Dune Part 1."

"Wait," I said. "How possibly does that compare to the long trek to Mount Doom?"

"Because I had to listen to Wulf complain about how the movie wasn't like the book for literally six months. Six months."

Wulf raised his eyebrows, shrugged, giving Sabielo a cheeky look of "I don't know what she's talking about."

"It was a long time," said Avalon.

Wulf scrunched his lips, trying to hold something in. His mouth wiggled, going through odd contortions. He was going to blow. Then, in one breath, he did.

"When reality is framed as a hologram and we're all one consciousness and my Wulf avatar is off, time is emergent and not fundamental. Time doesn't exist; it's just part of the holographic projection. Rovelli is of this belief. Time is derived from the relations of thermodynamics and interactions. Even in the Wheeler–DeWitt equation, there is no time. Time only emerges when the subsystems within the universe are examined."

Avalon and I broke out laughing.

Sabielo asked, "What was that?"

"A science explosion," I said, smiling. "If he doesn't get the words out, his brain will explode."

"Like you don't have history explosions?" retorted Wulf.

It felt good to laugh.

Avalon was the first to peel off from the group and headed down a cut-through street that led to her home. That left Wulf, Sabielo, and me. Wulf's Street was coming up. He offered for them to walk me home, but I declined the offer.

I pulled out my mace from my backpack and held it up. "I'll be fine." I was tired of seeing the two of them flirting anyway. The sooner this thing between them was over, the sooner things would be back to normal.

Before turning off, Wulf said, "I'll call you after I show Sabielo my grandfather's lock. I still want to discuss that quantum physics problem with you."

I nodded.

As we went our own ways, he said, "One more thing, Lot. Knowing you, you'll probably fall asleep before I call. Be sure to turn on your VAR before you do. Those noise-canceling sleep machines make it easier."

"Yes, Dad," I joked. Message received.

As I kept walking, my footsteps started to echo, a noise alone. Beyond that just silence. The trees' shadows stretched across the street as if they were crawling towards me. Something cracked to my left, a sharp, clean snap. My heart quickened, thudding hard against my ribs. I gripped my mace tighter and slid the trigger to unlock. *I wish Rex were here.*

A car drove slowly past. The glow of its tail lights in the mist cast a blood-red glow that hung in the air.

Up ahead, something stood motionless on the corner, watching. As I got closer, the dim streetlight behind it spilled just enough light to trace the outline of a small figure. Eyes fixed on me. Too small to be human who could walk, too human-shaped to be anything else.

Chapter 35

Standing on the corner was a little child, maybe 2 years old, staring at me. What was disconcerting was the absence of any child-like expression. The child was neither quizzical nor afraid. The posture was that of a self-assured adult. As I got closer, I looked around for any parents, but there wasn't a soul.

The child wore a long nightshirt and didn't seem worried that I was nearing. "Are your parents around?" I asked.

A tiny hand was held out, beckoning to be held. The other hand pointed at something farther up Kings Highway.

I opened my palm and gently wrapped my fingers around the tiny hand. A stream of peace and love flowed up my arm, and all my anxieties disappeared.

Without a word, I knew we were going to take a little walk. I'd walk anywhere to continue to feel this way. We walked up Kings Highway, past Strawbridge Lake, past the bus stop, and crossed the road to the Cowperthwaite home.

Earlier today, the librarian at the Library Company of Burlington handed me a book with a section on the outstanding works of Job Cowperthwaite. We stood out front of his home, originally built by his father, Thomas, in 1742.

I'd been taught that Job was pro-women, pro-education, and an abolitionist. A generous benefactor who had even converted one of his bedrooms in his home into a school, complete with coat pegs for the students.

The child turned towards me and slowly took my other hand. I could feel the child's desire for the gold gilt that had been painted over Moorestown's history to be washed off. For the decay beneath that, being the true history, to be given light.

I was shown four documents. The first was from the Quaker Meeting Minutes from 1776, when Job would have been about 30 years old. It stated that:

> "Job Cowperthwaite had been accused & it was generally believed, that he was ye father of a Bastard Child & that he neglected to take friends advice to clear up ye reproach."

Generally, this meant he wouldn't agree to either marry the mother or, at the very least, provide for the child.

The second document was a manumission by the brothers Job and Hugh Cowperthwaite of their shared enslaved girl Hannah Acorby in 1787.

The third document was part of John Hunt's, a Moorestown Quaker Minister and carpenter's, journal from May 15, 1813.

> "I went to the burial of Job Cowperthwaite, who died very suddenly. A very hard drinker, a worthless, base man many ways. I have dealt very closely and plainly with him, and he has always seemed to respect me and has been very kind to me. The people behaved orderly, still and quiet, but there seemed no more concern than if it had been the burial of a horse. There seemed no openness for to say any thing scarcely, yet I had some little remarks and felt no condemnation nor much satisfaction."

I was confused. Who was Job? The genteel land-owner who started the first school in his home, or the drunkard, womanizer, who didn't take care of a child conceived out of wedlock, who once owned a slave, and who didn't stir up emotion in people who attended his funeral.

I looked at the fourth document. It was a list of some of the people who voted in Chester Township in 1807.

The child ran her finger down the list and pointed to the name Ann Cowperthwaite, the daughter of Job, as one of the women from town who voted. I remembered Sabielo telling me about some women being able to vote in Chester in 1807. Sadly, later that same year, the law was changed to white male voters, and these women lost the right to vote. Many of these women voters were members of the same Quaker Moorestown Meeting that Alice Paul, the suffragette, attended a century later.

I looked down at the child to ask questions, but I was alone. Left with more questions than when I arrived.

The sense of peace vanished with the child.

I pulled the mace from my backpack, thumbed the safety off, and tried calling Mom. No missed calls from her, just an ache in my gut that said I shouldn't be alone on my walk home. My call went directly to voicemail, followed by the ding of an incoming text.

"Is everything okay?"

"Yep. Just letting you know I'm heading home. Be there in 10."

"Are you walking home alone?" Even in text, I could feel her worry.

"Of course not," I lied. I really need to stop lying.

I gripped my mace tighter, finger tapping near the trigger. I wanted to be ready, but was leery of macing someone by mistake. I've only accidentally maced one person.

My dad might take issue with the word "only."

Last winter, I was sound asleep when mom and dad came to check on me. I heard someone creeping into my room. Half asleep, heart pounding, and sure it was an intruder, I maced my dad right in the face.

I learned three things that night. One, high-powered mace cans shoot farther than I thought. Two, sleeping with mace in my hand is a bad idea. And three, even the calmest, kindest dads have their limits ... especially when eyes are burning out, and lungs are coughing from being sprayed.

As I passed a darkened street, a prickle crawled up my spine. That feeling like someone was behind me.

I glanced back.

Nothing but shadows.

I slowed my steps, listening. It was too quiet.

"Croak."

I turned. It was just a lost, lonely bullfrog with high hopes of mating. *Very sexy,* I laughed. I really needed to go to bed.

As I neared the lake, the place where Parisol had been taken, that's when I heard it. Footsteps ... behind me. Fast and getting closer.

Panic flared in my chest. There were no headlights. No neighbors on their porches. Just me and whoever was back there.

There wasn't time to run.

My hand trembled as I turned, finger poised on the mace, ready to spray.

Chapter 36

As I spun around, the mace spun out of my hand and landed somewhere in the dark.

A flashlight was beamed into my eyes and was lowered to the grass.

"Lottie. What are we looking for?" It was Keefan's voice, peaceful and flowing, like a stream gliding over the stones. My heart slowed in its warmth.

"Ummm... Just my can of mace."

He swept his flashlight across the grass, then paused. "Here it is," he said, crouching to pick it up. When he straightened, he handed it to me slowly, tilting his head slightly ... studying me like I was a puzzle.

I looked like a wreck. Yet, I was too drained to care.

"Can I walk you home?" he asked.

The question caught me off guard. My brows pulled together. "Sure," I said with a bit of hesitation.

Keefan and I were chums in early elementary school, until... well, until I shut down. Then, when I started to emerge, sort of, I was put with Avalon and Wulf.

That was forever ago.

We walked in awkward silence. As we turned onto my street, Keefan asked, "Whatever happened to us?"

"Nothing that I remember. Just drifted apart." Another lie.

"Do you remember when we were in the little-kid swim class at Sunny Brook?" Keefan asked. "You started that splash fight?"

"Oh my gosh, yes!" I laughed. "And we totally ignored the lifeguard's whistle. Ended up dragging the whole class into a full-on water war."

"Our parents were so mad when we got kicked out of class," he said, cracking up.

I was laughing too hard to speak. "And ... and then we got red slushies at the snack bar," I managed between giggles. "And spun each other around so fast that red juice came out of your nose!"

Keefan doubled over, laughing. I couldn't stop either. Laughter poured out without my permission. My stomach hurt, and my eyes were watering. But it felt so good.

Really good.

Keefan stopped and looked at me. "When's the last time you spun like that?"

"It's been a while." That summer ages ago, to be exact.

What's he up to? I glanced at him, then kept walking. He fell in step beside me.

"Let's twirl," he said. "For old time's sake."

"Here?" I asked as we reached my front yard.

"It's dark out. No one's watching. Just two friends," he said, reaching out lightly and grasping my hand, "having fun."

Something fluttered in my chest. Every cell in my body was awake.

I took a breath as he reached for my other hand.

Before I knew it, we were leaning back and twirling ... laughing, faster and faster. The years blurred. We were kids again, weightless. Except now, Keefan was taller. Stronger. Our weight difference larger than before.

Too large a difference.

I lost balance and he hit the grass with a soft thud. Hands still connected, mid-flight, I landed on top.

For a heartbeat, neither of us moved. He was warm. It felt like I was home.

I picked my head up off his shoulder, Keefan's face inches from mine. His breathing was as ragged as my own.

I rolled over and lay back in the grass, longing to still feel his warmth. Both still feeling silly, we dissolved into laughter.

I scrambled up, brushing grass from my clothes. "I need to go in," I said, still breathless, still grinning as I took the steps two at a time. "Thanks. I needed that."

Before he could respond, I slipped inside, closed the door behind me, and walked on air down the hall in pure bliss.

Chapter 37

As I stepped into the kitchen, Rex nudged me from behind with his Grumpy Gator clenched in his jaws, tail thumping the wall.

"Sure. I'll play," I said, reaching for the toy.

But he dropped it, nose twitching, circling me instead. Sniffing like he'd picked up the scent of something strange. Someone else.

I laughed, still a little breathless from spinning. My head felt light. Dizzy in the best way.

I grabbed a glass from the cabinet and flipped on the little kitchen TV. Scrolling across the bottom of the screen was: "Breaking News: 3rd young woman found murdered wearing white dress."

Crash.

My glass hit the floor.

Heart pounding, I turned up the volume just in time to catch the tail end of the segment.

"...police have not released any details. A news conference is scheduled for early tomorrow morning."

Please don't let it be Parisol. I cried.

I cleaned up the broken glass and dragged myself upstairs. My legs felt like they were filled with concrete. Everything felt heavy.

In my room, I collapsed face-first onto the bed. Empty. Hopeless.

Bzzz. Bzzz.

Dad's name lit up the screen. I sat up, heart thudding, bracing for the worst.

"Hello," I said, trying to sound normal.

"Hi, Princess." His voice was soft. "We wanted to let you know as soon as we heard. The police just called. The young woman they found ... it's not Parisol."

A dam broke.

The tears came in heaving waves. Relief, guilt, fear, all twisting together like a knot.

"Do you want to come over here?" he asked gently. "Or I can come home? We're all feeling the ups and downs. It's a lot."

In the background, I heard Mom's voice: "Is she crying?"

Her words only made more tears spill down my face.

"Rex and I are just snuggling in to watch a movie," I lied. "We're good."

"Too late," Dad said. "Mom's already on her way for a hug."

With that, I heard the deck door slide open.

Footsteps on the stairs.

I couldn't look at her.

If I did, I'd fall apart.

Mom climbed into bed beside Rex and me, wrapping her arms around me as my body shuddered beneath the weight of tears.

After a while, maybe an hour, she turned on Netflix to distract me. We watched *The Adam Project.* I cried on and off through the whole thing.

"Mom," I whispered, "how did they know the third young woman wasn't Parisol?"

"The police said the body had been there a while," she said gently. "They think she might have been the first victim."

When the movie ended, we put on a comedy show. Not many laughs, though. We were a tough audience tonight.

I realized I was keeping her from the work she was doing at Aunt June's, so I closed my eyes and pretended to fall asleep.

But in my mind, I was wide awake, running through the documents we'd seen in Sabielo's dad's office. The ones I'd snapped photos of. I wanted to review the police notes from the interviews with Dax, Eris, Whisp, and Galen. And the background checks on the people who'd driven down Haines Drive during the time when Parisol disappeared.

Eventually, Mom kissed my forehead, slipped out of my bed, turned on the alarm, and locked the deck door behind her.

Once the house was quiet, I sat up and opened the photo album on my phone. For the next hour, I combed through every picture ... except the coroners' reports for those two young women. I wasn't ready to read those right now.

Nothing stood out. Every person interviewed had an alibi. Dax was at home, confirmed by multiple video cameras, GPS, and texts. Eris was at home per her phones GPS until she went to pick up Parisol. She was in full view of video cameras at the lake the entire time. Whisp, who was from a neighboring township, was at a dance class. And Galen had filled his car with gas and then played basketball at Maple-Dawson Park. The police had confirmed his presence at the gas station and park with several people.

All of the drivers who drove down Haines Drive when she disappeared had clean records. I added all the new information to our electronic corkboard, but nothing stood out to me.

I sighed and lay back down, wrapping my arm around Rex, who had claimed most of my pillow with his big head. I grabbed my VAR out of my backpack and turned it on, setting it to voice-activation mode.

Curled around Rex, I fell asleep stress-petting his ears.

Chapter 38

My tongue lay dry and limp, glued to the roof of my mouth from thirst. Every breath breezed by my throat like fine-grain sandpaper.

Creee-eeaakk... The basement door groaned open above me.

I froze. I didn't dare breathe.

Sometimes he just stood up there, listening. Other times, he came down with ice chips in a tin cup. I prayed for the prior.

Creee-eeaakk... the door groaned again.

"Pfffffhhhh." I exhaled through my nose as the door clicked shut above.

His footsteps trailed away from the door.

I hated when he came down. Hated when he pulled the tape from my lips. I wiggled my tongue trying to get to my lips, but it was useless. They were raw and cracked from him pulling off the tape. When he'd put on the new tape, the glue burned my open sores.

Wait. I realized I was in the zone with Parisol. In that realization, I was no longer part of the action; instead, I was watching it.

Balancing on the thin line of conscious entanglement between being with Parisol and being in bed, I remained still, eyes closed to avoid being booted.

I whispered softly, trying to be emotionless, describing what I saw:

The basement is nearly pitch black. Just two faint lights. One is a tiny green LED on the water heater. The other flickers from the battered old flashlight in Parisol's hand. He gave it to Parisol along with a book about how wives were created to obey and please their husbands.

A chain fastened around her waist is bolted to the wall behind her. There is no slack. Not even enough to roll over. Her wrists are shackled to the chain at her waist. The chains are too short to bring her hands to her lips to remove the tape.

She's lying on a sun-faded cushion, the kind meant for an outdoor wicker couch.

The basement door is above her, the stairs descending down along the wall to Parisol's left. It's a small basement. The house might be eighty years old. Maybe older.

The ceiling barely clears six and a half, maybe seven feet. In one corner sits a stained laundry tub, with a long hose coiled around the faucet. Next to it sits an old washer and dryer. In the middle of the basement floor is a drain.

There is one basement window, high up on the wall. A black trash bag is duct-taped on the inside of the window, sealing out every trace of light. Further on this side of the window, two metal bars run horizontally, meant to keep intruders out.

Between Parisol and the window stands a rickety old table, its legs uneven. Restraints hang from both sides.

On the wall nearby, a single nail holds a whip.

Just beside her, several pieces of paper are taped to the wall. Most are about sin, obedience, and the role of a "godly wife." One is a faded illustration of a wife being whipped by her husband, copied from the pages of an archaic text. Two more show old illustrations of people being whipped at the Cart's Tayle.

Beneath them, written on a piece of paper in black ink, is a passage from Deuteronomy 25:2-3

If the guilty person deserves to be beaten, the judge shall make them lie down and have them flogged in his presence with the number of lashes the crime deserves, but the judge must not impose more than forty lashes. If the guilty party is flogged more than that, your fellow Israelite will be degraded in your eyes.

I couldn't help but think of all the cases in the old Burlington County Court Book where the penalty was thirty-nine lashes. Was that to avoid going over forty by mistake?

I felt a light pull. I hugged Parisol in spirit, and whispered:

"I am with you. Hang in there."

With that, I was pulled back into my body.

I shook my head. It took me a second to get my bearings. I sat up and made sure VAR had caught my whispers.

I grabbed my pencil and journal and wrote:

Listen to VAR audio

I was with Parisol

Wednesday, September 21, 2022, 11:48 pm.

Day 4, Thursday, September 22, 2022

Chapter 39

3:20 a.m.

Tossing and turning, I'd drifted in and out of sleep, my mind stuck on Parisol. But the thoughts wouldn't stop there. They twisted, bounced, and multiplied between intermittent dreams. They leaped to the three young women in white dresses, murdered.

Four others followed them, and yet another four. Thick and fast they came at last, and more, and more, and more.

My mind rolled onto Mary Driver, whipped down High Street, stripped of any future. The enslaved woman, whipped to death in the mini-garden. And the horrendous murders of the two Lenni Lenape women.

I thought of the death of women's right to vote in New Jersey in 1807. I thought of the young woman killed by her ex-fiancé, and the little girl who was buried in the neighbor's dirt basement. I thought of Carolyn Majane, who was last seen alive at the old Friendly's.

I thought of all the people who were whipped while tied to the old buttonwood tree. I thought of the rapes that occurred against young and old women when the British and Hessian troops moved through town. I thought of the cruel teacher who slithered into the position, getting kicks out of physically punishing children. I thought of the children labeled "bastards" at birth who grew up thinking their births were shameful ... that they were innately shameful.

My mind cried out, "Stop!"

And for a second, just one fleeting moment, everything went still.

And in that flicker of stillness, I remembered what I'd forgotten. I had a job to do.

I pinned the transcript from the VAR recording to the digital corkboard. Only one task remained on my screen: the coroners' reports for the two young women in white dresses. *I'm not sure I can do this.*

My mouse hovered over the thumbnail of the first report. *Do I really want to go here?* I wondered.

No, I don't, I thought as I clicked.

The images loaded slowly. I skimmed the report until my eyes caught on a line: "... was whipped. Thirty-nine or forty lashes. ... Cause of death: knife wound. ... Died approximately three days after disappearing."

Air slipped between my pursed lips as the words sank in.

Teeth clenched, I knew I needed to open the other report, but I didn't want to. I took in another breath. "Click."

My eyes soon found "whipped with more than three dozen lashes. ... The whipping happened just prior to death. Cause of death: stab wound to the abdomen with penetration of the small intestine and associated hemorrhage. .... Died within three days (maybe four) of being taken."

I bit my lip as I tried to stop myself from doing the easy mental math. But I failed.

F—k!

My emotions started bubbling up. My bottom lip quivered.

This wasn't the time to fall apart. *Pull it together,* I told myself.

I called Wulf and Avalon, waking them with a fifteen-minute warning of an emergency meeting on VoilaVid.

That gave me just enough time to head downstairs, pop in a mocha pod, wash my face, and return with a granola bar.

I opened the app. Wulf joined a minute late. Avalon appeared two minutes after that. Both were bleary-eyed and blinking.

"What's going on that couldn't wait till morning?" Avalon asked, rubbing her eyes with the palm of her hand. "It's four a.m."

Wulf yawned. On the nightstand beside him sat his grandfather's lock. my mind went to Wulf and Sabielo working on the lock. ... I swallowed at the thought and pushed that emotion, whatever it was, down.

I brought them up to speed on my review of the photos I'd taken at Sabielo's house and what the VAR had captured. I took a gulp of coffee, and then I recapped the coroners' reports. We all knew what the evidence added up to, but nobody dared say it out loud.

"So what do we do now," I asked, my voice cracking, "with the hours we have left? I've gone over the evidence again and again, and I still don't know where Parisol is, or who took her."

"Let's dive back into the evidence together," said Wulf.

"We can cross off Galen, Dax, Eris, and Whisp as being involved," I said. "They all have alibis."

Wulf pulled up the electronic corkboard and put lines through those four.

"I really thought it was going to turn out to be Dax," said Avalon.

"Me too," I nodded.

"It looks like the police spoke with all the drivers who passed by that part of the lake between 7:32, when Dax arrived, and 9:14, when the police arrived. Let's review those interviews as a team," said Avalon.

After reading them and the police notes, we looked at each other, hoping someone had an idea where to go from here. But we just ended up staring at each other.

Wulf broke the silence. "While the police took all those drivers' statements and did a complete background check on all of them, from their notes, it looked like they were focusing more intensely on the time between 8:49 p.m., when Parisol's last text was sent, and 8:58 p.m., when Eris drove into view of the camera to pick up Parisol."

During those nine minutes, two drivers went by. The first driver was a man whose passengers included his twelve-year-old daughter and her three friends on their way back from a soccer game. The other car was a ninety-two-year-old grandmother on her way back from the grocery store.

We extended our compass to reading all the statements from drivers who passed between 7:32, when Dax arrived at the lake, and 9:14 p.m., when the police arrived at the lake. The problem was that they all appeared to be good citizens with no more than speeding tickets in their background checks.

My head was spinning with all the facts. I was trying to stay focused, but I felt useless. I couldn't see any threads to pull on.

"Let's go back to your journal entries," said Avalon.

She pulled them up. They were:

Taken. Wet. Head hurts.

Emotion: Panic.

Monday, September 19, 2022, 8:46 pm.

Cart's Tayle...Parisol.

I was with Parisol. She's alive!

Emotion: Petrified

Tuesday, September 20, 2022, 11:59 p.m.

Listen to VAR audio

I was with Parisol

Wednesday, September 21, 2022, 11:48 pm.

We were all stumped. Staring at the corkboard. Occasionally, opening pins.

Then it hit me. "Cart's Tayle is on the electronic corkboard three times. It is in the journal entry from Tuesday night. It is documented in the VAR's recording from last night. And it's up there under the first time I was pulled back in time to witness history, where Mary Driver was whipped at the Cart's Tayle."

"But how does that help us?" Wulf asked.

We all went silent. I was losing hope on this thread and had started scanning the rest of the corkboard.

"From that recording, this guy sounds like a total religious extremist," said Avalon. "What if we focus on looking on the internet for religious cults in the area, the ones that believe that all 'women were created to be subservient to men' nonsense?"

We all started searching. But there weren't any groups like that nearby.

"How about we look at the social media of the people who drove past the lake between 7:32 and 9:14 p.m., specifically looking for any extremist religious views?

A man who women might have rejected because he comes off as mentally ill," said Wulf.

"Why are you focusing in on men?" asked Avalon.

"On the VAR, Lottie said something about the flashlight "he" had given Parisol," replied Wulf.

We all got to work. I took the first third of the list of drivers and was having no luck. I was examining the last one's social media posts. She was a mom who had been on the way to the mall to meet her friends for dinner. It gave mom vibes, but that was it.

"Oh my God, guys," Avalon whispered, her voice shaking. "I think I found something." She shared her screen of the posts made by the driver, Maves Woodbead, on JistWire.

There were multiple Bible posts, many of which focused on doom, threats, and warnings. He had several long-winded whines about women being disrespectful of men today, rejecting them when God had made women to be at men's command. He took a "how dare they view" of women who rejected him.

Avalon dug up a post on another platform where he quoted from an old treatise regarding the whipping of women who dress promiscuously, have relations outside of marriage, or disobey their husbands with thirty-nine lashes at the Cart's Tayle.

I grabbed Maves' address off the police list of drivers; it was just 3 miles away. I pulled up the satellite view of his house. *We could easily bike there*, I thought.

"Lottie, does the house match your description from the transcript from last night?" Avalon asked. "Does it have a basement window?"

I pulled up the street view. "I can't really tell from the front. The rectangular small footprint is correct. It's a rancher with no fence, but I wouldn't have known that from the basement with the window covered."

I drove up and down the road in street view, stopping between his and his neighbors' houses, trying to get a better look. The houses were very close. He had a gravel driveway, just wide and deep enough for one car. The house was only as deep as his old brown 70s Cadillac. A boat of a car.

There weren't any basement windows on the front or sides of the house. I went to the street view of the neighbor behind to see if I could see Maves' backyard, but I had no luck.

"Can I take over?" asked Wulf.

I nodded yes.

He took control of the street view and drove around the block across the street. There was a house on the corner with the same footprint as Maves'. All the houses looked like they had the same builder.

He turned the corner and made a U-turn to come from the other direction. From this side, we could see the back of this house, which was the same model as Maves'. And from the back view....

"It has just one basement window," I said.

"Where?" asked Avalon, squinting at her screen.

"Do you see the two steps leading up to the back door? Look seven feet to the left of that." The window is at ground level.

"Oh, I see it."

"That makes it highly likely that Maves' house also has one basement window."

"Great. Let's call the police and get Parisol home," said Avalon.

"And let them know what?" I asked. "That I have these weird dreams and occasionally get whisked off to see historical events happen in real time. And, oh yeah, that Sabielo broke her father's trust and showed us the police files. And that I broke Sabielo's trust and took pictures of them? And..."

"Enough. I see your point," said Avalon. "So how do we proceed?"

"We could go over to Maves' as soon as possible and wait for him to go to work and break in and get Parisol out," I said.

They both looked at me, shocked. "Do you have better ideas?" I asked.

They thought about it.

"It sounds risky. But I'm not sure what else to do either," said Avalon. "We could gather up Wulf's lockpicks and a bolt cutter from the garage and then head over there."

I squinted at her, wondering if she was being sarcastic.

"Wait, I mean, Lottie, you should bring your backpack," she giggled.

At this point, there was no denying those items were in there.

"So you're okay with breaking in? Just not with lying?" I asked Avalon.

She shrugged.

We changed topics and went into strategizing mode.

In the end, there were four steps to the plan. Bike over, wait for the serial killer to go to work, break into his home, and free Parisol. What could go wrong?

Chapter 40

When we reached Maves' street, the three of us stashed our bikes in the brush near the stream. The air smelled like wet grass. Dew clung to our shoes as we crept around the corner, hearts thudding, wishing Maves had already left.

Hopes dashed. His car sat in the driveway.

7:30 a.m.

Too early.

Avalon had found a recent photo of him tagged at a bookkeeping convention. His name tag read: *Maves Woodbead, Bookkeeper, Dankworth Brown Bag Manufacturers.* She'd already called the company's main line. An automated recording said they opened at eight.

So we slowed our pace, trying to look casual. Chatting just loudly enough to blend in.

Avalon's job was to look for signs of a dog ... chew toys, a bowl, anything. We'd brought hot dogs just in case.

My job was to scan the property for visible security cameras.

Wulf had the harder task: detecting hidden cameras or Wi-Fi signals he could potentially tap into. He clutched a small device in one hand, glancing sideways while pretending to laugh at something I'd said.

No dog. No cameras. No visible Wi-Fi, nothing hidden either, according to Wulf's scanner.

Two houses down, my phone buzzed. Mom.

Of course. She was probably watching my GPS.

We'd only left her, Dad, and Aunt June about twenty minutes ago. When Aunt June heard that we were taking the day to bike around town, she invited us over for a big breakfast. I think she needed a distraction. Something light, something joyful. We did our best to give her that.

I answered, trying to sound breezy. "Hi, Mom. What's up?"

"I just wanted to hear your voice. I'm a little on edge today. Where are you?"

As if she didn't already know.

"We just passed the Velvet Swoop Ice Cream Shop a block back. Heading toward that little park with the hill."

"Why that one?" she asked.

"We wanted to get a little farther out of town."

"Just... no bringing home a turtle this time."

"I promise nothing," I said, laughing.

Mom was going to be a problem.

When we reached the corner, the one with the best view of Maves' house, I left Avalon and Wulf and kept walking. At the park, I ducked behind a bush and slipped my phone underneath it and then returned to them.

By 7:55, I was getting antsy.

"What if he's not going to work today?" I asked, trying to keep my voice steady.

By 8:15, my nerves were unraveling. "What if he's hurting Parisol right now?"

Wulf pulled out his phone and dialed Dankworth's. He dropped his voice an octave and asked to speak with Maves. The receptionist said Maves was out for the day and offered to transfer him to someone else.

Not good. We hadn't planned for this.

We racked our brains, but every idea felt flimsy and unlikely to work. And time was bleeding away.

"What if we call the police," I suggested, "and say we were walking by and heard Parisol screaming?"

"No lying," Avalon said firmly. "I can't be part of that."

"I'm with Avalon," Wulf added. "If the police go in guns blazing, and Parisol's not there... and someone gets hurt? I couldn't live with that."

"But you both believed in what I saw...what I felt ... in my dreams and visions."

"I do believe," Wulf said. "I trust you. But I haven't lived it. And I can't make a move like this based on something I didn't experience myself."

I swallowed hard. "This might be the only way to save her. I'll go alone if I have to... but I don't want to."

"You won't be alone," Wulf said gently. "If you make the call, I'll stay. I'll tell them I had earbuds in and didn't hear anything myself."

I turned to Avalon. "And you?"

She shook her head. "If you lie to the police, I'm out. I can't be part of that."

"You're willing to let Parisol die?" The words came out sharper, almost a yell.

"We don't know that!" she snapped back.

And that was it. Without another word, she turned, went back to the stream, grabbed her bike, and rode off.

It was just Wulf and me now.

"You've got this," he said quietly. "You're stronger than you think."

"Are you sure you can't back me up on the lie?"

"I just can't. But I'll stand with you, and vouch for your character."

We walked back toward the Velvet Swoop, away from Maves' house. I didn't want him to see a police car pulling up.

Wulf had me rehearse what I was going to say.

Then I took a breath, picked up the phone, and dialed 911.

Chapter 41

I didn't give the 911 operator much information, just said, "I need to speak with an officer". This was a conversation best had face-to-face.

My hands felt shaky. Wulf reminded me to just say what we'd practiced.

But before the police arrived, a familiar unmarked car pulled into the parking lot.

"Wait. What is he doing here?" I asked, my voice rising. "This isn't even his jurisdiction."

Detective Huerta stepped out and walked over, his expression unreadable.

"Avalon called me," he said. "Told me I should be here for this. Said you have información about Parisol."

A small rush of warmth bloomed in my chest.

Avalon's way of showing support.

I nodded.

A squad car pulled in just behind him. Detective Huerta introduced himself to the officer, and mentioned he was the lead on Parisol's case in Moorestown. He said he knew us both, that we were good kids from good families, and asked if it would be all right to sit in.

The officer gave a brief nod. "That's fine."

"Wulf and I were walking past a house on our way to the p—park," I began, my voice catching, "when I heard Parisol screaming for help... from inside."

Crap. The stutter was back. I forced myself to slow down.

"I know what I heard. It was her. Wulf had his earbuds in. He didn't hear anything. But I did. I'm certain it was her."

The officer tilted his head. "How do you know it was Parisol?"

"She lives directly behind me. We grew up together. We're... close."

My lip trembled. Tears welled up despite my efforts to hold them back.

Not now. Not the time for tears.

But they came anyway, sliding down my cheeks as I tried to steady my voice.

"What house was it?"

"The fourth one on the right," I said, pointing. "We looked it up. It's owned by Maves Woodbead."

"Maves Woodbead?" the officer repeated, brows lifting. "He's a member of my church. Volunteers a lot. I highly doubt he's a kidnapper."

He turned toward Detective Huerta and lowered his voice, though not nearly enough.

"More likely she's emotional and imagining things."

As if I weren't standing right there.

Detective Huerta met my eyes. I stared back, pleading silently.

Then he turned to the officer. "Would you mind knocking on the door? Just ask a few questions about the reported screams."

The officer sighed. "I guess I could do that. You can come with me to ease your concerns. But don't ask any questions."

"I understand," Detective Huerta said calmly.

The officer told us to stay put.

Fat chance.

The moment they climbed into their cars and started talking into their radios, Wulf and I took off, booking down the street.

We stopped in front of the neighbor's house next to Maves', just a foot this side of the rusted bumper of Maves' old brown Cadillac.

The officer and Detective Huerta pulled up in their cars in front of Maves' house and spotted us. Their faces said everything. As they stepped out and headed toward the front door, Wulf and I dropped low, crouching behind the car. We peeked over the trunk, eyes locked on the porch.

Only ten feet away, we could hear their conversation clearly as they walked up the cracked walkway.

I set my backpack down and held my breath. That's when we heard it. 'Swoosh.'

Tires hissed against pavement behind us. Wulf and I spun around.

Avalon coasted up on her bike, dropped it onto the neighbor's lawn, and ducked behind the car beside us.

She placed her hand on my arm. I laid my hand gently on top of hers, eyes never leaving the front door.

"This is just a wild goose chase," the officer muttered. "I feel for her, losing her friend and all. But she's wasting our time."

He reached out and pressed the doorbell.

Silence.

Twenty seconds dragged by like hours.

Then—

"Squeak."

The front door began to open.

Chapter 42

"Hey Hank! What are you doing here?" Maves asked, his voice a mix of friendliness and surprise.

"We got a call that someone heard a teenage girl screaming from this house," the officer replied.

Maves' hand shot up to his mouth. "That's crazy. As you can hear, no one's screaming. It's been peaceful here all morning. Not even a lawnmower or leaf blower."

He's lying! She's here! I screamed in my head.

The officer glanced back at Detective Huerta, who made a small motion with his finger, silently urging him to get inside and look around.

The officer turned back to Maves. "Would it be okay if we came in and took a look around?"

"Really, Hank?" Maves crossed his arms. "I'm shocked you'd ask that. You know me better than that."

I started pacing behind the car, too panicked to stay still.

"Even so," the officer pressed, "we got the call. We'd really like to confirm nothing's wrong and put the report to rest."

Maves took a step back. And then another.

"I'm going to have to decline, 4th Amendment and all," he said shuffling his feet. "No warrant, no look around ... even if it is you. "

Crap. Crap. Crap.

Maves stepped back inside and closed the door. The deadbolt clicked.

No!!!!

The officer and Detective Huerta turned and began walking toward their cars.

What are they doing?

What can I do? What can I do?

I dropped to the ground, yanked open my backpack, and pulled out my auto escape tool.

I sprinted around the side of Maves' house and into the backyard, dropping to my knees at the basement window. Swinging with everything I had.

Glass shattered.

Shards rained down.

I reached in and yanked at the black plastic bag that had been covering the inside of the window. It didn't give.

I shoved my hand in deeper trying to loosen the duct tape fastening the bag to the inside of the wall.

It gave and I pulled it through.

And there before me... were Parisol's eyes. Wide. Frozen. Petrified.

She was restrained on the rickety table, duct tape across her mouth. Her eyes pleaded for help.

"Parisol's here!" I screamed. "She's here!"

Thump-Thump-Thump.

He was running down the basement steps.

And then I saw it.

"HE'S GOT A KNIFE!" I screamed, yanking at the bars unsuccessfully.

He was going to kill her, and there was nothing I could do.

Parisol's eyes locked onto mine, begging.

I held her gaze. *Don't look at him. Just stay with me.*

CRASH. A shoulder hit mine, and I was knocked to the ground.

BANG! My left ear exploded in pain.

Sound vanished. The world was a swirling haze.

I turned. Detective Huerta came into view, his gun still raised. The smell of smoke in the air.

I tried to push myself up with my right hand, but it wouldn't work.

Dead weight.

I planted my left hand into the grass and forced myself up to my knees.

Detective Huerta raced to the back door and flung all his weight at it over and over again. Kicking at the lock until he was in.

Wulf raced towards me.

I turned and looked through the shattered window.

Maves lay on the floor, blood spreading around him like spilled paint.

The table Parisol had been tied to had collapsed next to Maves' body. She was still strapped to it, her head twisted awkwardly to the side, lying in the expanding pool of blood. Hers or Maves', I could not tell. Her golden hair was soaked red.

She wasn't moving.

Chapter 43

I couldn't take my eyes off Parisol. I watched her body, begging for any sign of movement.

Please move.

Detective Huerta bounded down the basement steps and dropped to her side.

Wulf tried to help me up from my knees. I pushed him off. I couldn't stop watching through the bars.

He became more insistent. Some muffled hearing returned to my right ear.

Detective Huerta pressed his fingers to Parisol's wrist. I leaned in closer, barely breathing.

He pulled a radio from his breast pocket. "She's alive. We need three ambulances."

Cool morning air rushed back into my lungs.

She's alive.

Wait—three?

Wulf gave up trying to get my attention. He slid his hands under my underarms and lifted me to my feet. Then, in one fluid motion, he pulled off his shirt.

I stared, confused.

"You've cut your hand," he said.

I looked down. Blood sputtered from dangling flesh. I didn't feel anything. It was as if my hand didn't exist at all.

There was so much blood. The air reeked of iron. It was grotesque.

Wulf wrapped his shirt around the wound, winding it tighter and tighter. Further up my arm, I could feel the pulse, thudding hard, like my body was trying to send more blood to the injury.

As he was tying a knot, the blood began soaking through his shirt. First a crimson dot, then a quarter, then more. The blood continued to soak through his shirt as he doubled the knot.

Avalon ran over, took one look at the blood on my clothes, on the grass and shards of glass, and seeping through Wulf's shirt, and turned and puked.

Wulf lifted my arm above my head to slow the bleeding. I swayed, dizzy.

He shouted something at Avalon.

Then he scooped me up in his arms.

Avalon, still gagging, grabbed my wrist and held my arm up high.

As Wulf turned with me in his arms, I caught a glimpse through the basement window. An EMT had reached Parisol's side.

Please let her be okay.

Wulf carried me to the front yard while Avalon held up my arm.

The front yard was swarming with people going in and out of the home. The street was thick with emergency vehicles and police cars. A crowd of gawkers was growing by the second.

An EMT spotted us and rushed over.

He directed Wulf to put me down on the bumper of the ambulance and said he'd be over shortly to take my information. "You'll have to wait until the two people in the basement are taken by ambulance before you'll have your own."

Wulf lowered me onto the bumper gently. My legs dangled. He sat to my right and took over, holding up my arm. Avalon took the spot on my left and slipped her fingers through mine.

I realized I was rocking. No idea how long I'd been doing it. I didn't care to stop.

A news crew arrived and started debating where to shoot from. They decided I was the visual hook.

A mic drifted toward my face.

Avalon jumped up, blocking it. "Buzz off," she snapped. Not her normal response to cameras.

The EMT soon returned and asked if he could take a look. Wulf, still holding my arm up, advised him not to, as it was a gusher and only just now had slowed down.

I heard everything, but I didn't respond. I stayed silent, still rocking.

The EMT turned to Wulf and Avalon. "Do either of you know how she got the injury?"

A police officer stepped up, notebook in hand.

Wulf gave them a quick rundown. "Lottie heard Parisol screaming from within Maves' house when we were walking to the park. She called the police. The homeowner wouldn't let the police in without a warrant. The police started to walk away. She was afraid Parisol would be murdered soon, so she broke the back basement window and reached her hand through, pulling the black bag that was duct taped within, out, injuring herself on the broken glass. When she saw through the broken window that Parisol was down there and the homeowner was coming at Parisol with a knife, she screamed for help. Hearing her screams, Detective Huerta came running and shot Maves through the broken window."

Wulf turned back to the EMT. "Her ears should be checked. I believe her hearing might have been impacted by the gunshot. Also, be sure a trauma counselor is called in."

He was talking about me.

I knew it. I just didn't care. Over the police officer's radio came a shaky voice, "We found a white dress in the suspect's closet. Matches the description from the other cases."

Avalon noticed what was going on around, jumped in front of me, and turned her head towards the EMT. "Do you have a blanket we can hold up to block the view of those recording?" Avalon nodded towards the news crew and the crowd of gawkers, phones in hand, facing us.

The EMT grabbed a blanket and tossed it to Avalon.

Wulf and Avalon held it up like a privacy curtain. Wulf stayed inside the blanket with me, still holding up my arm with his other hand.

Avalon was on the outside of the blanket, telling people who had questions to go away.

It was nice to have a layer of privacy where I could rock and only my friends could see me. Not that being in view had stopped me from rocking.

Wee-woo. Wee-woo.

A second ambulance pulled up.

I could hear a little struggle going on outside the blanket. "I need to get in," said an elderly, frail female voice. "My baby is inside."

"Who is your baby?" asked an officer.

"Maves lives here," she sobbed.

"Bernice, you shouldn't be here," I heard the officer's voice from earlier, the one who went to church with Maves, say.

He walked off with her, trying to comfort her. His voice was shaky with emotion.

Avalon lifted a corner of the blanket as someone approached.

Through the opening, I heard my mother's voice: "Thanks for calling us."

Then she stepped inside.

"Hi, Princess."

I swallowed and whispered, barely perceptible, "Hi, Mom."

A tear slid down my cheek.

She sat down beside me and gently took over arm duty from Wulf. He lowered his tired arm and shook it out. He then replaced the blanket-holding hand with the other, giving that one a good shake. He moved outside the blanket.

Mom leaned her head against mine. She felt my rhythm and matched it, rocking with me.

Just being with her made it easier to breathe.

Wee-woo. Wee-woo. The other ambulance drove away, siren blaring.

The EMT peeked around the blanket. "Your friend's on her way to the hospital. And the man, ... well, he's no longer in need of a ride. This chariot is now yours."

Chapter 44

I was content in my little blue paper cocoon. Dangling twenty inches above my face was a screen streaming "Fate: The Winx Saga, Season 2."

I hope Parisol won't be mad that I'm watching it without her.

I glanced to my right. The blue paper wall, through which my arm disappeared, was still up. I didn't care what they were doing on the other side.

This was the most peaceful place I'd been all day. No questions. No pitiful looks. No gawking. Just Bloom and Stella mid-tiff playing over the headphones.

But the peace didn't last nearly long enough. The doctors soon declared that all the glass they were going to find had been removed. Any remaining minuscule pieces would rise to the surface over time. Blah, blah, blah, stitches. I zoned out.

There were only two things I needed. One, to see Parisol. And two, to lie in bed, shades drawn, bingeing on shows for a week … or maybe a month. The first was out of the question for today, as Parisol was on the ICU floor and only immediate family was allowed.

Back in my ER room, Mom and Dad said Aunt June wanted me to call her. I tried to remember where I left my phone. *Crap, it's still under the bush at the park.*

"Can you dial her for me?" I said, holding up my bandaged right hand. I didn't feel up to chatting with anyone, but I needed to hear how Parisol was doing. I needed to know.

"Hi, Aunt June."

"My Hero who brought my Parisol back to me," she gushed in a whisper.

I swallowed hard. I couldn't get into emotions right now, or the dam would break. "How's Parisol?"

"She's doing very well. They are rehydrating her with an IV. The swelling in her brain is already starting to come down. There doesn't look to be any permanent damage. She's expected to wake up in the next day or two. All of her signs are very good."

"W...Was she stabbed?" I asked hesitantly, holding back a tear.

"No. Not at all."

I paused and took a breath.

"Was she ... whipped?" I asked, turning my face from my parents, who would be in pain seeing the tears welling up in my eyes.

"No, Sweetheart. She's fine." I dropped the phone onto my lap as the tears burst out, and I put my left hand over my eyes. I could no longer control it. Sobbing. Waves of tears.

Mom picked up the phone. "She's good. Just an explosion of happy tears."

Dad and Mom were coming in for hugs, but I put my palm up for them to stop. The world was too loud. A volcano of emotions.

I put on my headphones and turned on the Winx Saga.

I was almost through another episode when peace was shattered again. The perky nurse came in and turned on the local news, saying, "You've got to see this."

There I was, well, actually, my hair was. The news station was playing a video of me sitting on the bumper of the ambulance with my arm up over my head, bleeding through Wulf's shirt, with a smiley emoji over my face, and my hair sticking out all over, as if my finger had been in an electrical socket.

"You're famous," she happily exclaimed.

Chapter 45

Not exactly what the girl who wants to be invisible wants to hear.

Dad stopped her, taking the remote before she could turn up the volume. "Thanks anyway," he said, turning off the TV.

I lay back down, but now I was ruminating on my uncombable hair. One in ten million had the syndrome. I'd rather have won the lottery.

"Knock knock," said a well-dressed woman in a suit as she opened the drape.

No more! My brain yelled, overwhelmed.

I was putting my earphones back on to drown out the intruder when I heard, "I'm Hattie Caflisch, Dax's mother," she said proudly, as if that were a good thing. "And Director of Public Relations here at Saint Rita's."

She turned towards me. "I wanted to check in and see when would be a good time to set up an interview room for you with the media. They are all calling me," she said with self-importance. "And want to interview the girl who stopped the serial killer," she said, almost salivating at being the media's connection.

Before I could say no, Dad interjected, "Absolutely not. I've been blocking their calls all afternoon."

"I understand," she said, clearly not understanding, as she started rattling off the names of TV personalities whose shows had called, trying to book interviews.

Seeing that wasn't working, she changed her approach and tried to win me over. "I'll take off my PR hat and put on my 'make every patient happy hat'."

I highly doubted she was concerned with every patient's happiness.

"What can I do for you?" she asked me.

I decided to shoot for the moon.

"I want to see Parisol."

She put her hand up to her chin in thought. "I can do that. I just need to get Mrs. Bonneville's approval. I was up to see her earlier. My son is dating Parisol, so I think I can get her to say yes."

I turned to Mom. "Please dial Aunt June and hand the phone to Mrs. Caflisch."

"Aunt June?" she asked cocking her head.

Mom handed her the phone, "like family, but even better."

Of course, Aunt June said yes.

As Mrs. Caflisch started to wheel me out of the room, she told me, "Your parents can handle the checkout instructions and catch up with you in the lobby."

Dad handed me a little box of tissues and his phone.

I nodded thanks.

I was anxious to see Parisol. My punishment was listening to this pompous narcissist drone on while she pushed me through the halls. "I'm sure you know my son Dax, Captain of the rugby team. Even he isn't getting into see Parisol today. I want you to know how lucky you are......"

Bzzz.

I looked at dad's phone. A text from Sarah. "Here is the trauma team I recommend calling in while in the ER. I'm also available to chat. I'd skip Dr. Nosepicker, the hospital psychiatrist. He's worse than useless."

I zoned out. She pushed me into the elevator and pushed the button for the seventh floor. "I just need to stop by my office for a second," she said, with a sly grin.

She pushed me into a suite of grand offices. On the far side was a large conference room. Within, three people were chatting, and another was on the phone. I recognized one of the people as a news reporter.

All activity within the conference room stopped when they saw her, ... well, actually, when they saw me. Their eyes were glued to me like vultures, and I was their prey. Another soundbite to pull at the heartstrings.

She went in and chatted with them for a minute.

"What's she up to?" I wondered.

They didn't look too happy. One of them handed her something small. She came out all fake smiles, and off we went.

Her self-inflating chatter was gone. Instead, she was now shooting background questions at me.

"How long have your family and Parisol's been close?"

I thought about how to answer, while not turning her off and stopping her from taking me to see Parisol.

"A long time," I answered

"How long?"

"Years."

She was getting flustered. "Yes, but exactly when and how did you meet?"

"I've just always known her."

"You mean your families were friends before you were born?"

"I guess."

Her phone vibrated. She answered, "Yes, darling."

I could hear Dax's frustrated voice on the other side.

"I understand you want to see her, but not today. Nobody is getting in to see her today," she winked at me.

"How's she doing?" he asked.

"She's doing great. They expect her to wake up in the next day. All is good."

"Isn't there a string you could pull to get me in?"

"Not tonight," she said curtly. "I've been invited to dinner by some special people," she turned around to glance at me, "and I'm not going to miss it."

Dax sounded anxious.

They hung up, and she went on with her next question. The game was afoot. For this next one, I would try to drag it out to five minimal answers. The game went on for several rounds, her not knowing we were even playing.

She stopped pushing for a second, clearly annoyed at being the middleman for the media's questions, and said, "Here's the business card for the producer of the Thornbroque Show." She paused for a reaction of aww. Instead, I yawned.

"Mindy takes tips if you ever want to just chat." As if she knew "Mindy" personally before today.

"What's the Thornbroque Show?" I asked, fully aware of the show.

"You'd recognize Earl Thornbroque."

She grabbed her phone and tried pulling up his picture, but the elevator arrived, and she wheeled me in. She tried to pull up his picture in the elevator, but she had no service.

As the elevator doors opened, I noted that directly across from the elevator doors were the ICU doors. She stopped and held up her phone. "Here is a picture of Earl Thornbroque," she said, showing me her phone.

"Oh yeah. I think my grandpa watches that show."

She threw up her hands in defeat, scanned her badge, and the ICU door swung open.

Fear entered my body as she wheeled me in. I braced for the drama often depicted in ICU units on TV shows, expecting Parisol to look as if she were on death's doorstep.

Instead, it was very quiet on the floor, except for the whir of strong, forced-air flow machines coming from several rooms. I could see Aunt June standing next to a bed through a large window in a room just across from the nurses' stations.

She came out and greeted me, joyfully hugging me, without saying a word.

To Mrs. Caflisch, she whispered, "Thank you. I can take it from here. I'll call an orderly to wheel her back down."

Dad clearly prepped Aunt June.

"Are you sure?

"Yes," said Aunt June, "we're good," as she stepped behind the wheelchair and pushed me in, shutting the door behind us. I could see Mrs. Caflisch go over to the nurses' station and have words with the charge nurse before disappearing.

I swallowed hard and forced myself to look at Parisol.

Chapter 46

The first thing that struck me was the EEG cap, tight against her scalp. It was covered in tiny silver rivets, spread out evenly, like some strange crown. From the left side spilled a thick bundle of cords onto her pillow, which snaked down and into a monitor that blinked and hummed.

I pulled in a slow breath, as Sarah's voice rang in my head: *Look for the positive things.*

No breathing mask, that was good. She had an IV dripping clear liquid into her arm, a few wires trailing from under the blanket that I presumed went to a heart monitor, and a small clip on her finger measuring oxygen.

All the displays glowed green.

Green was good. It had to be.

Up close, the bruise on Parisol's forehead was blooming into a deep purple, and she looked thinner than I remembered. The only other change was her hair. The blonde strands that peeked out from beneath the EEG cap were now a shade of pink.

A chill ran through me. Maves' blood, even after being washed from the surface, was still embedded within her locks. It had seeped in.

I slipped my fingers around hers and willed her eyes to open, pouring every ounce of hope into that touch.

Her slow, even, peaceful breathing continued. The sound of slumber.

I reminded myself, she's not in distress. Just sleeping. Her brain was simply... taking its time to heal.

I repeated it like a mantra, trying to keep the knot in my chest from tightening, pushing the worry down where it couldn't spill over.

Aunt June asked if it was okay if she stepped out for a minute to grab something from the vending machine. I figured she was giving us a moment alone. Then again.

"Can you grab me something too?" I was famished, having not eaten anything since her breakfast this morning.

"Of course."

She whispered something in Parisol's ear as she headed out and closed the door behind her.

"Oh, Parisol," I pulled her blanket up higher. "I hope you can hear me."

I lay my head on her shoulder and took her hand. Enjoying the peace that she was here, alive. Safe and sound.

"Parisol, do you know what I'm thinking of right now?" I asked.

"Being in Brigantine," I answered. "Waking up in our room to the sound of a seagull. Opening my eyes and lazily watching the sheer curtains move gently with the light ocean breeze. The smell of someone cooking in the kitchen. Breakfasts just smell better down the shore."

I closed my eyes. It was peaceful here in the quiet with the white noise whir coming from distant air flow machines. I was thankful for the tranquility the day had finally brought.

I continued talking to Parisol. "We'd paint our toes in the morning, only to immediately walk on the beach barefoot and mess it up. It didn't matter. Nothing matters down there. And that summer we discovered racy romantic reads," I giggled.

Everything was better in Brigantine. Everything moved slower there, tasted better there, was tranquil there.

I felt someone move her arm. I rubbed my eyes and looked up. The nurse was taking Parisol's pulse. "I'm sorry. I need to take her vitals," said the nurse. "You two looked so cute taking a nap together."

"Don't worry, I only sent one picture to your parents." Aunt June whisper laughed.

My fingers were still laced with Parisol's unmoving fingers. It felt good to have her near.

I looked out the window. It was dark. "How long was I sleeping for?"

"Three hours."

I grinned. *I really needed that.* I felt refreshed and more capable of handling the world.

The nurse looked up at me. "The night staff will be coming on soon. They will not be happy you are here; it breaks several rules." She opened the cabinet and placed a sheet and a pillow on the couch under the window. "Your Aunt will be staying with Parisol overnight, and I'm sure she will keep you updated when Parisol wakes up."

I smiled, and the nurse headed out the door.

"Your mom and dad are downstairs waiting at the café just outside the security desk," said Aunt June.

She tossed me a bag of chocolate-covered pretzels. I tried to catch it with my right hand. Utter fail. This was going to take some getting used to.

"Sorry. I forgot about that."

I laughed, feeling more like myself.

I leaned over to Parisol and whispered, "I'll be back tomorrow. I'll find a way. Sweet dreams, Sis."

The orderly came in, and I kissed Parisol's cheek goodnight. As he pushed me towards the door, Aunt June approached, gave me a bear hug, and whispered, "Thank you."

I nodded, tears pooling in my eyes. It was that kind of day.

Outside the room, I asked if I could stop for a second to speak with the nurse. He pushed me up to her.

I whispered, "Parisol's hair is normally blonde. Right now it's pink, stained with Maves' blood. It would be good for Parisol's mental health if she didn't see a mirror before that shade of pink was washed out."

"I agree. They brought her up like that. I had no idea." The nurse made a note.

As the orderly pushed me away, the nurse's desk phone rang. "Yes. Yes, I know how close you two are. ..... No, you can't come up tonight. Only immediate family in the ICU. .....Yes, I know who your mom is..."

Chapter 47

We sat at the dinner table, each lost in our own thoughts, the weight of the last few days still being absorbed.

In front of us were three oversized takeout bags from Great Taste, bulging with enough Chinese food to feed a dozen ravenous teens. Dad should never be allowed to order takeout. I stared at the bags, shook my head, and laughter began spilling out. It was not that funny, but more a release of everything from the last week. My giggles were contagious; Mom and Dad couldn't help but be sucked in.

As the laughter died down at the table, I noticed the living room curtains were drawn closed. Normally, they were open. Tonight, they were keeping out the media glare. The same reporters who had been helpful outside Aunt June's, pushing Parisol's story, had now driven around the block and were positioned like vultures, hoping to score an interview with me.

One even knocked on our door mid-dinner. I thought Dad was going to lose it. The note he hung on the front door was clear: "No Interviews. Don't Knock."

Rex nudged my leg, tail wagging.

"I understand," I said, petting his head.

"Still out there?" Mom asked.

"Just one,"

"I'll take Rex," she offered, already grabbing the leash.

"I can take him, Hon," Dad said.

"Nah, I'll do it. You're likely to deck the kid who looks like he just graduated from college. Best if I go until your protection mode simmers down."

The doorbell rang. Mom went to answer it. It was Wulf and his dad dropping off my bike. Wulf gave me a hug and slid my phone into my left hand. Wulf was the best! They didn't stay for long. Some beet stew, they needed to race home and eat. Poor Wulf.

"Wanna watch a movie, Pumpkin?" Dad asked.

"I'm wiped. I think I'll just zone out upstairs."

Before I could escape, Mom and Dad caught me in a surprise bear hug.

"How long are these hug ambushes going to go on for?" I asked, muffled in the squeeze.

They both shrugged. I doubted they knew.

Upstairs, I collapsed into bed and finally started The Wheel of Time. Wulf had been bugging me for weeks to watch it. This was going to be my long weekend of uninterrupted bingeing, so I might as well try.

I was fast-forwarding through yet another overly dramatic fight scene when my phone buzzed. A text from Avalon, with a few pictures from the candlelight vigil.

"Just got back. They thanked all the work of the police, fire, and emergency services. Eris, Galen, Sabielo, and Keefan asked about you. Dax, of course, ignored us."

"How is your crush?"

"He's fine... like really fine."

I ignored that.

"Want me to come by?" Avalon asked.

"Not tonight. I'm exhausted. I feel like I could sleep for a straight twenty-four."

"Got it. No early-morning calls."

T hat little troll was on TV again.

In that instant, I realized I was balanced on the edge between quantum consciousness and home. I hoped VAR was still on from last night. I began to whisper.

I stabbed the little troll with my remote control, killing her in my mind. Had she walked by just a few hours later, this entire nightmare would've been over. I should've taken her out earlier when she was a nuisance. I won't make that mistake again. There is always more insulin.

WHAKK!

The door from the garage to the house slammed open, hitting the wall and leaving a doorknob hole in the drywall.

There she was ... completely trashed. Mother of the year.

I reached my hand into the garage for the button to close the garage door and noticed her car atop of the trash cans.

"Nice park job, Mom!"

"Sarcasm?" she slurred.

"No," I muttered, rolling my eyes.

She staggered under the kitchen light. "Is your top on backwards?" I asked, "Wait, I don't want to know."

Then it hit me. This will work.

"Hey, Mom. Let me help you," I said, slipping her purse off her shoulder and onto the hall floor, just out of view of the security camera.

Getting her up the stairs was like herding a wet cat. She collapsed on her bedroom floor, and I left her there. Dad could deal with it if he came home.

Back downstairs, I dumped her purse contents on the floor.

"Where is it...?"

There.

I took it and slipped it into my pocket, leaving the rest of the mess where it fell. She wouldn't remember a thing anyway.

Back in the kitchen, I grabbed my sandwich from the fridge and peered into the cheese drawer where Grandma kept her pens. There were two. I snatched one and hid it underneath my plate.

This was going to be easy. She just can't be allowed to wake up.

Back in my room, I shoved Grandma's pen underneath the ink pens in my backpack and leapt into bed with my sandwich.

My toes snuggled in the clean sheets. I love Thursdays when Francis changes the sheets. Given how often I wear flip-flops, she should change them more often than that.

I texted Francis, "I want clean sheets on Mon and Th."

What else do I need to remember? I wondered.

Oh yeah. Visiting hours start at 9:00. I set my alarm for 8:00.

But she might wake before then. *Maybe I should go up now.*

But no, I can't. If I am seen during the day, people will think it's normal. If I'm seen in the middle of the night, it will stand out as odd. Plus, her Mom is sleeping in her room.

I glanced at the wall across from the bed. Francis had hung the quillocrane that had arrived. The taxidermy eyes were chilling, despite it being dead. I couldn't wait to be part of them.

Life was good.

I felt like puking. Swimming in the black current of ick that resided in this consciousness disgusted me. Repelled, I lost my balance and fully returned to my body.

I grabbed my pencil and journal and wrote:

Listen to VAR

Is Parisol still in trouble?

Thursday, September 22, 2022, 10:23 pm

Day 5, Friday, September 23, 2022

Chapter 48

"Lottie, I thought we were done with 3 AM video calls. This better be important," said Avalon.

"Me too. But circumstances changed. At least I waited until 3:00 a.m. to wake you up. I wanted to at 11:00."

We sat together, listening to the VAR recording. Avalon and Wulf both agreed that the audio sure seemed to mean that Parisol was still in danger. But why? And who? None of it made sense.

From the looks on Avalon and Wulf's faces, it was clear they were onto something, but struggling to put it into words.

I looked at my notes. Little troll.

Then it hit me.

"Wait... is little troll me?"

"Crazy," said Wulf, "but I think yes."

"Ouch. And this person is saying they should have taken me out?"

Panic washed over me. Someone actually wanted me dead. A bead of sweat ran down my temple.

"And you don't remember who this person was?" Wulf asked. "No distinguishing vocal patterns or linguistic markers?"

"No. What you hear on the VAR is what I remember. Anything else is now gone."

We replayed the audio again, listening for anything, a tone, a phrase, a slip. But nothing new surfaced.

"What even is a quillocrane?" Avalon asked, yawning on the screen.

"It's a huge, ravenous crane that originates from the Caribbean," Wulf said. "Doesn't usually come this far north. But when it does, it devours all the prey in an area, leaving the other animals to starve. Then it moves on."

A lightbulb went off in my brain.

"That's it. The Quillocrane. It's the mascot for Preddington University."

They both looked at me quizzically.

"On Spirit Day, Dax was wearing a Preddington Quillocrane shirt. I took it to mean early acceptance, and probably a rugby scholarship."

"But... why would he want to hurt Parisol?" Avalon asked.

"I don't know," I said. "Not yet, at least. We can figure it out on the way."

"On the way?" Avalon blinked. "You want us to go? As in ... stop Dax?"

"What's the alternative?" I asked. "We don't protect Parisol?"

Twenty minutes later, we had a plan. Not a great one. But it was something.

The Plan

We'd bike to the hospital. Avalon would lend me her E-bike, since I only had one working arm. She'd ride my regular bike. We'd ditch the bikes in the woods behind the hospital.

We'd stay connected through a call and have earbuds in.

I'd be stationed out back, far away from Dax and the media, wearing a hat and hoodie to disguise myself if anyone happened by.

Avalon would take the Emergency Entrance, just in case Dax tried to sneak in that door.

Wulf would enter the main public lobby and watch for Dax to come in that entrance. From past visits, we knew the lobby had lounge seating and tables, an entrance to the little café, and the security check-in to access the rest of the hospital.

There were several one-way doors from the hospital that led into the public lobby. But they didn't open from the lobby side. Wulf would hover near one of those doors. When someone came out, he'd slip in before it shut. From there, he'd make his way upstairs and position himself near Parisol's room, watching for Dax.

That's where our plan ended. Incomplete. Full of holes. But it was all we had.

If the plan didn't work and Dax got upstairs, I was the emergency button. If pressed, it would blow up my life, but it also had a chance of keeping Parisol safe for twenty-four hours, giving her more time to wake up.

Chapter 49

We arrived at 8:00 a.m., an hour before Dax would arrive for visiting hours. After stashing our bikes in the back woods, we searched for somewhere to sit and review our plan.

Looking at Wulf, I realized he was still carrying my backpack without a word of complaint. "Hand it over," I said, reaching out my left hand.

The weight sagged immediately. My left arm wasn't used to carrying the full load, and the bag hit the ground like a ton of bricks. One-handed wasn't going to work. I slid my arm through the strap and swung it onto my back. Getting the second strap over my right shoulder was another battle. I could move my arm, but every motion had to be deliberate. Nothing could brush against the thick gauze that wrapped the stitches zigzagging across my right hand.

There was no pain, only the strange sensation of absence, as if my brain no longer believed my hand existed. Yet, I could see my hand. It existed.

Trees and overgrown bushes surrounded us, bunnies and squirrels darting between them, but no benches or tables. We followed the concrete path leading to the employee entrance out back. A thick fence of tall arborvitae was just five feet past the entrance.

Inside was a peaceful garden with picnic tables and benches, empty for now. It was a lovely spot for medical staff to get a break from patients. We sat, and I put my backpack down. A song sparrow serenaded us.

"Why don't you just stay here?" Avalon asked me. "With your Phillies hat on and hoodie up, nobody is going to recognize you."

I nodded, but my anxiety was rising at the thought of being alone.

We created a conference call and tested it for clarity.

Avalon left for the Emergency Entrance, Wulf for the Main Entrance.

And I sat by myself. But not entirely alone, the song sparrow was still singing.

My phone buzzed. It was a text from Keefan. 'How are you doing? Rumor has it, you're unavailable for spinning this week.' I laughed, remembering how the stars sparkled as we spun, then swiped left. This wasn't the time.

"Miss, you can't stand here," I heard through the earbud.

"My mom is being dropped off by her neighbor. I just want to help her in," said Avalon.

"No worries then. I understand."

"Was that a lie I just heard, Miss Duvois?" I asked.

"You are a bad influence, Miss Aaraniah."

"Can I have a large mocha coffee, please?" Wulf asked.

We laughed. "No wonder you volunteered for the lobby," Avalon said.

The conversations grew quiet. At 8:20, I began to hear footsteps, fast and purposeful. A woman swiped a card and let herself in the employee entrance. By 8:29, a swarm of employees streamed through the door, oblivious to my presence. By 8:30, there was no more foot traffic. Not a soul but me was out back.

At 8:34, employees who were just getting off work started heading out the back door toward the employee parking lot. The stream gathered momentum, then tapered to nothing.

Not one of them peeked their head into the garden. *Not a bad spot,* I thought.

Snap.

A twig from the woods broke.

My heart jumped. The songbird went silent. My hypervigilance engaged.

I grabbed my mace and eyed every potential escape route. I also identified the thinner sections of bushes, where I could squeeze through in a pinch. But my mind also had me watching those places for a bad person to enter through.

I identified three places I could hide.

Having prepared for what would probably never come, I felt the grip of my anxieties start to ease.

"Guys, it's getting crazy in here; some of the media are getting angry," said Wulf. "There must be sixteen news trucks here covering the Maves serial murderer story. They all want the scoop on Parisol."

"That is crazy," said Avalon.

"I'm going to try and get closer to the security desk and listen for any more news," said Wulf.

While they were busy, I started to go through the information in my mind. What was Dax's connection to all this? Why did he want Parisol not to wake? I turned over the facts in my mind over and over again, looking for answers.

I didn't know why Dax would want this, but I couldn't ignore what I'd learned from the zone.

"Your mother hasn't arrived yet?" I heard in my ear.

"No, and I'm starting to wonder if she got lost," said Avalon.

"Follow me. Let's check to see if she was already taken back to see a doctor."

"Thanks!" said Avalon, unable to say no.

"It sounds like Mrs. Caflisch, Director of Public Relations, had several meetings scheduled for this morning, and she has called out sick. Nobody knows what to do with the press or whether to release a statement. It's a mess," Wulf said.

"Yep, your mother hasn't arrived yet, Miss Duvois."

"I'll go back and wait outside for a little. Thanks for your help," said Avalon.

"You used your real name?" asked Wulf.

"Lying is new to me. Give me a break."

"All of the TVs in the lounge are turned to local news. Lottie, they are talking about you," said Wulf.

I opened up the local news app. There I was, my emoji face with my fuzz sticking out all over the place. I turned up the volume.

"We've learned more about the girl who broke the window to get her friend out when the police were walking away. People close to her said, 'The two girls are like sisters. Like family, but better.'"

"Frackin' Mrs. Caflisch," I muttered. "My mom said those exact words in front of her yesterday."

"Avalon, ten minutes until his arrival. Be on the lookout," said Wulf.

"Yes, sir."

I needed a momentary distraction. I was angry at Mrs. Caflisch. I took a drink of water and opened the hottest meme app. It was always good for a laugh.

I scrolled through the top ten. At number one, water shot out my nose upon seeing Frizznado, the new superhero. My hair with a cape.

"What was that noise?" asked Avalon.

"Just looking at a funny meme."

"Whose got the cushy assignment now?" asked Wulf.

Crack!

Another branch broke.

My head turned toward the sound. I glanced at the exits and the thin areas in the bushes where someone could push through.

I unlocked my mace and approached the bushes to peek at what made the noise.

I could now hear footsteps. Slow, methodical, with purpose. Getting closer.

"F—k," I whispered so softly I didn't think they'd hear it.

"What's up?" Wulf asked.

"D...Dax came through the woods and is now on the em....employ...ployee path.

"Hide, Lottie, hide," Avalon gasped in my ear.

Chapter 50

As he came closer, I watched him through the bushes. I couldn't move. Even the thought of shifting felt dangerous. He might hear my breath, my heartbeat, or the shuffle of my shoes in the leaves.

His words slid into my head:

> "I stabbed the little troll with my remote control, killing her in my mind. .... I should've taken her out earlier when she was a nuisance. I won't make that mistake again. There is always more insulin."

A shiver ran through me at the casual way he thought about murder. My murder.

Every step brought him closer to discovering me and to reaching Parisol in the ICU.

Parisol, I thought, *wake up. Tell someone what happened. It's time to wake up now.*

He slipped a hand into his back pocket and pulled out a card. It looked like the employee key cards the staff used during the shift change. *Of course. That's what he'd stolen from his mother's purse last night.*

"Everything okay?" Wulf's voice asked softly in my ear.

I couldn't answer. He was too close, just three steps from the door.

He slowed and scanned the area. On just the other side of the bush, I held my breath.

Then he turned back and swiped the card.

I was relieved I hadn't been seen.

But then other thoughts flooded in. *What about Parisol? Wulf and Avalon still hadn't found a way up to her floor.*

The lock clicked. He pulled the door open and stepped inside.

As it began to swing shut behind him, a wave of guilt and dread filled my heart.

Before I could think, I stepped out from behind the bush and lunged my left hand into the door latch. As the door slammed on my hand, I winced in pain, and pried the door open.

Walking into the hospital's stale, air-conditioned chill, I tried shaking off the pain as I started after him.

What am I doing?

I hadn't realized my footsteps would echo down the hall. He stopped and turned.

"What the eff are you doing here?"

I lifted my bandaged arm, forcing myself to breathe so I wouldn't stutter. "Just an ap...appointment and visiting Parisol."

"Well, don't get in my way," he snapped, eyes hardened against me.

"What didn't you understand about hiding?" Wulf's voice scolded in my ear.

I scanned for security cameras. Nothing. The fluorescent lights hummed overhead.

I matched his pace, step for step. When he sped up, I sped up. When he slowed, I slowed. He wasn't slipping past me, and he wasn't getting near Parisol.

Failing to shake me in the hospital's maze, he switched tactics.

He turned around and started to walk next to me.

I nodded his way, pretending to be happy he joined me.

"Why does everyone walk around you on eggshells?"

There was no safe way to dismiss his question without my inner child coming out, so I ignored him, pretending I didn't hear.

"You know everyone's wondering what happened. It's all anybody talks about."

I kept my eyes forward.

He moved in closer... too close, the antiseptic hospital smell mixed with his sweat. I could feel his stale hot breath on my cheek in the cool corridor.

"How old were you when you changed?"

I wanted to run. I tilted my head and started rocking my head as a coping mechanism. I forced a smirk, pretending I had this. But I didn't. Inside, I felt weak and small. My feet were ready to bolt.

"Lottie, ignore him. The sociopath is just trying to bait you," Avalon said in my ear.

In my peripheral vision, I could see him searching my face for any change indicating that his questions were hurting me. A glint of a target hit.

Don't you cry Lottie. Don't you give him that satisfaction. I thought.

I turned to my right and smiled at him as we continued walking.

"Was it painful?"

"Focus on my voice, Lottie. I am here with you. Nothing can hurt you," Wulf said, as Dax kept baiting.

They talked over him, walling me in with their voices. My heart swelled with love and warmth. A tear formed in my eye at the thought of being loved.

Dax mistook the tear for proof that his daggers had landed.

"Were pictures taken? I'd love to see them."

Finally, the hall was getting more crowded. He was thinking his questions were landing. I needed to snatch victory.

I took an earbud out and motioned to it. "Sorry, did you say something? I turned up the music."

He looked baffled.

"Didn't you have a var...... I mean, a par.. party this summer?" I asked.

"Already on it, Lot," Wulf said.

Why? Are you jealous you weren't invited?" Dax said.

"I'm not one for parties."

"You know, I'm going into psychiatry in school. I can't wait to get to work."

We turned another corner. Empty.

"Maybe you can introduce me to whoever messed you up. It would be nice to study a maestro at work."

"It's the little things that can lift up or destroy," he said.

He paused as another person walked by.

"Take Turkel, for example."

He meant Tuck.

"A few little things here and there are going to impact him for the rest of his life. Then, while torturing him, seeing you disturbed by my actions, was the icing on top."

"He's sick," Avalon said.

"Oscar is a different case. A little push here. A little push there. He'll now do anything I ask. Had I not been there to train him, he would have turned out to be a volunteer in an animal shelter."

"Lottie, he's just trying to scare you off. He doesn't know you," Wulf said.

I breathed in goodness and exhaled.

After a stretch of silence, he turned to face me again. "Are you stalking me?"

"Why would I do that?" I asked. "I'm... j-just going to take the elevator your mother showed me yesterday, up to see Parisol."

He knit his eyebrows, realizing I could reach Parisol on my own. "I know a shortcut. Follow me," he said

"Don't do it, Lottie," Avalon said.

"It's a trap," Wulf said, panicked.

There was no good alternative. I needed to stick with him and slow him down, even though I knew it was a trap.

"Lead the way," I said, wanting him in front where I could keep an eye on him.

We reached a heavy steel door.

"Lady first," he said with a smirk, motioning me forward.

Hell no. If I went first, he could stab me from behind or shove me to whatever was on the other side. Maybe the door would dump me outside.

"I don't go in for that crap," I lied.

He hesitated as someone walked past, then pushed the door open and went through. It looked safe enough. I could see people in the room.

I followed.

SH-T.

Chapter 51

As the door closed behind us, I realized we were near the bathrooms at the far end of the hospital lobby. On the other end, down by the security line, was a throng of media. A row of empty wheelchairs was lined up near the front door.

I spun around and reached for the door, but there was no handle on this side.

Dax grinned as the lock clicked into place, having won the battle.

I looked around, concerned he might have won the war, too.

A news reporter stepped out of the men's room. I yanked my hoodie tighter, trying to shield my face.

Dax laughed, clearly enjoying my predicament.

Across the lobby, I spotted Wulf. He looked relieved to see me in one piece. But he kept his distance to preserve my cover.

The TVs mounted around the lobby were streaming news. In the corner of each screen was a picture of Maves. The reporters were digging into his background.

I followed Dax toward security, veering around the line for coffee that flowed into the lobby.

"Who are you here to see?" the guard asked without looking up.

I glanced at the screen above us. The news was playing the video of me from yesterday, the one with my wild hair and emoji placed over my face. I dropped my gaze, fearing I'd be noticed. Craving to be invisible.

"My mom, Mrs. Caflisch," Dax said.

The guard looked up. "She's here? Everyone is looking for her. Rumor was that she called out sick. We need her to fix this," he said, gesturing to the media circus.

"I'm sure you'll see her soon."

The guard wrote "Floor 7, Caflisch" on an orange pass and handed it to him.

Dax stood there waiting, clearly hoping I'd get denied. In fact, he was already gloating.

"Who are you here to see?" the guard asked.

"Parisol Bonneville," I said meekly, not wanting the media to hear.

"Are you family?"

"We're sisters," I whispered.

He began writing on an orange pass when Dax leaned in. "She's not a real sister. She's just a neighbor."

The guard looked up. "Is that true?"

"Well... sort of."

"I'm sorry, miss," the guard said, his tone firm. "Only immediate relatives can enter the ICU." He turned his head and called, "Next."

Dax smirked, soaking in my rejection. At the far end of the security desk, another security guard held the door open for approved visitors. Dax walked toward the open door.

I didn't move. The people behind me grew antsy.

Think. Think. Think.

I needed to act. Fast. And unfortunately, what I needed to do was the exact opposite of what I wanted to do. I looked at the cliff before me and jumped.

I threw back my hood, yanked off my hat, and shook out my hair. It sprang to life in all directions.

"I'm Lottie Aaraniah," I announced loudly with fake confidence.

Chaos erupted. Reporters rushed forward, microphones in hand, cameras going live. Everyone started shouting questions. I wanted to cry. I hated this. But I pretended to be good with it.

"Hang in there Lottie. You've got this," Wulf said.

The second guard released the door to help with the mayhem. It began to swing shut, just as Dax neared.

Dax lunged for the door, trying to grab it before it closed. But he was too late. It clicked shut right in front of him.

Booyah. I thought, smirking at Dax.

The media was getting louder.

"Lottie, how long have you known Parisol?"

"How did you end up on Maves' Street?"

"How did you know Parisol was in the basement?"

They all wanted to get their soundbite.

The guard at the desk stood up. "I saw you on TV earlier this morning. How's your arm?"

"Healing."

"Would you mind signing an autograph for my granddaughter?" he asked.

"Of course. But I've never written left-handed before. I hope she's okay with chicken scratch," I laughed.

While I fumbled through the signature, he wrote me up a pass to see Parisol in the ICU.

"But she's not family," I heard Dax whine as he kicked the air in frustration.

The second guard cleared a path for me through the crowd as he made his way back to the door. He opened the door and held it for both Dax and me.

If Dax had been pissed earlier, now he was on fire, ready to explode. His neck was bright red. Sweat beaded at his temples. He hated losing.

He still scared me, but a little piece of me was happy to watch him lose.

Unlike the staff corridors, this hallway was crowded. I wasn't nearly as afraid here. At least he couldn't taunt me in public.

But as we turned towards the elevators, I immediately noticed we were the only two waiting. The last thing I wanted was to be alone with him in an elevator.

I pushed the button to call the elevators and wondered if the one on the right or left would arrive first.

A woman joined us, stepping near.

Phew.

The elevator to the right of the button dinged. The doors slid open, and we all moved toward it.

Then came a second ding, and the elevator to the left of the button opened.

The woman veered off, choosing the other one.

I glanced at her elevator and then at Dax's.

I must be nuts, I thought, stepping onto the elevator with the narcissistic sociopath who hated me.

"Gutsy move," he said.

It felt like both a compliment and a threat.

The doors slid shut. Panic rose in my chest. I breathed through it, wiggling my toes.

Parisol, you need to wake up. Dax is coming. Please wake up now. I pleaded.

I had to stall. I reached forward and pressed both seven and ten.

"Why'd you do that?" he asked.

"Because you said you're visiting your mom," I replied, motioning to his orange pass. "It says floor seven."

"I'm seeing Parisol first," he said as he pushed twelve.

"She's on eleven," I said as I pushed the button. Another lie.

"Stop pushing the buttons!" he snapped, stepping in front of the panel to block me.

He was unraveling. He began fidgeting with something in his front pocket.

Was it the insulin? A knife?

I glanced around, wishing someone, anyone, would get on the elevator with us.

He saw me watching his hand, and it thrilled him. He liked disturbing me.

The small space suddenly felt cramped as I watched the digital numbers above the door slowly climb.

At floor seven, the doors opened with a soft whoosh, and a woman stepped in, bringing the scent of coffee with her. She pressed fourteen.

"You know what, Dax," I said. "I think she's actually on floor nine."

"Lottie, don't," Avalon said in my ear.

I tapped the button. *Parisol, Dax is coming. It's time to wake up. Please wake up.*

Dax shifted from foot to foot, forced to wait for the elevator to stop at several unnecessary floors. But too soon, the elevator dinged at floor twelve.

Across from the elevator, the ICU doors stood propped open, nothing like yesterday when his mom used her pass to buzz us in. The cleaning team moved in and out, changing sheets and ferrying loads between the rooms and the linen cart parked just outside the ICU doors.

Dax leaped out of the elevator. He had some sort of plan in mind.

I raced to keep up with him, my heart hammering against my ribs. Three steps off the elevator, he stopped so suddenly I nearly collided with him.

Standing at the nurses' station, right across from Parisol's room, was a familiar figure in a wrinkled business suit. My stomach dropped.

"Mom?" Dax's voice cracked with disbelief. "What are you doing here?"

Chapter 52

Mrs. Caflisch didn't even turn to acknowledge Dax. She was too busy raging at the staff.

"Just tell me what's going on up here," she half-yelled. "Fenton thought it was important enough to have someone call me in, so clearly you are in need of my help."

"Actually," Wulf whispered in my ear, "I said, 'Fenton, the hospital's General Manager, is pissed, and she needed to go directly to the ICU to handle an urgent issue. And after that, she needed to take care of the media circus in the lobby.'"

"It wasn't any of us who called," said the ICU's managing nurse, who was so helpful yesterday. "It's been quiet all morning... that is, until now." She glanced around pointedly, trying to get Mrs. Caflisch to notice the patients who were sleeping.

"I'm just trying to throw a wrench into Dax's plans," said Wulf into my ear.

"More like you are trying to throw a Hattie Hurricane into the mix," laughed Avalon.

Mrs. Caflisch opened her mouth to fire back, but stopped, looking like she might toss her breakfast instead. Her skin had a yellow-green hue. Although she held onto the nurses' station, her body swayed like a first-time sailor without sea legs. Clearly, she hadn't planned on showing up to work in this condition.

Aunt June came out of Parisol's room and stood in the doorway to watch the commotion. Seeing me, she waved and then gave a quick swirl of her finger at her temple, indicating Mrs. Caflisch was nuts.

Dax stepped into his mother's view, pulling her out of her fixated rage and waking her up to her surroundings.

"Darling," she said with an over-dramatized hug and a kiss, complete with a dramatic smooch sound.

Noticing me behind him, she ran over as if we were best friends, not a stranger she had just met yesterday.

Over her shoulder, I could see Aunt June shrug and smile. My eyes took in the area, running through my normal threat assessment. Two individuals were in the room at the end of the hall, stripping the sheets. My gaze continued to pan, finding the exits and hiding spots.

"Did you see me behind the door?" asked Avalon in my ear.

I revisited the area I had just panned and located her through the crack of a door. The man in the room's bed was sound asleep. I glanced elsewhere and gave a quick nod.

"We really need to have a long chat," Mrs. Caflisch said. "How about over some coffee in the private dining room?"

"Maybe later. I need to visit Parisol and Aunt June," I said.

Dax came between us and put his backpack down against the nurses' station. "Mom, what are you doing on this floor?" he asked, not hiding his irritation.

"Working." She looked at Dax and me, and I could see her mood shift. "Why don't you both join me for coffee?" she said. There was a plan brewing behind her eyes. Maybe instigating a media interview with Parisol's boyfriend and Parisol's sort of sister. *Never going to happen.*

I still needed a plan. My backpack was getting heavy. In one move, I let it slide behind me onto the floor as I leaned backward against the nurses' station to rest. I looked around, taking in the area.

A great idea popped into my mind. Well, maybe. At least it was something to try. I picked up the backpack with my left hand and began walking over to Aunt June.

"I saw that," whispered Avalon in my ear.

Aunt June gave me a hug, and we walked into the room. Dax and his Mom continued chatting, not even noticing my absence.

Parisol was peacefully sleeping, and her hair was no longer pink. I looked out her window at the nurses' station and smiled at the Managing nurse.

Aunt June quickly brought me up to speed on Parisol's condition. She had slept through the night. The only change in Parisol had been an increase in occasional leg movements. Once, she even thought she saw Parisol's finger move.

I put my hand in my pocket and took out Foxworth, Parisol's Fennec Fox that she won at the Saint Charles Carnival a dozen years ago.

"I'm so glad you went over and grabbed Foxworth," said Aunt June.

Whenever we had a sleepover or went to the house in Brigantine, Foxworth came too. I snuggled him in under her forearm. The corners of her mouth turned up slightly.

"Her neurologist said that these small movements are encouraging signs that she's improving and getting closer to waking up," said Aunt June. "This morning's CT scan showed a reduction in brain swelling."

"I have a favor to ask you," I said sheepishly.

"Anything. Just name it."

"Can I have twenty minutes alone with Parisol?"

"Of course. That will also give me a chance to grab something to eat. Do you want anything from the cafeteria?"

"Yes, a breakfast sandwich, please. ... And do you mind asking that nice nurse from yesterday to keep those two, Dax and his mother, out of here for twenty minutes for my personal time?"

"I understand. I will handle it," said Aunt June. "Call me if there is any change." She closed the door behind her.

With the click of the door, my heart began racing. I had twenty minutes. This was my chance to stop him.

"I'm still working my way up," said Wulf.

"Dax is still chatting with his mother," said Avalon. She was keeping an eye on him from her hiding spot.

I walked over to the chair next to Avalon and moved it over two feet into the corner. People walking by couldn't see into this corner, neither from the window in the door, nor from the large window to the hall.

I placed the backpack on the chair and reached for a small medical glove.

My left hand shook as I tried to put it on. It was nearly impossible without using my right hand. I threw it out and grabbed a large glove. *Breathe*, I told myself. *You've got this.*

Everything took three times as long with just one hand. I placed my right elbow on the backpack to hold it still while I nervously unzipped his large middle pocket.

Crap, it wasn't there. Where was it?

I glanced at the clock. My pulse hammered in my ears as voices continued to drift in from the hallway.

Next, I tried the front exterior pocket. The zipper stuck for a terrifying moment before giving way.

There it was. The insulin pen meant for Parisol, with a white pharmacy label wrapped around the barrel: 'Margaret Caflisch.'

Now to empty it. *But should I?* If he found it empty, he'd just look to hurt her in another way. But then again, maybe it will give her enough time to wake up.

I walked over to the trash can, keeping my back to the window, and pushed the injection button. The insulin streamed out. I repeated the steps multiple times until the pen was empty. I then wiped it off, put it back in the backpack, and threw out the glove, all the while wishing there was something else I could do.

Returning to Parisol's bedside, I gently picked up her hand.

"Parisol, I need you to wake up."

Nothing happened. I tried again, shaking her hand slightly.

Again nothing.

I really didn't want to go down this path, but I didn't know what else to do. She needed to heal, not to be poked into remembering the trauma before she was ready.

"Parisol. Dax is outside. He wants to hurt you. You need to wake up."

There was no movement.

Bzzz.

The side pocket of his backpack lit up. I put on another glove and slid out his phone. On the screen was the beginning of a message from his dad. "Hi, Dax. I." I clicked on the message to see the rest, but it asked for a PIN.

What would Dax use as a password? I tried "DaxC", but that didn't work. I tried "Evil", but no luck. Eight tries left before the phone locked. I was disheartened.

From the hall, I heard Mrs. Caflisch's voice get louder. "You don't have a choice. I need you to stick around today and give me a ride to the dealership."

Then I remembered Parisol grabbed Dax's phone from his backpack at the game. When she saw the text from Whisp, she opened his phone and read all of Whisp's texts. Parisol must know Dax's PIN.

I went back to Parisol and rubbed her arm more urgently. "Parisol, please. I need you to wake up." Nothing. Her breathing remained steady and deep.

The conversation in the hall grew louder. Time was running out.

I tried moving her arm. "Parisol, Dax is here. I need the PIN for his phone. Please, I'm begging you." My voice cracked. Still nothing.

Desperation clawed at my chest. I leaned closer, whispering urgently in her ear. "Remember at the rugby game? When you grabbed his phone? What was the code?' I squeezed her hand. 'Please. Give me something. Anything."

The elevator dinged in the hallway. Thirty seconds later, I watched an elderly man of maybe ninety wheel his squeaky old rollator down the hall to visit his wife on the other side of the nurses' station. He was small, shrunken from his many years. I could barely see his head over the counter.

I moved Parisol's arm up and down in large movements now. Time was running out. But, no response.

Ding.

The elevator bell announced another arrival on the floor. The elevator dings weren't so loud yesterday when the security door was shut between the ICU ward and the elevator.

One of the cleaners was now wiping down the nursing desk countertop. Hopefully, they'd have that door shut soon.

"What are you doing here?" I heard Dax ask.

"I got a call that Lottie wanted to chat," said the deep voice.

It took me a second to place it. It was Detective Huerta.

"Wulf," I said, frustrated.

"Too early for the cavalry?"

I held Parisol's hand, thinking this could be our last moment together. I was out of ideas.

I was losing hope when I felt it: the faintest pressure against my palm. So light I almost missed it.

Then it came again. Deliberate. Rhythmic.

Tap tap taaap taaap taaap

Barely perceptible but unmistakably deliberate. It was Morse code, our old dinner game.

dot dot dash dash dash

dash dash dash dot dot

dash dash dot dot dot

dot dot dot dot dot

It translated into 2875. I repeated "2875" out loud to myself as I put a glove on my left hand and then ran to his backpack.

"Control," said Wulf in my ear.

"What?"

"On a keypad, the numbers 2875 spell out CTRL. Dax wants to control people, their emotions, their heartache."

I typed in 2875, and it unlocked, just as I heard the door handle turn. Detective Huerta walked in. I was in the corner of the room, wearing a glove, holding a phone, my mouth dry with fear. *Not suspicious at all.*

I whispered to the Detective, "Shut the door," and waved him over. I explained quickly: "Dax attacked Parisol at the lake and left her for dead. Maves found her unconscious on that rock and took advantage of her condition. Repeat victimization."

He looked at me quizzically. I wasn't sure if it was because Dax had already been ruled out or because I'd used the term "repeat victimization."

"But Dax isn't done. He's been faking his alibi and came here to kill Parisol, so that she doesn't wake up and tell what happened at the lake."

His brows furrowed. "We cleared Dax. He was home all evening."

"Dax used the delayed text app on his and Parisol's phones to cover his tracks."

"But Dax was home when Parisol's phone received texts from Eris and her mother, and there were responses from her phone back to them."

"Dax changed into dark clothes and snuck out his window to avoid the security cameras. Dax stole Galen's E-bike, that lives on the side of his house under the overhang, and biked back to the lake. He used Parisol's phone to respond to those texts and further set up his alibi."

His face had a look of "that's the craziest thing I've ever heard." *Crap. He's not believing me.*

I needed to change course. "I can write you up a timeline of how he did it later. But how to prove it to you now? Hmmm."

Dax opened the door, "Time's up. My time to be alone with my Sweetie."

Detective Huerta glanced back at him. "Vámonos. Can't you see Lottie is having an emotional moment?" He patted my back.

Dax grunted and shut the door behind him.

"We have the same backpack. I accidentally grabbed his, and inside I found his grandmother's insulin pen. I believe he was planning to use it to kill Parisol. I just emptied it into the trash can and put it back in his backpack, so he couldn't use it on Parisol."

He scratched his head, still disbelieving.

"How can you prove all this? He'll claim you put the empty pen in there to frame him."

I looked down at Dax's phone in my hand. I opened the texting app and showed him the texts.

"Yes, I've already seen these."

I then opened the delayed texts sent history, hoping they'd be there. That I wasn't crazy. It took a few seconds for it to open.

And there they were. With both the time they were originally entered and the time they were scheduled to send."

He grabbed the phone out of my hand and stared. "Dios mío!"

Then I remembered, Parisol.

"Parisol is just waking up. She used Morse code earlier to tap on my palm and chat."

"I don't know Morse code," said Detective Huerta.

"Y is a dash, dot, dash, dash."

"Put your hand under hers. Ask if what I said is true - she can tap 'Y' for yes."

"Hi, Parisol, it's Detective Huerta. Did Dax hurt you?"

He held still, waiting.

There was nothing. She didn't respond.

"Don't look now, but Dax is looking in the window," I said to Detective Huerta.

Detective Huerta said, "dash, dot, dash, dash."

He squeezed Parisol's hand and gasped, fully recognizing the situation.

"Don't you worry, Parisol. I'll keep you safe."

He picked up Dax's backpack and phone and headed out the door.

"Dax, I have a few questions."

Chapter 53

"Woohoo," Avalon whispered.

"Are you breathing easier now, Lottie?" Wulf asked.

"A little. It's going to take my body time to let go of the tension."

"I slid through a door and I'm on my way," said Wulf. "This place really is a maze. Hopefully, I'll find the elevators soon."

I took Parisol's hand. "Great job, Parisol. You're safe now. You can rest," I said. My bottom lip trembled. "I love you, sis! I'll be back in a minute."

I swallowed hard and shoved down the emotions one more time. I could fall apart later. Right now, I needed to see Dax get what he deserved.

I opened the door and found the cleaning crew mopping the hallway in front of Parisol's room. I stepped carefully, placing each foot gingerly across the wet floor.

Mrs. Caflisch was yelling.

"What do you mean Dax needs to go with you to answer some questions? He's not going anywhere with you. We know our rights."

"There are just a few things Dax can help us clear up," Detective Huerta said calmly.

"Is he under arrest? If not, we're leaving."

"I'm simply trying to get to the bottom of things."

Dax stood a little farther up the nurses' station, jittery, like he was ready to bolt.

I reached next to Dax for my backpack, forgetting how heavy it was for my left arm. I staggered slightly, but managed to get it up on my left shoulder.

Looking at him in the eyes, I said, "Sorry, Durkel. I opened the wrong one."

Dax froze. Mouth open. Processing.

That's when Dax spotted what was in Detective Huerta's hands: his backpack in one, his phone in the other.

His gaze snapped to me. Fury radiated from his eyes.

"What have you done?" he hissed.

"It wasn't my fault," I shrugged with a huge smile. "They do look alike."

As I spun around to make my dramatic exit, I heard Detective Huerta say, "I do have probable c—"

In that instant, I was yanked back, hard. My backpack hit the floor.

Something jabbed into the side of my neck. Sharp.

I thought it was a knife. I waited for the warmth of blood to trickle down my skin, but then realized it was the other insulin pen. He must've taken it out of the fridge this morning and slipped it into his pocket.

"Dax, you don't have to do this," said Detective Huerta, voice low and steady.

"Don't hurt my son!" Mrs. Caflisch screamed at Detective Huerta.

He ignored her. His eyes were locked on Dax.

"Mijo, right now I only have questions," said Detective Huerta. "Take the insulin pen out of Lottie's neck so we can talk."

"Back up," Dax snapped. "Or I'm going to inject her."

"I'm here with you, Lottie," Wulf whispered in my ear. "Focus on my voice. I'm just waiting for the elevator."

The tears I'd been holding back all day finally broke free, sliding down my cheeks.

Detective Huerta, the nurses, and the cleaners all looked at me with deep sadness.

The old man with the squeaky rollator peeked from behind a half-closed door, his phone recording the whole thing. He looked heartbroken. But he didn't stop recording.

"How much?" Wulf said in my ear.

I stared forward, wondering: Would I die instantly if he injected insulin straight into my neck?

I really didn't want to find out.

"Everyone back away or I'll do it!" Dax shouted.

"Dax, put down the insulin pen," said Detective Huerta. "You haven't done anything yet. It's not too late."

"Don't say anything, Dax," his mother screamed.

"We're going to go down the elevator," Dax growled. "If anyone tries to stop us, I'm injecting her."

Mrs. Caflisch shrieked, "Stop encroaching on my son!"

Was she serious? Did she not see the needle jammed in my neck?

"Incoming guys. Be ready to jump," Wulf whispered.

Whatever he had planned, I wasn't ready for it.

Dax yanked me backward toward the elevator. Each step sent the needle jiggling painfully within my neck. I could feel a tiny trickle of blood streaming down my neck.

Ding.

Whooosh. The elevator doors started to open.

As the doors spread wider, I heard Wulf's voice, singing the cheesy, overplayed song he'd been torturing me with all summer long. Off-key, obnoxious, and impossible to miss.

Dax started to spin us around, and all I could see was a massive teddy bear wearing a "Congratulations" sash and dozens of blue balloons coming off the elevator. As we turned further, the needle slipped out of my neck for a second, and his grip loosened.

I didn't wait.

I ducked my head and drove my elbow into his groin. As he doubled over, I dove away, sliding across the wet floor.

The bear hit the ground with a faint thud as Wulf launched himself at Dax. Avalon went for his right hand that was still holding the insulin pen, while Detective Huerta tackled him full on.

BEEP BEEP BEEP. The screeching hospital siren went off.

"This is not a test. The hospital is on lockdown," said a stern voice over the loudspeaker.

A little late.

Dax's mom screamed over the sirens, "You are hurting my son."

Detective Huerta came up out of the pile with Dax handcuffed behind his back. Wulf stood too, then reached down to help Avalon.

As she got to her feet, we all saw it... the insulin pen stuck into her thigh, just below her shorts. As she looked at it, she began to fall and was caught half by Wulf and half by the giant bear lying on the floor.

She was only out for a second.

As she came to, Wulf and I joined her, sitting in the middle of the floor with the bear.

"That was your best faint yet," he joked.

I glared at Wulf.

"What? Too soon?" he asked.

One of the nurses picked up the insulin pen and examined it. "It was discharged," she said, bringing it to the head nurse.

"It's long-acting insulin," she said.

Detective Huerta walked Dax and Mrs. Caflisch into the small conference room and closed the door.

Meanwhile, another nurse pricked Avalon's finger. "Sixty-two," she announced after reading the blood sugar monitor.

"Yes, requesting emergency medical team now," said the third nurse, speaking into the phone, "to ICU."

"You'll need to be monitored for the next twelve hours," she told Avalon. "But in the meantime, let's get you sugared up."

She returned moments later with a blanket that she laid on the floor. The head nurse and tech followed her with a sugary picnic feast of graham crackers, ice cream cups, ginger ale, apple juice, and brownies that were all laid out before us.

Avalon, shaken up, started to scarf down a little bit of everything.

Squeeeeak.

I glanced up to see the elderly man with the rollator slowly wheeling himself closer, still recording us with his phone.

"I think my five seconds are up. It's your turn," I whispered to Avalon.

She turned toward him. "Want a brownie?"

"Yes, please. I hope you don't mind my recording. Gertie would be heartbroken to have missed the takedown of the bad guy," nodding to his wife who lay sleeping.

"Can you send me a copy?" Avalon asked.

"I would, but I don't know how."

She held out her hand for his phone and replaced it with a brownie. She tapped away and returned his phone.

"This is the most exciting thing I've ever witnessed," he said.

She gave him a second brownie, and he wheeled away.

The nurse returned, pricked Avalon's finger again, and smiled. "Normal."

"You mean I'm not going to die?" asked Avalon.

"Not a chance," the nurse said. "But your fingers are going to get pricked a few more times over the next twelve hours. We're going to keep your sugar levels on the high side of normal today."

The nurse turned to me. "We are also going to want a little of your blood too, since the same needle pierced both of your skin. Best to rule out any chance of transmitting anything to your friend."

Ding. Ding.

Both elevators opened at once. Police poured out the first, the emergency medical team out the second. One whisked Dax away to jail. The other was here to whisk Avalon to the ER.

Avalon picked up her phone and dialed. "Dad," Avalon said firmly, "I need you to get someone to watch Mom. I don't want her here. This is about me right now."

I nudged Wulf. "You should go with her."

"Are you sure?"

"Yes. I'm going to visit Parisol."

Wulf caught up with the ER team as they wheeled Avalon onto the elevator. That left me alone on the floor with the bear and our sugary picnic.

While gathering up the wrappers on the blanket, a pair of blue sneakers walked up to its edge. My gaze panned up.

Aunt June had one raised eyebrow and was holding up my breakfast sandwich. "Looks like the lockdown didn't slow you down," she laughed.

"You have no idea," I said, scooping up the bear as I stood.

She put her arm around me, and together we walked into Parisol's room.

She had one eye half-opened.

"Any snacks?" she whispered.

Two weeks later.
Friday, October 7,
2022

Chapter 54

Rex zigzagged along the water's edge. I followed behind, peeling off my sweatshirt under the mid-morning sun. Seventy-seven degrees and breezy, a perfect day for a late start.

Spotting a bird far out, Rex dove in and barked for me to follow. I dipped my toes in and yanked them back, shivering. Not today.

I kept walking and daydreaming in the sunshine. Rex would catch up.

BANG!

My brain rattled as my wet, ecstatic snuggle bug collided with my legs.

I laughed, brushing the sand off my thighs.

"Rex, you play too hard," Mom called out from farther up the beach.

"He's fine," I said, rustling his damp fur.

Parisol, Aunt June, Mom, and I arrived in Brigantine a week ago after the doctors suggested that Parisol needed a quiet place to rehab. Off-season, the island's pretty empty. The perfect place to hide from the media and just veg.

I backed away from the incoming wave and continued walking. A seagull's long cry echoed over the waves.

We'd had a deal with the moms forever. They set up the beach chairs in the morning, and we take them in before dinner. Dad came most nights, since it's only about an hour drive from home.

Parisol sat bundled in a fuzzy blanket, her body lightly shivering. Ever since she came home from the hospital, she'd had trouble shaking the cold from her bones.

I sat down beside her. She didn't notice; her eyes were lost in the ocean waves, her mind somewhere farther than that. I took her hand. She looked up and smiled.

This weekend was about having fun and slowly getting back to normal. Parisol was asked to invite friends, but she declined. I can't say I was unhappy that she didn't invite Eris.

I invited Avalon and Wulf to join us. Somehow, that grew into Sabielo being invited too.

The trauma team told us not to chat about Maves or Dax or any of that yuck in front of Parisol. Yet, if she wanted to bring it up, we knew to listen.

Aunt June's voice broke through the peaceful off-season beach tranquility. "What time are they arriving?"

I glanced at my phone, startled by how late it was. I looked towards the street and saw them unloading Detective Huerta's car.

"Now," I said, jumping up. Rex followed.

"Shout if you need extra hands," said Mom.

My heart picked up pace as I crossed the sand toward the street. My emotions were running high, yet nothing was wrong. I gulped down the emotions and threw on my neutral mask.

When I reached the car, Avalon's hands were full. I took the little cooler from her with my left hand and turned to walk back to the beach.

"You're not getting away that fast," she said, giving me a bear hug.

"How's the hand?" Avalon asked, nodding toward my right arm.

"Stitches dissolved," I said, holding up my hand. The red-purple zig-zag scars were a little Halloween-esque, but I was assured they'd fade some.

"Can you feel anything yet?"

"Not yet. Nerves take a long time to heal," I said. "My doctor will evaluate the need for a nerve graft in the spring. Until then, I'm a lefty, and PT starts next week."

I looked at Sabielo and Wulf giggling as they rounded the car. Wulf's hand slipped naturally into Sabielo's. I felt adrenaline pour into my veins, wanting to pick a fight over ... well, over anything.

I turned away and told myself, *I'll eventually get used to that.* Then I glanced back, my fake smile screwed on.

Sabielo looked uncomfortable. I wasn't sure if it was because she felt left out of Maves and Dax's takedowns, or if it was just her first time being here with this group. She was the one with the lifelong dream of working for the FBI, and actively studied and trained for it. Without her sharing sensitive information, including the drivers' names at Strawbridge Lake, we would never have searched Maves' social media and figured out it was him. Yet, she would never know how important her contribution was.

I went over and hugged Sabielo. A long hug.

She hugged me back and we stood there for a minute. As we let go, I asked Wulf, "Are you playing hooky?"

"Mom called it in as a mental health day," he chuckled.

"There's been a lot of those lately," I said.

We set up a few more chairs on the beach, and everyone sat down and started to catch up. After a little while, an awkward silence settled in. Nobody knew what to say to Parisol.

Avalon broke the silence by jumping up, grabbing the bodyboard, and running toward the water. "Last one in has to shake out the sandy towels."

"Av," I shouted, hoping to warn her about the cold water.

Too late. She was already up to her thighs when her brain registered the water temperature. She turned to run back to the beach, just as a frigid wave rolled over her back.

"What's the water temp?" Sabielo asked.

"Sixty-nine degrees," I said. "Not ideal for hot water lovers."

Avalon was back in a flash, squeezing the water out of her hair and wrapping a towel around herself. "It wouldn't be so bad getting out of the water if there weren't a breeze." She moved her chair up close to Parisol, who smiled and shared her blanket.

Sabielo looked at Wulf and me, raised an eyebrow, and sprinted for the water. "No sandy towel duty for me," she called out.

Wulf took the challenge and chased after her, the two of them going all out.

Did I just see that? Did he just slow down that last step and let her win? I had to laugh. He wouldn't have done that for anyone else.

The two of them swam out. "Can any of you toss out the bodyboards?" shouted Sabielo.

Then Sabielo playfully shoved Wulf. "I can last longer out here than you."

"I'll take that bet," Wulf said. "While you might have the edge with more body fat and a better surface-area-to-volume ratio, the fact that you're wasting energy treading water increases your heat loss through convection. My feet are firmly on the ground, which gives me the overall advantage."

"What do you mean ... more body fat?" Sabielo asked, splashing him.

"I'll grab the extra boards from the car," said Detective Huerta. "Lottie, can you help me carry a few things?"

"Sure," I said, standing up.

As we got out of earshot, he asked, "¿Cómo estás, mija? How are you holding up?"

"I'm fine," I lied, knowing I'd just stuffed it into a cardboard box and put it with the others in my mind.

"I'm still trying to piece together everything from those few crazy days. Can I ask you a few questions?"

My heart rate quickened. There were things I couldn't explain.

"Do I need a lawyer?" I jested.

"Of course not. Just a few missing little details."

"Fire away."

Detective Huerta stopped walking and turned to face me. "I was wondering, how did you end up on Maves' street that day?"

My stomach tightened. I kept my voice casual. "Just luck, I guess. We wanted to get away from town, and the park seemed like a good option."

He nodded slowly, but his eyes stayed on mine. "And you just happened to pick that particular park?"

"It was the closest one that was in another town," and that was true. I hoped I looked more relaxed than I felt.

"Funny how these things work out sometimes, no?" he asked.

"Yep."

"I was also thinking it was odd that when we found Parisol, her mouth was taped."

"Why's that odd?"

"Because you heard her screaming just twenty minutes before."

"Maves must have put the tape back on when he heard her yelling or after he heard you ring the doorbell."

I wonder what Parisol told him about the tape over her mouth. Did she remember?

I needed to be careful. Sabielo might be feeling left out, and her dad clearly knew things were off.

I grabbed two bodyboards from the back of his car and wedged them under my left arm. While he was rummaging through a pile of blankets in the back seat, I walked away.

Once back at the chairs, I added the third board to my arm and headed toward the water.

They were treading water, carefully keeping their noses above the surface. "Which ones do you want?" I shouted.

"The yellow one, please," said Sabielo.

"Picking the one with the best control," Wulf said with a nod. "It doesn't matter, I'll still win."

Wulf turned towards me. "I'll take the red one. Can you bring them out to us?"

"Not a chance," I laughed. He knew my throwing stats.

I tossed them, and they went up high and out about eight feet. The wind caught Wulf's, and it backtracked, landing just two feet from the water's edge.

I gave him a devilish little smile, shrugged, and walked back to the chairs. I could hear him whine as he dashed for his board as the wind picked up.

I sat down and checked my phone. Another text from Keefan, I smiled. Not that I'd answered any. This one said, "I'm not giving up."

I went to swipe left, but paused, remembering when we twirled and how I fell on top. I was lost in the moment. I texted back, "hi," giggled, and put down my phone.

Detective Huerta joined us. "Look who I found." Beside him stood Galen.

Parisol looked up. "I thought you'd never get here."

Everybody tried to hide their shock and pretend they knew Parisol had invited him .... happy she was chatting with anyone.

Avalon stood up. "Want to take a walk?" she asked me, giving up her seat next to Parisol to Galen.

We strolled down the sand, and I motioned over my shoulder. "How are you with that?" I asked regarding Parisol and Galen.

"Pfff. I'm fine," she said, waving it off.

She pulled out her phone and showed me the video of her grabbing Dax's arm and getting jabbed with the insulin pen. It was up to two million views.

"It's crazy. Right!?" She asked.

She had three companies pursuing her for endorsement deals. One of them was the teddy bear manufacturer.

I swallowed before asking my next question. "Any updates on the case against Dax?"

"Through the grapevine, I heard that discussions were taking place between the AG and Dax's attorneys. Sounds like he might be considering an insanity defense. They've got him up at the Center in Trenton for evaluation."

I pursed my lips. Forty-five minutes away was too close for my comfort. And how secure was a state psychiatric hospital for those in the legal system?

Reading my mind, Avalon spoke up. "Stop that," she said, putting her arm through mine. We walked around the northern tip of the island.

When we got back, Wulf and Sabielo were still in the water, but sharing a bodyboard now. I grabbed my phone and lay on the towel behind the chairs, desperate for any distraction. Emails, it was. I paged down, deleting junk, trying not to notice the sound of Sabielo's laughter carrying over the waves. Delete, delete, delete … until an email from the Gloucester County Historical Society stopped my finger mid-swipe.

I clicked on it thinking it was their monthly newsletter, but instead it was a response to my question regarding Mary Driver.

The horror of teenage Mary being whipped down High Street popped into my mind, while her stepfather got off with a fine.

I paused, thinking I wasn't in the right mindset to find out what happened to her. I knew the odds were stacked against her. I'd rather imagine she had a good life, than know for certain she didn't, so I clicked the email closed.

I then deleted a few more messages and stared out over the horizon. It was a beautiful day. Yet, my mind kept wandering back to Mary. The chance of any documents existing from the late 1600s and early 1700s regarding her was highly unlikely anyway.

I clicked the email back open.

> Hi Lottie! So glad to hear from you. Yes, I was able to find information on Mary Driver. She was the last case from Gloucester that was tried in the Burlington County Court.

My hands trembled as I read. I didn't want to hear that Mary had a tragic short life.

> The Gloucester County Court was established separately from Burlington on May 26, 1686. All Gloucester County cases from then on were supposed to be heard in our court. But there was some malfeasance (or possible mix-up), and a judge and sheriff who were friends with Mary's stepfather had Mary and him brought to Burlington to be tried for the 1687 case.

Poor Mary. Convicted in a town where people didn't know her well. No one to give her a break.

> There was a big outcry in Gloucester, but by then, a special session of the Burlington Court had already punished Mary with the whipping, and fined her stepfather. It was ultimately decided that there was nothing Gloucester County could do.
>
> Mary's father, Samuel Driver, died in 1685. Her mother, originally Anne Parker, then Anne Driver, became Anne Tradway when she married Henry Tradway in Burlington on Nov 8, 1685. The quick remarriage was quite common back then, due to economic necessity and social pressures.
>
> Mary Driver married William Chester Sr. and they had children. When Mary's brother died, he left his estate to Mary and her siblings and made Mary's husband the executor of the estate.

Wait what? I read it over again. Mary not only survived the whipping, she got married, had children, and had close siblings.

A happy tear rolled down my cheek. She was loved. She wasn't alone.

Mary was still alive on September 30, 1727, when her husband died, leaving a large estate and property to her and their children.

I did the quick math. *Mary, you would have been in your 50's at the time. You outlived most other women of the day.*

I continued reading the email.

Mary's descendants have continued to multiply. Not only in New Jersey, but around the country.

Joy bubbled up from deep inside. Tears streamed down my face.

Her legacy continued. Freedom gained.

I walked into the ocean, reached down and splashed cold water on my cheeks, washing away the happy tears and hiding my emotions.

My feet and ankles tingled from the cold water.

That's when I saw it. One of those old-fashioned, large wooden ships with a mast and several sails. As it grew closer, I could see a cannon on its deck.

"Look, everyone. One of those replica tall sh..."

I stopped mid-word, realizing the laughter behind me was gone. I spun around.

My family, friends, and the houses had disappeared from the shore, replaced by a thick forest of massive pine and cedar trees. As the beach grew farther away, I turned and found the six-gun sloop looming large overhead.

My essence floated up. A hundred men were running around and working on the deck, mast, and sails.

"Splice that line before it parts!"

"That tackle's gone slack!" shouted another.

"I need oakum, tar, and the caulking iron!"

Everyone was hustling. The smell of men laboring in the sun, with no access to showers, permeated the air.

THUD!

Silence fell over the men as the captain's heavy boots announced his arrival on deck.

He moved with patience, a tall predator playing with his prey. His long, jet-black beard hung to his waist, braided roughly and tied with black ribbons. Smoke curled from the lit fuses underneath his black hat.

Another ship came up alongside. Grappling hooks pulled it closer, boarding planks were thrown across the gap. The quartermaster, cook, and a few others boarded the second sloop. This one had far fewer men, but was fully stocked with wine and other provisions.

Black Beard's voice cut through the chaos. "Avast! Tonight we feast. Tomorrow we weigh anchor for ye Del-a-wahr Bay."

The crew shouted a hearty "Huzzah!" The fiddler struck up an ominous tune, and barrels of wine were uncorked. As crews finished their work, they fell to drink, their shouts of laughter and debauchery rolled south across the deck and toward the Delaware Bay.

References and Fluffles' Warrens

The References and Fluffles' Warrens are available online via the below QR Code. With all the pictures, links, and references, it became too large and cost prohibitive to include in the book. Hosting it online also gives me the ability to add/fix references. If you spot any errors, corrections, or missing sources, please drop me a note on my Contact Page.

QR Code to References and Fluffles' Warrens